Fallen Woes

The Fallen Favorites, Volume 4

Amelia Rose

Published by Amelia Rose, 2025.

• • • •

First paperback edition October 2025

• • • •

ISBN: 9798990211773 (eBook)
ISBN: 9798990211780 (Paperback)
Written by Amelia Rose
Cover design by Amelia Rose
Book typeset by Draft 2 Digital

Want to set the mood for this book? Here's a playlist of songs that fit the vibe and the characters of this book:

"Vicious" – Bohnes

"Shipwreck" – Letdown.

"Make Hate to Me" – Citizen Soldier

"Wild Things" – Lø Spirit

"Burning Down" – Alex Warren

"You've Created a Monster" – Bohnes

"Devil Inside" – Citizen Soldier

"Karma" – Letdown.

"Evil" – Letdown.

"Poison" – Hazbin Hotel

"I Say No" – *Heathers: The Musical*

"Wind and the Spark" – Andy Black

"Train Wreck" – James Arthur

"Achilles Come Down" – Gang of Youths

"Down With My Demons" – Lø Spirit

"Dangerous" – Set It Off

"Don't Threaten Me with a Good Time" – Panic! At the Disco

"Freak" – Demi Lovato & YUNGBLUD

"Free" – KPOP Demon Hunters

"Bleeders" – Black Veil Brides

To listen, open Spotify and scan the code below:

(and Trigger Warnings)

The thing I hate most about being permanently stuck in the body of an eighteen-year-old: everyone always underestimates me.

No one expects me to be responsible. No one expects me to address any situation with a level head, or without *emotion*. Even if my head is in fact level. Even if—though I have plenty of emotions—my approach to everything is coolness and swagger, they never expect such a thing from youthful, beautiful me.

Yeah, I'm comfortable calling myself beautiful. I've been called beautiful my whole life, from birth to the day I was killed and transformed and to *this* very day. I've always been beautiful, I will always *be* beautiful, and people will never expect anything else from me.

Most see my face, with its vaguely feminine features, and its striking gray-green eyes, up against my shoulder-length dark brown hair and think "angelic." Surely nothing but innocence and boyish ineptitude could lie beneath, right? Surely there couldn't be a twisted, corrupt soul within, *right*?

I *have* a soul—and I clarify because I know a man who had his soul *eaten*. He's a miserable sight: so hollow. It was impossible to get any kind of rise out of him past annoyance. No fun.

I'm not soulless, but time and experience have left my soul shredded and blowing around the recesses of my body like razor wire. Poetic, right? Don't worry, I'll try to keep the metaphors to a minimum. They aren't really my style.

What is my style though? Clothing-wise, let's go with skater-chic. I spent too many years in expensive clothes—in cravats, waistcoats, and three-piece suits—that now I don't give a crap. No, today I'm more of a worn-out gray or black skinny jeans, T-shirt, and ratty Vans kind of guy.

My style in other aspects of my life, though? While similarly blasé, it's more *uncaring* and reckless. I stave off the boredom of immortality by pleasuring humans and Lapsi—and the occasional witch—and by tempting fate with various thrills. The more dangerous and harmful the thrill, the better, and I skate through the decades mostly without *caring* about anyone or the state of the world.

I'm not unfeeling—like my soulless acquaintance. I *feel*. I simply, actively, *don't care*. Trust me, it was better that way.

Ah, shit, I used the past tense there, didn't I? Oh well, you caught me. I *didn't* care, but maybe now I do. A little.

Much as I hate it, I do care a little now. About a select few people. "Why hate it, Mason?" you'll ask. Well, you'll see. You'll see what caring for people did for me—for them.

This isn't exactly the story you're used to. The tone's a little different, and the trigger warnings...well they're trigger-warny. My past is brutal and violent. I don't sugarcoat many things. So expect that. I am a very sexual being, and I'm pansexual, so I have sex with women and men and, really, *any*. I'm not aggressive about it, I don't pressure anyone, and I *hate* those who do. Those monsters deserve the worst deaths.

FALLEN WOES

Over the centuries, I was sexually abused, groomed, and turned into a killing machine, and in my recent past there's more sexual trauma, and not just to me. So be wary of that on these pages, but I *promise*, justice is served to the assailants. My family, including my child brothers, dies. A kid *nearly* dies. I swear a lot and talk about dick—mine and others'—and pussy a lot. There's *plenty* of sex in here, and there's also love. Sweet, new, devastating love, with a bittersweet ending—translation: there isn't a happy ending.

This isn't a love story. This isn't a grand adventure. It's a redemption arc. *My* redemption arc, and it's incomplete.

I'm telling it now because, well, recent events in Oregon have shown that the world is changing around me, and I'm not sure yet whether it's changing for the better. So before it changes further, I figured I should get this tale of woe and redemption onto paper. It's a few years old, though. Back before Oregon. And again, it's bittersweet, so don't expect a Happily Ever After.

Now, enough circling and obfuscating.

My name is Mason Gravesdale, born in 1820 and died in 1838.

Enjoy my story. Or don't. I don't care.

The night started, as my nights often do, with a dark ceiling, dark sheets, and a dark hunger. I don't need to sleep more than a few hours a week—if even that. So I wasn't exactly asleep, just lying there, looking up at the dark ceiling and starting to feel that familiar, stupid itch in my retracted fangs.

I might not have been sleeping, but the woman beside me was. It was understandable; she was exhausted. We'd thoroughly enjoyed each other for the past several hours. Even if she wouldn't remember it, I was the best—and the longest lasting lay—she'd probably ever have in her life.

You see, I, as a Lapsus, can keep going until fully satisfied, and then some. My women—and men sometimes—always come first. And in the women's cases, *multiple* times before I ever bury myself in them. I may be selfish. I may be uncaring. I may be a lot of...unsavory things...but no one can say I'm not a giver.

But now it was time for her to go. The itch had started in my teeth, and the hunger would set in soon. I'd already fed a little on this woman hours ago—before the sex—and I shouldn't take more from her. As a rule, I don't like to feed on someone twice.

FALLEN WOES

Without disturbing her, I shifted off the bed and stepped into my black jeans. The girl's purse was by the door where she'd dropped it. I fished her phone from its depths and, as always, purged her phone and social accounts of any pictures she might have snapped of me. I opened her web browser and was thankful that she was still logged in to a common shopping site. I had three guesses for her home address.

I shifted to the most likely option, which was a house rather than an apartment, and tracked her scent to where it was strongest. A distinctive buzzing behind a closed bedroom door made me pause for a second. Smirking, I continued down the hall to what was surely the girl's bedroom and closed the door. From there, I returned to my dark room, lifted her carefully into my arms, and shifted us back to her room.

I'd barely placed her on the bed when the door opened with a low creak, followed by a strangled shriek of surprise.

"Who are— What are you doing here?" a young woman demanded breathlessly from the doorframe. She drew in a sharp gasp. "*Mer*? Oh my god, what are you doing here?"

Despite the sudden interruption, I didn't turn around immediately. I covered my date's naked form with a fuzzy blanket from the foot of the bed, allowing her a little modesty while she snuggled deeper into her pillow. But as I did this, I noticed things I'd missed on my first trip to this room.

Her scent was there, yes, but fainter than it would have been if she *lived* there. On the blanket and her sheets, I smelled more laundry detergent than her scent, meaning she hadn't been there in a while. I glanced around the room without turning my head, noting how the room, devoid of personal touches, seemed more guest room than anything else.

I'd guessed wrong. This might have been her space at one time, but it wasn't her current residence. At least it seemed her family still lived there, and the girl behind me was her sister.

Mildly amused by my minor mistake, I turned from the sleeping girl and faced the door with an easy, confident grin.

"She had a few too many tonight, and I guess told the Uber the wrong address," I lied easily. I held my hands up in surrender while pressing into her mind to ease her concerns. *Nevermind that I'm shirtless and she's naked, even though we've only been here for less than a minute.*

I crossed the room to her, and my grin slid sideways and turned sultry as I took in the new arrival.

She was the girl's sister, most likely, but she was taller and curvier than the woman I'd been fucking for the past few hours. Her dyed-blue hair was twisted into messy buns, and she wore nothing but an oversized T-shirt that just covered the delicious V of her thick thighs. Her age and family resemblance were obscured by a translucent skincare mask. Face mask or no face mask, I was dying to take a bite out of those creamy, bare thighs.

"Sorry to surprise you and then run out of here," I said calmly, sauntering toward where she'd pressed herself back against the doorframe to fearfully let me pass. I stopped directly in front of her and offered her a less-than-innocent flirtatious smirk. "But we should let Meredith sleep."

FALLEN WOES

I leaned an arm against the doorframe, over her shoulder. She was taller than me, but it didn't matter. I was experienced in the doorframe-lean with people of all heights, sizes, and genders. Her eyes hadn't left my face since I'd turned to face her. This was typical.

She shuddered when I idly rolled the hem of her shirt between my fingers but didn't push me away or step out of the doorway.

"Aren't you a little young?" she asked, finding her voice at last.

"I'm older than I look," I said automatically, tamping down on my instant annoyance at the question. This boyish face was beautiful but off-putting: a perfect blend of feminine and masculine. It was alluring and confusing at the same time. My curse. But lucky for her, she'd never find out just how *cruel* this angelic face could become. "Older, and way more experienced than you'd think..."

I inched even closer, and my fingers brushed her thigh, light enough that it could've been accidental. She didn't pull away and I grew even bolder. I tapped two fingers gently against the damp fabric covering her clit, and she uttered a small gasp. Rather than jerking away from me, she swayed forward. I probed her mind just enough to gauge whether I was pressing my luck too much and should just leave, but she was *pulsing* with sexual energy. She'd already come once, from the scent of her, and I'd have no issue convincing her to come a few more times for *me*.

"We would have announced our arrival, but we were a little busy...and so were you..."

"I don't know what you—"

Her words died on her lips when I hooked a finger under the fabric of her panties and gently tugged the soaked fabric away from her swollen, stimulated clit.

"There's no shame," I murmured into her neck, willing my fangs to stay hidden, even though her racing pulse was tantalizing—both in her throat and against my fingers. My cock was throbbing inside my jeans, and I ground my crotch gently against her leg. "Women pleasuring themselves is one of the hottest things...we can continue with your vibrator if you want, or we can do it with my cock. It's up to you."

I pressed my middle finger into her entrance and brushed my thumb against her clit. My touch was light, but she tensed and clamped her mouth shut around a surprised moan.

"Oh, god, *cock*, yes please! But—now?" she sputtered, grabbing my wrist to pause my teasing. She gestured with her other hand at the mask obscuring her face. "I'm, uh, let me take this off first?"

"I don't mind it. I like it even," I told her honestly, cupping the side of her face and angling it toward mine. I'd done plenty—*plenty*—of weird stuff. Fucking a woman in the middle of her skincare routine was hardly weird.

I captured her lips with mine and pulled her against me, laughing softly as my nose brushed her face mask and the scent of floral moisturizer assaulted my nostrils, melding with the delicious and intoxicating scent of her arousal and her sister's behind me. With a barely stifled moan, I lifted her and pulled her back into the bedroom with me. She gasped in surprise but linked her ankles around my waist instinctively.

"How are you—" Again, her words failed her as I set her on the edge of her sister's desk. I separated from her just enough to undo my fly. I pulled her panties aside and angled my dick at her entrance.

"Right here? She'll hear us—"

"She's out cold, I promise," I assured her. Truly, my focus was divided between the beauty in front of me and keeping Meredith *extra* asleep with a bit of mesmerism. It would quickly drain my remaining power, but at that moment I didn't care. I ghosted my fingers across her clit, and her mouth formed an adorable O shape. "Besides, doesn't the threat of her waking and seeing us make it that much more *thrilling*?"

On the last word, I pressed all the way into her, and her hands gripped the edge of the desk. Her back arched and her legs tightened around my hips.

I made sure she came twice before I reached my own climax. When we finished, I laid her on the bed next to her sister and put her into an easy, relaxed sleep. But before I left, I peeled off the face mask and wiped any residue from her face with a damp towel from their bathroom.

Back in my apartment, I picked out a clean black shirt, kicked the woman's clothes into the corner of my room, and collapsed onto my dark sheets. I was still thrumming with energy, and *thirsty*. It was midnight where I lived, but the night was still just starting in other parts of the world.

I tugged on my hair and silently prayed that I'd fully purged her phone of images of me. Meredith had been a little too obsessed with taking selfies with me, like she was convinced I was some celebrity. There was a time when I was almost a celebrity. Then again, maybe celebrity was the wrong word: I was *notorious*. My handsome face and debaucherous nature inspired a beautiful playwright named Oscar Wilde and his character Dorian Gray. All because I was pretty, and reckless. And because, for a time, I traveled with a rotting painting.

Why the painting? It wasn't vanity, and it didn't contain my cursed soul. It was just sentimental. It wasn't a solo portrait but a portrait of my family. It was the last thing I had of my family, aside from their inflated inheritance, and it had been finished just before they died. By the time I showed Wilde this piece of my heart, it was rotting. Why? Well, England is damp, and a bitch left it somewhere without protecting it from the elements.

After its final destruction, I left England and never looked back. And aside from that classic bit of literature, all my celebrity and notoriety vanished with me.

Now, more than a century later, in the age of social media thirst traps and influencers, I envied humans for the first time. All because *they* could put their faces out there and be lauded for their beauty. Unlike their beauty, *mine* wasn't fleeting, but after twenty years of photos documenting my changelessness, the praise would turn to suspicion, envy, and hatred. But still, I wanted what *they* could have.

What eased my mind was reminding myself that I wouldn't get the kind of admiration I wanted. I was frozen as this picture of boyish youth: forever beardless and innocent-eyed. My thirst traps would only garner the attention of groomers and pedos. And while I knew Lapsi who relished preying on predators, it wasn't *my* MO. I preferred the classic Triple F: flirt, fuck, and feed.

Nah, it was best for me to stay off social media. The last thing I needed was my face showing up on the wrong person's feed, the wrong *woman's* feed. Because unlike me, I know *she*'d never shy away from doom scrolling. She'd be looking for the next me, and then find...me.

My teeth gave another twinge. Letting out a frustrated growl, I rolled off the bed and stretched before strolling to the full-length mirror by my closet. I gave myself one last once-over—thanks to that conditioned vanity—but, alas, the same cursed angelic face and coy smirk stared back at me beneath straight, dark hair that fell to my shoulders. If I wore more than just black, my eyes would appear more green, but my monochromatic color palette tonight made them more of a slate gray.

With one last eye roll at my reflection, I turned and shifted away from my apartment. I brought myself to a bar district about a hundred miles from my apartment and in a different time zone.

I chose a loud bar with flashing lights and a dance floor. A man was carding at the door, but I breezed past him with a whiff of mesmerism. The atmosphere shift from the street to the club was jarring, and I nearly backed out as the strobes flashed in my eyes and the pounding, reverberating beat hit my sensitive ears. But I kept going, straight onto the dance floor, even though I'd hardly equate the thrashing bodies to *dancing*.

I was born and raised in Regency England, where dancing was often the main form of semi-regular evening entertainment. They were complicated, folksy, multi-step dances, and there had to be twenty different kinds. But today, people on dance floors just kind of...jump around. If that.

I sidled up behind a woman twice my frozen age, placed my hands on her hips, and pressed my chest against her back.

"*Mind if I dance with you, sweet thing?*" I asked her, both aloud and telepathically.

She tensed as I first touched her, but she didn't smack my hands or pull away. *Good. Good,* I thought, as a pleased smirk spread across my lips. Like the girl I'd just fucked, she was curvy and taller than me, but her hair was cropped short and smelled like orchids. Her shoulders were bare, and a spotted animal print—cheetah, maybe—was tattooed over her left shoulder, down to her elbow. I couldn't stop myself from kissing a spot on her shoulder where the tattoo started.

When the song ended, she faced me, curious about who'd dared come up behind her at a club. She froze when she saw my face, her expression a mix of appreciation and disbelief. As if she couldn't believe someone as attractive as me would give her the time of day. They all *always* wore this look. I call it *The Pause.*

I never understood The Pause. I'm attractive, yes, but it doesn't mean that others are less attractive next to me. I might not *care* about humans. I might brush their existence off and use them only to satisfy my hunger and my lust, but they're all beautiful. And their beauty is fleeting and ever-changing—it was so different from mine.

I could take this woman home with me and convince her of this—convince her that she was attractive and sexy, but my social battery was about dead. I just wanted my meal and to go home and watch TV.

"How about we get out of here?" I asked the woman, waiting the proper few seconds for her to recover from The Pause.

Shorter on patience than usual, I didn't wait for her to respond or to question whether she should leave with a stranger. With a little brush of Lapsi mesmerism, I put the thought into her head to follow me.

I waited until we were several feet from the entrance of the club before grabbing her waist and pulling her to me. She resisted for a split second but relaxed as I pressed my mind into hers, calming her. I pushed her gently against the wall and cupped a breast in each hand as my fangs extended and pierced her throat. After a second, she let out a shuddering sigh of pleasure. Anyone passing by would avert their eyes, because people generally looked away from PDAs.

I hadn't gotten anywhere near the point of no return when the sudden presence of another Lapsus jarred me out of the woman's mind. Cursing, I pushed away from her and turned toward the intruding Lapsus. The woman slid unceremoniously to the ground with a groan, but I hardly registered her, thanks to the new arrival.

She stood only a few feet away, staring fixedly at me, with her head tilted to the side. Her long blond hair was fitted into loose curls, pinned back at her crown. She wore a black mini skirt and a white tank top with a long gold costume necklace hanging to her navel. Her red, rosebud lips were turned up into a cunning smirk.

Rosaline.

She looked as beautiful as the day I first saw her. And as deadly as the night she changed me. As my sire, she could track me and drop in whenever she wanted. She just tended to stay away for *longer* than this.

"Hello, Mason," she cooed in her deep, sultry voice. Her head tilted the other way. "Miss me, my love?"

I held up my middle finger as aggressively as I could, and disappeared.

CHAPTER 2

One hand tightly gripped the rim of the bathroom vanity and the other a large, jagged shard of glass—though I couldn't remember what it came from.

Without breaking eye contact with myself, I pressed the shard into my forehead and dragged it down, all the way to my chin. I growled through the pain as the glass dug a deep channel into the precious features of my cheekbone and lip. I slashed another deep gash diagonally from eyebrow to chin, fully marring the face that halts people in their tracks. The face that drops panties and hardens dicks. The face that caught Rosaline's eye and cost me my home and my family.

Rosaline. Rosaline. Rosaline.

Rivulets of blood poured from the nightmarish gashes into the sink, and I stared hard at the damage, relishing it. But it didn't last. The exposed red muscle disappeared as the skin knitted itself back together. Soon, the only hint that I'd cut my face open was the wet blood on the side of my head and in the sink. My hand tightened further on the glass shard in my anger, cutting into the thick flesh of my palm. I let out a roar of frustration and threw the glass into the corner, then ran a hand towel beneath the tap.

Slowly and deliberately, I cleaned up my mess and slumped to the floor, drawing my knees up to my chest.

In many parts of Regency England, a man was not technically considered "independent," nor did he actively socialize and court women, until he was twenty-one. But my area of the country was more lax. I was attending parties and social gatherings by my seventeenth birthday, and my sixteen-year-old twin siblings, whom I refused to be separated from, were considered "out" at this same time.

I had four siblings in total. The twins, Clara and John, were my best friends. Henry was eleven and Michael nine. While I was closest to the twins, I was close to, and responsible for, all of them. The parts of me that died with them never resurfaced.

I missed "sword" fighting with my youngest siblings and teaching them to read. I missed cheering on Clara's talent for complex math equations. Because of the stupid gender roles of the time, her genius would never realize its full potential. She'd been born with the brain, and John was born with pianist's fingers. They were both bound for lives of unsatisfied desires.

And I, as the oldest, would inherit a fortune without having to work for it. All I had to do was marry and carve out a fraction of happiness while hunting, smoking, entertaining, and dancing. It would *look* like a life of comfort and pleasure, but really I'd spend most of my time worrying about my younger siblings and hoping to make them happy.

I liked one thing as much as teasing my siblings: teasing women. At seventeen and eighteen, I wasn't actively courting women yet, but I sure enjoyed teasing and flirting with them.

I spouted poetry in their presence and showered them with doting compliments, and in turn, they would blush and bat their eyes. That was the extent of romance in that time—such poised and chaste times—and, admittedly, so *dull*. Until Rosaline.

She started coming to balls in the winter of my eighteenth year, and she caught my eye immediately—or rather, she reeled *me* in. She was a better match for my teasing than any woman I'd danced with before. She didn't blush easily, and I craved her amused smirk and the cunning, intelligent gleam in her eye. I kept asking for dance after dance, just to touch her hand again or brush her hip with my fingers.

I shouldn't have been surprised by her letter the following day—she was the boldest woman I'd ever met—but I was. Our letters were innocent enough at first, but they quickly grew debaucherous. She had *me* blushing, at least at first, but I quickly learned how to turn it back around on her. I lived for her daily letters and to see if she approved of my sultry descriptions from my previous letter. There wasn't a word for it back then, but I can see now what she was doing: *grooming* me.

The next time we saw each other was at a fancier ball, and she wasted no time making good on her written promises. I followed her lead without question, into a secluded corner of my neighbor's home, and she coaxed my dick out of my trousers. She went to her knees in front of me and took me between her rosebud lips. She took all of me, eagerly, and encouraged me to put my hands to her head and hold her there. She didn't complain when my grip messed up her carefully pinned curls. Everything she did was to make me feel like *I* was the one winning. *I* was the one in control. But she had the power the whole time.

After the head, she wanted more, and, hell, I wanted more too. I'd had a taste, and she was offering a feast. I found a spare bedroom where no one would bother us, and *she* pulled me inside. We kissed and she instructed me on where to touch her and what to do to get her stimulated and ready, while my cock recharged with another eager load.

The actual act of bedding her was less intimate than I'd expected, and brief—it was my first time after all—and didn't seem all that satisfying for *her*, despite me following her instructions. I wouldn't realize until later that she was playing a longer game with me.

She clawed her way in subtly back then, but she stopped being subtle a long time ago, I grumbled silently, pulling on my hair. *She's dropping by to drag me back, and drag the monster back out of me.*

It'd only been a handful of years since the last time Rosaline and I tumbled together, and usually she gave me more rope before dragging me back—often she gave me so much rope that I fell into the trap of thinking she was done with me forever. When she yanked on it, I kicked and screamed and fought, but not really. Most times, it was just easier to crawl back into the monster's skin and ride it out. Especially after nearly two centuries, I was *tired*.

But this time I *needed* to fight more, because it hadn't been long enough. I'd barely done anything this time to repent. Instead, I'd fallen in with a Lapsi biker gang and ridden out the guilt and shame on several hundred miles of highway. The gang wasn't Rosaline's level of wild and savage, but they were far from tame. At least a lot less people died.

After a few more minutes of stewing on the bathroom floor, I stood and shifted to my bedroom, where I changed into a clean shirt and a dark denim jacket. I was still rattled from my run-in with Rosaline, and I needed wide open spaces and fresh air, preferably somewhere public. Though witnesses wouldn't stop Rosaline. They hadn't before.

I shifted west, to a random California beach I'd been to a few times. A few groups were scattered along the beach, but the darkness hid my sudden appearance. I dropped heavily to my knees, dug my hands into the cool sand, and stared out at the lazy waves.

Out of the corner of my eye, I watched a family packing up their things for the night. The two parents folded a blanket between them and picked up two large tote bags. An older sibling roughhoused with two younger kids, simultaneously riling them up and corralling them after their parents. The sight pierced me, but I couldn't look away. It drew me back into my dark thoughts of the past.

After our short tussle, and saying goodbye to my virginity, we rearranged our clothing—and her hair—and we wandered the dim hallways of my neighbor's house.

She took advantage of my blissful daze and came clean about what she was. A Lapsus. An immortal Descendant of Cain that must live on human blood. Before I could fully register this and laugh in her face, she offered me a seat beside her for eternity. I was still riding a euphoric high, and I'd have done anything she asked, within reason. But *that* was outside of reason. I thought it was a joke, so I laughed.

Her eyes darkened and a cold, calculating expression replaced her cunning smirk. She pushed me against the wall with impossible strength and flashed a humorless smile, extending one of her four fangs and pressing its razor-sharp point into her beautiful bottom lip. She made her proposal again.

I recoiled and tried to push her off balance so I could get away, but I ended up knocking a porcelain vase off a pedestal display in my struggle. The shattering sound of pottery echoed in the hallway, sure to draw people to us. She hissed and bashed my head into the wall.

By midday the next day, my head injury and the broken mess in the hallway were completely forgotten, because my little brother Henry was sick. I wouldn't have thought it had anything to do with Rosaline if she didn't visit me in Henry's bedroom that night and repeat her offer. In my sick worry over Henry, the events of the night before had become a half-remembered dream. I'd imagined her savagery, surely. So I warily laughed her proposal off again. I don't remember anything else of that night.

Henry was worse the next day. He was pale, lethargic, and had no appetite. The doctor didn't know how to cure it. But it wasn't a wasting disease. He was being bled.

Rosaline came again that night while I paced by Henry's sickbed.

She made her offer. I refused, angry this time, but she kept pressing it. She said she would kill Henry and everyone else in the household if I refused again—and she seduced me—all in the same conversation. I'm not proud of it. I'm still horrified over it, but I bedded her again, this time on the floor of my baby brother's room while he lay dying.

Maybe I thought fucking her again would satisfy her and she'd leave. Maybe I just wanted to succumb to a few minutes of distraction. Maybe she raped me through coercion. Maybe. Maybe. Maybe. Most certainly *she* was the one in control the entire time. It was the first mindfuck that I chose to bury, and it wouldn't be the last.

Only when she was hovering over Henry's nearly lifeless body, fangs extended in full view, did I finally say yes.

The details of my change are gone. Like losing my virginity, it was unceremonious, dark, and brief. I woke to a world that was too bright, too loud, and full of smoke.

I shot to my feet just as the upper frame of Henry's bed collapsed. I dove for him, but it was too late. His throat had been slashed from ear to ear, but he hadn't had much blood left to bleed. I reeled back and stumbled out of his room, into Michael's, then the twins' separate rooms, then my parents' suite. Dead. All dead, just like Henry. My childhood home, and all its inhabitants, was burning to the ground.

All I'd ever wanted was for my brothers to stay kids forever—to make the wonders of childhood last as long as possible—and for the twins to reach contentment, but I'd never gotten to see any of that.

By the time I shook myself from these thoughts of the past, the retreating family was long gone from the beach. I let out a mostly silent groan and chucked a handful of sand at the retreating surf before plopping my ass down onto the sand. I brushed sand from my knees and hands and ran them through my hair again. When I lowered my hands, something else caught my eye, to the right this time.

A group of late teens was standing around an LED campfire. They were loud and obviously drunk. A pair had sprinted toward the surf, while a few others egged them on and snapped photos that wouldn't turn out in the darkness. The ones remaining by the fake fire were dancing to some terrible music playing softly—thankfully—from their speaker.

They were all paired off, except one. A pretty teenage girl in braids and a purple sundress was looking my way. When I glanced at her, she swayed and moved her hips suggestively. She beckoned for me to join them.

I was surprised she could see me at all. My eyes are better than a human's eyes, so with the full moon, it appeared only dusk to me, but there was no way she could see my face in this near-midnight darkness. At best, she could see a dark figure in a dark jacket with long hair who'd just thrown a handful of sand into the wind in a tantrum.

What, does she think I'm some broody bad boy having an emo moment? I scoffed. She wasn't wrong to think that, but I wasn't in the mood anymore to flirt, especially not in a crowd of people. I offered her a disinterested smirk but remembered she couldn't see the details of my face and instead shook my head.

Her lips turned downward into an exaggerated pout, and she tossed a braid over her shoulder. She danced a little harder, as if to show me what I was missing. I snorted at her confidence and realized I was biting my lip at the display.

FALLEN WOES

You know what, fuck it. I got to my feet and faced her and her friends. If I was going to be caged again in Rosaline's thrall, I should go down fucking, shouldn't I? She was pretty and confident, and maybe—just maybe—for her, The Pause wouldn't be surprised or flattered, but *feral*.

CHAPTER 3

I strode down from the sand dune—only a Lapsus could manage to do that with any semblance of grace—toward the group by the silly fake fire. The beckoning girl backed away from her friend group, still hinting for me to follow her, and turned and ran toward the pier.

Running in sand is difficult, even for Lapsi, but I managed. If I were feeling cruel, I'd shift directly to the pier and catch her while she thought I was behind her. But I was *never* in that kind of mood anymore. Instead, I trailed after her, steadily shortening the distance between us, until we were beneath the pier, near the water. I caught her by the waist and pulled her, laughing, to me.

"Caught you," I murmured as her hips met mine. Her heart was racing from the exertion, reminding me that my meal had been interrupted—and bringing Rosaline's face to my mind again. *Ugh.*

"I didn't expect you to be my age," she said in a gasp, running her hand through my hair and tugging on it.

The usual annoyance at the comment about my age didn't surface. Instead, it gave *me* a Pause.

"What, you just casually flag down strangers on the beach, hoping for a *daddy*?" The incredulous question was out of my mouth before I could stop myself. Despite my bafflement, my hands gripped her hips, lifting her dress higher up her legs. "I could be a serial killer, you know."

"Maybe, but my gut tells me they don't make serial killers as pretty as you." She shrugged and slipped her arms around my waist, beneath my jacket.

Oh, you'd be fucking surprised, I thought darkly. She probably saw me as an emo boy her age that she hoped she could demean with her prowess. I was willing to let her underestimate me, then shock her with exactly how good a lay I am. But it turned out she was underestimating me in a different way. Little did she know that I *was* a dangerous fucking killer.

"Please, pretty boy, kiss me and make me moan so loud my friends all hear me."

I huffed in shocked amusement and resisted the urge to look around for a hidden camera. I cupped her jaw with one hand and pressed my lips roughly to hers. She melted into me while I deepened the kiss and parted her lips. My hand moved from her jaw and clasped her neck, squeezing the sides with the gentle threat that I could do far worse.

This girl was either a feral freak in the sheets or she was absolutely dumb. Her lack of self-preservation was going to get her killed. I could have been a drunk, a thug, or a pedo and rapist. At best, she could get stuck with herpes for the rest of her life, at worst she'd end up in a plastic drum. If I was even a fraction of my former self, I would teach her why she shouldn't be so flippant with strange men, and she would die terrified.

But I shrugged out of my jacket and put it around her bare shoulders to protect her back from the bird shit and barnacles on the pier's support beams. I gripped her throat again but moved and cupped her breasts, nuzzling my lips into the bend in her neck. Her still-rapid pulse made my teeth throb. I nibbled playfully on her collarbone, and she groaned in pleasure, her hands buried in my hair.

I dropped slowly to my knees and ran my hands up her thighs and under her dress. My fingers hooked around the sides of her bikini bottoms, still wet and sandy from swimming in the surf, and gently pulled them down and over her ankles. Kissing a trail up her inner thigh, I lifted her leg over my shoulder, giving me perfect access to the pulsing artery where her inner thigh met her hip. While my fingers stroked her sensitive folds, I locked my lips over her artery and my fangs tore into the tender flesh.

She shuddered and moaned against me, not realizing that while I was teasing her clit, I was also devouring her lifeblood which, thanks to Lapsi mesmerism, was almost as pleasurable as an orgasm. I drank only a few mouthfuls and moved my mouth to her tender core, prodding her entrance with my tongue and swirling it around her clit. She keened and bucked her hips forward, but before she reached her orgasm, she grabbed a handful of my hair and pulled me away.

"I want you to fuck me hard," she said breathlessly when I was back on my feet and pressed against her.

She reached for the front of my jeans, but I grabbed her throat again, more forcefully. While her hands clasped mine in surprise, I used my free hand to undo my fly and pull my dick out. Releasing her neck, I grabbed her hips and lifted her against the pillar until she was poised just over my dick.

Maybe this is a prank and she isn't actually coming onto strangers in the dark, I told myself while I thought again about how stupid she was to be so trusting. Maybe her friends were in on it and were about to jump out of the shadows, their phones out, filming us. If that were the case, I'd just disappear, and this crazy girl would miss out on a great time.

I hesitated for a beat, to see if anyone would jump out, but when no one did, I pulled her down onto me and thrust upward in the same motion, giving myself over to the promise of a feral fuck.

With a keening whimper, she gripped my hips with her thighs as her walls stretched around me. She was tight and wet, and even though her entrance was gritty with sand, she felt *so good*.

"Yes, you're a hot young thing, aren't you?" I murmured into her neck, below her ear, thrusting on every other word. "You like being *fucked* by *strangers*?"

Before she could answer with words, I captured her lips in a rough, savage kiss, nibbling on her bottom lip while she tangled her hands in my hair. I thrust deeper into her, and she moaned against my lips before breaking the kiss.

"Oh, *fuck*." She threw her head back as her back arched.

I extricated her hands from my hair before she could pull any of it out and pressed her wrists into the pillar above her head, shifting to better support her without my arms.

"Oh, yes, yes, *yes*," I practically whimpered as the new angle changed the intensity of sensations spreading outward from my pelvis.

Fuck, I'm not going to last like this. If I wasn't careful, I was going to break my one rule and come before *she* did. I slowed my pace and tried to focus on the gritty wet-sandpaper discomfort of her sand-coated pussy, but she rolled her hips suddenly, as if sensing my hesitation, and I groaned. *Damn it.* I was going to come soon.

I released her wrists and again cupped the back of her neck, bringing her forward. With one more grunt that was supposed to be the word "fuck," I locked my lips on her throat and tore into her artery with my fangs.

Like before, I switched her pain receptors to pleasure with the slightest mesmerism, and she melted into me, floating on a cloud of bliss while I drank deep from her. The blood worked to fuel my stamina as well as offer my brain something else to focus on to slow my orgasm's approach. It was still too much of a race, one I was determined *she* win. I was a gentleman, after all.

I curved the fingers of my free hand around her soft, sandy mound and, on my next thrust, pressed two fingers deftly to her clit. She tensed, and a slow spasm rolled through her spine.

There we go, crazy girl, come for me, I murmured into her mind, knowing she was close. I swirled my tongue around the wound in her throat to heal it without a mark and pulled my face from her throat so I could watch her come.

She was just on the cusp, her eyes widening and starting to roll back, and I was right behind her on the wave, opening my mouth to cry out in ecstasy, when the cool metal of a blade pressed against my throat from behind.

Mid-thrust, and teetering on the cliff of orgasm, I froze and, without thinking, forced the girl's mind into a daze so she didn't panic.

"Release her, or the last thing you're going to feel is your dick going limp inside of her," a woman's voice hissed behind me.

The distinct scent of herbs and smoke reached my nostrils and pierced the pre-orgasm fog in my brain. *Witch.* And not just a witch: a huntress. They were rare these days but not unheard of.

"Joke's on you, then. This little knife-action just made me even *harder*," I quipped, my open mouth snapping shut into a crazed grin. "And she was just about to come, so if you don't mind."

Without moving against the knife, I worked my fingers against the girl's clit with just the right pressure to tease that orgasm out of her. As the girl's eyes rolled back in pleasure, I released her mind from its daze so she could feel every last sensation.

My satisfaction lasted only a second because the witch's grip shifted, and the sharp blade nicked my throat just enough to bleed.

"I said release her," she snapped, unamused.

With a growl of frustration, I withdrew my hand and pulled out of the girl. The witch lowered her knife from my throat so I could step back and set her back on her feet, but instead, I mesmerred the girl to sleep and dropped her to the ground like a ragdoll.

My back still to the witch, I took my time tucking my hard—still very sensitive—cock back into my pants and redoing the fly.

"That was fucking rude, *witch*," I grumbled as I turned around slowly, holding my hands up, palms out.

She was about thirty, and pretty, but in a deadly, frustrating way. Her dark hair was piled into a messy bun on top of her head, and her black sweatshirt was only partly zipped over her tactical vest and arsenal of knives.

"Don't you guys ever take a night off?" I teased her, lazily adjusting my still-hard dick in my jeans.

"If you all could take a night off from being assholes, maybe we would," she snapped back.

"Hey now, I was hardly being an asshole," I said, holding my hands up again. True, I'd *contemplated* being an asshole, but she didn't need to know that. "She was enjoying herself, wasn't she?"

"She's just a kid," she argued, narrowing her eyes in disgust.

"Yeah? And so am I," I purred easily. I loathed the look she gave me, like one would look at a child molester. I didn't want to tease her anymore; I wanted to snarl at her. "I suppose I should only make love to ninety-year-olds, then? Even then, I would be cradle robbing—"

She lunged, the silver knife arcing in a practiced killing stroke. I knocked the knife from her hand, and grabbed her wrist, twisting her arm painfully behind her back. She put up an arm to brace herself against the pillar, but it ended up pinned between her chest and the barnacle-encrusted wood.

I pressed myself against her, focusing most of my weight into my hips. I was still hard from being interrupted, and I pressed my whole length against her inner thigh so she couldn't help but notice it.

"I have no real beef with witches, but I'm not opposed to killing one that pisses me off." I spat in her ear as she struggled to wriggle free, but she couldn't.

Witches used to primarily be Lapsi hunters, though most of the bad blood got washed away before my time as a Lapsus. But, much as asshole Lapsi were still out there, some witches still hunted them down.

"Get off me, you fucking pig," she snapped.

She tried again to force her way out of my hold, but I pressed further against her, knowing it would make it harder for her to breathe.

"I wasn't going to kill her, by the way," I said, lowering my voice.

"Yeah right. I know who you are—"

"You don't," I hissed, still speaking low. "You really don't."

I pressed against her for another tense moment and disappeared.

CHAPTER 4

I was still in a justifiably *foul* mood the following day.

First I had my past dug up again when Rosaline made an appearance. I hate having to look at my past, and being flayed open by grief again.

Then, the run-in with the fucking huntress and the hatred in her eyes. Like I was a monster. While I *have* been one before, I wasn't one right then. I was a worm. A neutral worm.

I hated that the witch reminded me of the cruel truth that while I strove for neutral, really I was always one breath away from unraveling completely into the monster I was made into.

Needing to blow off steam, I shifted to one of my favorite skateparks right on the beach in Southern California. It was only a few miles from the beach where I'd encountered the huntress, but I wasn't about to let a measly witch scare me away from my favorite haunts. Besides, I also hoped that *not* killing her had earned me *some* grace.

I've been skateboarding since the early nineties, when clothes were baggy and Vans were clunky, and if you didn't skateboard with a beanie, even in one hundred degree heat, you weren't considered edgy enough.

FALLEN WOES

I'm a creature of extraordinary grace, dexterity, and reflexes, but the first several months of skateboarding were a struggle. After years, though, there wasn't much I couldn't do. I went up against Tony Hawk in several events—though people recognize me only *slightly* less than they recognize him today. I only beat Tony in a competition once, not that I couldn't beat him every time though. But I avoided fame and recognition as much as possible. Much as I wanted to be known and admired for something other than my *face*, I couldn't.

I was good though. I was able to take risks that others weren't, and taking risks made me feel alive. I'm not the dark, brooding type. Yes, I like the color black—sue me. But mostly I seek amusement and good times. Either through pleasure or through thrills.

I was in America for the first World Columbian Exposition in 1893, and I was the first to ride the Ferris wheel prototype. Which, as far as thrills, is *nothing* now, but trust me, in 1893, it was *something* great. The most extreme thing I've tried is HALO parachuting, and while it was a beyond-thrilling experience, my one true thrill-love is rollercoasters. The higher the drops and the faster the turns, the better.

But skateboarding was both the simplest thrill and one of the most challenging. Rocketing down a halfpipe or into a bowl brought the same feeling as a rollercoaster—if briefer—but you're closer to the ground, exposed to the world, and at the mercy of your own reflexes. And when pulling tricks—especially when you're upside down, with the skateboard *hovering* above you—time seems to *freeze*—it's exhilarating.

The Venice Beach Skatepark was a beautiful oasis of smooth gray cement surrounded by golden sand. It has several bowls, kickers, funboxes, and Nessies. And a large circular seating area to the side with a railing that, if you were good enough—and if no one was foolishly sitting there—you can grind all the way around.

I started off on the far side of the park, coasting lazily over the rectangular ramp into a small little hop. Using the momentum down the ramp to gain speed, I paddled myself forward with power that no human has. I closed my eyes for as long as I dared, enjoying the feeling of the wind through my hair and ears, not unlike a dog with his head out the window.

At this time of day on a Thursday, most skater bros were in school, so the park wasn't busy and, thankfully, no one was in the farthest bowl.

I placed my skateboard on the coping at the edge of the bowl and kept my weight on the back edge until I was ready to drop. Leaning forward, I shot down the curved cement into the bowl. I crouched low on the flattest part and shot up the other side, grabbing several feet of air and turning to rocket back down the ramp again.

I kept at this for a while, pulling more and more tricks every time I reached the lip. It was helping to blow off steam, and it helped to keep my mind focused on something other than Rosaline.

But when I was in the middle of a jump, Rosaline's face popped unceremoniously into my brain, breaking my concentration. My board didn't land correctly on the coping, and I crashed down into the bowl. My ankle hit first and folded impossibly under me. When I came to a rolling stop, my ankle was bent and facing three-quarters the wrong way. Jagged, fragmented bones stuck out of the broken flesh, puncturing a hole in my jeans and pointing into the air.

I yelled out in pain before I could clamp my mouth shut against it. I clenched my fists and struck them against the cement beneath me as the bone painfully set itself, pushing back into place, and the broken skin knitted back together. Once it was healed, I shot to my feet and stomped over to my board, which had skittered away.

I'd come here to distract myself, but she'd crept in anyway. And, even without her being here, she'd wrecked me. I brought my board down hard on the cement wall of the bowl again and again, yelling with each strike.

When I calmed, at least ten people stood at ground level, watching me with various levels of concern. Understandable—I'd bailed out horrifically and then thrown a violent tantrum. I gathered a substantial amount of power and thrust into the surface of their minds, making them ignore me. It took a lot to alter so many minds at once, but thanks to the girl on the beach, I was plenty fed.

I put the board back on the ground and peddled forward with Lapsi-strength, aiming the board at the narrowest transition of the bowl. As I approached it, a pair of legs dangled over the lip, right in my path.

I bailed for the second time in five minutes, but with less violence and injury this time. I rolled to a stop at the bottom of the ramp and sat up, fuming at the laughter above me.

"Graceful, Mason. Very graceful," Malcolm mocked in his Scottish drawl, still laughing.

"Fuck you, Malcolm." I got to my feet and retrieved my board again.

And I had fucked him. On many occasions. But I wasn't in a hurry to do it again.

"That's no way to speak to a friend," he chided. He held a hand down to me.

I ignored him and shifted out of the bowl, reappearing feet from him. He pulled up his legs and stood. He had been changed at an older age than me: somewhere in his late thirties. He was half a foot taller than me, with broad shoulders and muscular arms. He had russet-colored hair that grayed at his temples, currently pulled back into a bun at the top of his head, and a beard that I *envied* more than I ever wanted to admit.

"What are you doing here?" I demanded. He was not exactly a welcome sight. I'd last seen him three years ago, when I deserted the biker gang.

"Can't a guy just look in on an old friend?" Malcolm said with a jovial shrug.

"Not if he doesn't want you to." I turned away from him.

"There was some chatter about a woman found outside of one of *yer* haunts last night," Malcolm said behind me. His tone was casual, but I could sense the underlying reproach there.

"That so?" I asked, unconcerned. I wanted to forget everything about last night, except for the sex. The sex had been good.

"Yeah, a woman was taken to the hospital, missing plenty of blood, with no explanation as to...how she lost it."

Shit, I thought, closing my eyes. I was glad my back was turned from him so he couldn't see my reaction.

You either take the amount that a blood drive takes, *maybe* a little more, or you kill them and dispose of the body. Unexplainable mysteries attract far more attention than outright murders. This was more than Lapsi etiquette; it was survival 101.

"I got interrupted mid-kill last night by a huntress," I admitted as I turned and faced him. I was half-lying, blending the two experiences from last night into one. Even if I hadn't been intending to kill either woman, I wasn't going to admit that to Malcolm.

"Well, considering ye're still alive, then ye must have killed the huntress," he said, crossing his arms and shrugging dismissively. "In which case, ye should have gone back and taken care of the prey. No excuse."

I set my jaw. If what he said about the woman I fed on was true, he was right to berate me. But I had more control than he gave me credit for.

"Look, ye left us, that's fine," he said, holding up his hands. "And ye don't want to see me, despite how *close* we've been." My eyes narrowed at the reminder, but Malcolm raised his hands higher in innocence. "That's *also* fine. I recognize ye have haunts that ye frequent, and we're all able to respect that and give ye a wide berth...as long as ye cover yer ass, Mason. Don't be sloppy, and *don't* leave them drained enough to put them in a hospital. I don't like cleaning up after someone else."

I narrowed my eyes, out of patience. I'd barely taken any blood from that woman before I'd been interrupted. She hadn't been taken to the hospital unless someone else fed on my sloppy seconds.

"Cut the crap, Malcolm," I snapped, crossing my arms in front of my chest. "You're not here to police me about my leftovers. Why are you really here?"

A smirk spread over his face, but he didn't answer.

And how had Malcolm found me? He couldn't track me. He knew I skateboarded, but it was a hell of a guess that I would be at Venice Beach out of all the skateparks in the country.

Only one Lapsus could pinpoint me.

"How did you even find me?" I demanded.

"Rosaline told me where to find ye," he admitted with a shrug, confirming what I was afraid of.

God. Damn. It.

I really should look into getting some warding, I thought, not for the first time. And why didn't I already have wards? Probably because I was a nihilist masochist, and resistance was futile.

I didn't like that Rosaline was keeping these tabs on me, but even more concerning than her sending a stranger to corner me was her sending someone I *knew.*

"Well, you can tell her, as politely as you deem fit, to go fuck herself," I said, keeping my face as impassive as I could.

At first, Malcolm looked mildly surprised, but then his face broke into an amused smirk. He clicked his tongue at me reproachfully.

"So *rude*, Mason," he reprimanded playfully. "What did she do to ye to deserve such scorn?"

Murdered my entire family, for starters, I thought but didn't say.

"Just pass on my message, all right?" I said, taking a step back from him and turning to leave. "Good to see you again by the way."

"I'm not a messenger boy, Mason," he said. The thinly veiled threat in his tone made me pause.

"Yeah? Then what are you?" I challenged, turning back to him. "I'm not in the mood for threats or games. What do you want?"

"Rosaline wants to see ye."

"I thought you weren't a messenger boy," I jabbed viciously.

"I'm not *yer* messenger boy." His expression twisted into a smirk, like he was uncovering a juicy secret. "What is Rosaline to ye, Mason?"

"She made me." I set my jaw and held my head as high as I could. I had nothing to hide but nothing to be proud of either.

Malcolm let out a low whistle.

"No shit?" His grin widened and he looked at me with a new appreciation. "I knew I liked ye for a reason."

"You too?" I asked, trying not to sound exasperated.

Malcolm's grin didn't waver as he nodded. "Looks like Rosaline is responsible for both of our immortal arses," he agreed with a whistle, still looking amused. I'd admitted it as if it was nothing to be proud of. But Malcolm looked fucking proud.

"Yeah? And did she also murder your whole family after she changed you?" I asked, though I normally wouldn't divulge this to someone who irked me as much as Malcolm did.

"No," he said shaking his head. He looked smug. "She let me do the honors myself."

I managed to keep all the surprise and horror from my face, but every fiber of my being wanted to recoil. He'd murdered his own family and, judging by his age when he was changed, that probably included a wife and children. I'd known he was fucked up, and I'd thought for a while that we were the same *kind* of fucked up. But really we were very different.

I was a spiteful fuck as a response to what had been done to me. Malcolm had been a spiteful fuck to start.

"Great for you," I said with a shrug, swallowing my horror with some difficulty. "She didn't give me that privilege, unfortunately. She must like you better."

"I certainly hope so," he agreed, smirking again. He rocked back on his heels slightly. "Ye ever gone with her for a while?"

"Yeah," I admitted placidly, though my skin was crawling. "A time or two. You?"

"A few times in the past. And currently," he admitted, adopting my placid expression, but then he grinned again in territorial amusement.

"Only until you get tired of her, right?" I said, remembering my times with her. They were so...so bloody, and lustful, and menacing. She'd been the Blood Countess, after all. And Jack the Ripper.

"No, actually. She's the one that grows tired of me," he admitted, his grin spreading even farther with his meaning.

One of the biggest caveats to what makes us Lapsi *was*—past tense—the fact that we were predestined to be *lonely*. We weren't to belong with humans or with our own kind. Lapsi could only tolerate each other for a period of a few years before the physically irritating, chafing pain became too much and drove them apart. A few years back, a young Lapsus named Danielle somehow broke that part of the curse. So now there was nothing but *habit* stopping Lapsi from forming a true community.

But it hadn't been the Lapsi curse that forced me away from Rosaline—*hell*, it was half a century before I even heard of the painful caveat of the curse. Even though I couldn't resist her, and I was weak-willed around her, I *hated* her. Eventually the horror and revulsion finally drove me mad enough to free myself from her.

And here Malcolm was implying that it was *Rosaline* who eventually grew tired of *him*. Probably not by horror and revulsion, but some emotion strong enough to make her push him away. I was now more perturbed than ever by Malcolm. And I'd fucked him. So many times I'd fucked him.

"And she wants to see me." I said it like a statement, not a question.

"Yes, and at first I thought I would be jealous," he said, frowning as he gave me a level look. But his face changed and his head tilted. The same head-tilt that Rosaline did. *God damn*, how had I never made the connection before? "But I kind of enjoy the idea of the *three* of us. Together. Can ye imagine us sharing her?" He tilted his head the other way. "Or, rather, I think with her in the picture, ye would finally let *me* top."

My dominant footing faltered at the blatant threat. Without a doubt, up against both of them together, I wouldn't be the dominant one. It was bad enough being submissive to Rosaline, but the idea of subbing to Malcolm made me want to step back.

I managed to keep my unamused, dry expression fixed in place, but my hands clenched into tight fists at his threat.

"Yeah, try it and I'll fucking kill you," I warned him, my voice steady, even if *I* wasn't steady anymore. My dominant footing was wavering because I knew if Rosaline demanded it, I wouldn't have a say in Malcolm fucking me. She'd set men on me countless times before. Just one of many ways she fucked me up and over.

"Yeah, I'm dying to see if that tight little ass performs as well as that mouth does," Malcolm mused, stepping closer.

"It doesn't perform as well as my dick, I assure you," I said, standing my ground, though I was ready to beat him with my skateboard. "And you *know* my dick performs well."

"Easy, easy, Mason," Malcolm said, laughing jovially suddenly. He settled back into his heels and held his hands up. "Rosaline's not hoping to seduce ye—most likely. She's just gathering all her favorites around her for something big."

He wanted me to lean in, intrigued, or at least to question him, but I wasn't inclined. No doubt what Rosaline had in mind was something grotesque. *Blood Countess*, remember? And possibly at least *a hand* in Jack the Ripper.

I wanted no part in whatever she was planning or what she thought was coming.

"And apparently, Mason, ye're a favorite. And now I can see why," he said, looking at me appraisingly.

Suddenly, absurdly, it struck me how wild this conversation and its location was. He was a thirty-something-year-old burly Scottish specimen, and I, in all appearance, was an eighteen-year-old angel-faced kid at a skatepark on a beach, of all places. But for Lapsi, this was just a Thursday.

"And am I allowed to refuse?" I said at last, keeping my voice as even as I could, though I was about to either crack up laughing or retch in revulsion.

Malcolm looked surprised again, like he'd never considered that I'd slap her hand away. But a smirk stretched his lips to one side.

"Sure, ye can refuse. *That's* a message I can pass to her." He said it with a measure of appraisal and respect in his voice at my refusal to submit.

"You tell her that, then. Because I want *nothing* to do with whatever this is," I told him truthfully.

"If I didn't know ye better, I'd think ye were afraid, Mason," he said coolly.

"Not afraid." I'd never, *ever* admit if I was truly afraid. I leaned forward, to better emphasize my next words. "I *hate* her. I really do, Malcolm. And you can tell her that. Or, rather, you can tell her that she should come herself so I can tell her to her face that I *hate* her."

I took a step back, refusing to show, or even admit, that I was riled—possibly even scared.

The last thing I wanted was for Rosaline to drop in on me *ever* again. If I fell to her prowess again, I might not come back from it.

I needed to hire a witch who knew wards. I was done unconsciously leaving my back door unlocked. I wanted to protect what was left of my soul from Rosaline. And now Malcolm.

CHAPTER 5

Popular fiction likes to paint witches as uncommon, keeping to the shadows in small, tight-knit covens. It's really the opposite. They're everywhere, woven into every part of mortal society: economy, healthcare, education, philanthropy, etc. Yet they also have their own secondary society that operates similarly, but only among witches.

So it wasn't difficult for me to find a witch, even though I'd actively avoided them for eons. It wasn't exactly like going into a McDonald's and requesting a "Happy Meal with extra happy," but if I wanted wards, or a witch who could point me to another witch that did wards, I *guessed* that my best bet would be a federal building in any city.

I was right.

I chose a federal administration building in Boston at random. Mainly, I chose the East Coast to get as far as possible from my exchange with Malcolm, without crossing an ocean. I barely made it halfway to the metal detectors before the head of security approached me. I tried to look as disarming and nonthreatening as possible, putting my most angelic expression over my already angelic face, as I politely asked where I could find a witch that specializes in the kind of ward I needed.

Still looking displeased to be near me—was I still *that* notorious?—he opened an app on his phone. His cursory search directed me to a young witch in the same city of Boston.

I went to her immediately and pleaded my case on her front porch before she let me in. I didn't tell her any gritty details; she wouldn't have helped me otherwise. I merely told her that I was being harassed by my sire and wanted something that would prevent her from dropping in on me unannounced.

The girl was pretty and voluptuous, with bleach-blond hair in a side-parted pixie cut. She was dressed simply in jeans, a T-shirt, and a sweater cardigan over it. When she pulled the cardigan tight around herself, her stomach protruded flaccidly over her jeans: the telltale, deflated stomach of having just given birth.

I don't think she liked me, and I don't blame her: I'm not everybody's taste, and I don't strive to be. This was a business transaction, and it didn't need to be any more than that. I don't think her husband liked me either, but he drew my eye far more than the woman did.

He was a gorgeous, slim specimen with dark skin and a nose that didn't quite fit his ethnicity. And the fact that he was holding his swaddled newborn in his arms as he stood protectively beside his wife stirred my insides pleasantly, almost toward arousal. Pregnancy and parenthood perplexed me because I'll never experience them. I'd held my infant brothers more than my parents had, but I'd never felt like a *father* to them—more like a co-conspirator. Yet somehow, witnessing it turned me on? *What the hell?*

For the charm I was purchasing, she pricked my palm with a plain, non-silver knife and collected a little of my blood. Rosaline had given me her blood when she changed me. Her blood mixed with mine as a kind of signature: part of her was always within me, much to my utter chagrin.

The witch mixed my blood with some powders, which I couldn't name if I wanted to. She took a wide silver ring with a tiger's eye focal and painted the mixture into every crease and fold of its intricate, filigree-laden band.

I didn't like *wearing* silver. Silver is the only thing that can kill us, aside from fire and beheading. Even touching it, though not painful, is a mild irritation. But silver held enchantments when other metals didn't, so silver was something I was going to have to cope with if I wanted protection.

After painting the ring with the blood mixture, she placed it on an antique brazier and let it sizzle and smolder until the mixture cooked off—or rather cooked *into* the metal and semi-precious stone focal.

As it cooked, we all sat in silence, aside from the newborn, who made typical infant cooing and gurgling noises. Aside from motherhood and parenting making me uncomfortable, so did the sounds of babies, but for different reasons. It reminded me of my brothers when they were at that age and I was caring for them, cooing along with them.

This innocent little newborn was stirring up painfully sentimental memories in my mind, but what could I do? Tell it to stop? I guess I could've made polite, casual conversation with the pair of adult witches to drown out the sounds.

But instead, I sat in the uncomfortable non-silence, wishing more than anything that I could be riding a rollercoaster.

When the ring was finished, I stuck it on my right middle finger, and despite the immediate discomfort of the silver against my flesh, I felt immediately safer, like I could take a deep breath again. I paid them handsomely for the service, though she tried to say that it was too much. I insisted. They had a child now, after all, and every little bit helped.

After I left them, I wasn't sure what I wanted to do with myself. If I went home, I might end up cutting my face up again, and if I didn't limit that activity to once a week, it'd be concerning.

It was evening in Boston, but three p.m. on the West Coast. These days, I felt most drawn to sunny Southern California. Perhaps because the almost unending sunny weather was so different from the dreariness of the English countryside of my childhood and smoggy London of my early Lapsi-hood.

I shifted back to California, but this time chose a small town at random, half an hour's drive from the coast. It had a skatepark, and I was still carrying my skateboard around with me, but I didn't go straight to it. I wandered for a bit through the town, while—I suppose because I felt safer knowing I wouldn't be ambushed by Rosaline—my mind traveled back over the painful centuries.

I'd fled from my burning house but recovered enough of my wits to know I needed to plan how to *not* look like a murderer come morning. I shifted somewhere at random in England—shifting came instinctually, but it was baffling at first, to put it mildly. I booked a room, only so I could bathe and steal a fresh set of clothes.

An hour later, I returned to my village and drew the doctor out of his bed, claiming my baby brother's health was even worse. It nearly killed me a second time to pretend like I thought the kid—that my family—was still alive, but I had to.

I rushed with the doctor back to my estate. As we approached it, I stared at my hands so he'd be the first to see the flames. When he cried out in his surprise, I put on the mournful show I'd prepared, but the only lie in my performance was my *surprise*.

By the time we pulled up, my home was a beat away from crashing down in a burst of sparks. I let the doctor restrain me from running into the burning bones of my home. My weakness was a farce, but the screams that came from me and the harrowing sobs that racked my chest were real.

I wasn't considered a murderer. The fire wholly consumed the bodies inside, leaving no way to tell that they'd been murdered *before* burning. The injustice of it all burns me to this day, but my reputation and inheritance remained intact.

Everything of my father's that hadn't been destroyed was now mine. Two days after my family perished, the affairs of the estate were settled. The following day, I was alerted that the painter had finished our family portrait—another knife to my heart. I paid the painter double what my father had promised, took the painting, and left the countryside behind—unfortunately with Rosaline attached to my back like a leech. Later, I went to London, where I developed the black-souled, debaucherous attitude, mystique, and pleasure-seeking personality that later inspired Oscar Wilde.

I was eighteen, and as the sole survivor and heir, I was considered an adult. But prior to the tragedy, I hadn't spent any time *preparing* for adulthood and responsibilities. I enjoyed teasing women, but not courting. I'd spent more time than I should have visiting the nursery rather than learning how to manage an estate.

As the oldest, I hadn't been a child the longest of my siblings. When Henry, the second youngest was born, I became adult-adjacent, seizing much of the responsibilities of rearing him and making his—and then Michael's—childhood last as long as possible. In a sick way, I got my wish: they'd never be adults.

Overnight, I became an adult with an estate, income I didn't work for, harrowing grief, and power beyond that of any human. But all I wanted—still, two hundred years later—was to be a *kid*. I sought pleasure and thrills because those things are outside of what was considered *acceptable* adult behavior. Thrills and distractions made me feel almost like a child again.

My brooding sentiments propelled my feet toward the high school in the town just as classes let out for the day. *How convenient*, I chided myself with a groan.

But I didn't shift away. Part of me wanted to torture myself with the sight of so many people who looked like me: on the cusp of adulthood but still kids.

Truly, in the twenty-first century, "cusp" of adulthood keeps getting pushed out further. Twenty-four is seen as the new cusp, and eighteen might as well be the new twelve. But the kids leaving that school didn't see it that way. To them, they were adults because they foolishly *want* so badly to be adults.

They want to be done with school and with their parents. They want to abandon their childhoods for their lofty hopes and dreams. And they won't realize until too late that they should have held on longer. They'll regret rocketing so quickly to that falsely promised freedom that they wanted so badly.

I envied their hopes and their bright, arrogant faces. But I also cruelly—almost altruistically—pitied them. Because those hopes and dreams are harder to attain than they think, and that promised freedom will just shackle them to a society that expects them to work, pay taxes, and contribute, when all they want to do is *play*.

I watched everyone pile out of the open campus, cross the street, get into their various parents' cars, or start their walk to their homes. The boys played grab-ass with the girls, books were playfully smacked from hands. So many almost-adults juggling backpacks, lunch bags, books, and instrument cases.

The rivers of students thinned and sounds of football practice echoed from the other side of the campus. Behind the building closest to me came an eruption of a dozen brass instruments in warm-up: marching band practice.

I'd never experienced anything these kids had, and I'd never really wanted to, but still, it was fascinating and I wanted to observe it a little more. I walked up the drive and onto the campus.

California campuses are constructed like mini college campuses, without the dorms. The buildings are spaced out, with wide outdoor hallways, but the whole campus can be traversed in less than five minutes.

I walked along one row of lockers, sending the locks rattling noisily as I brushed them with my fingers. I passed the quad where students would eat lunch, which still smelled of milk, Mountain Dew, Cheetos, and—bafflingly—ranch dressing. I took a seat on a bench across from a row of green lockers, resting my skateboard across my lap.

With my clean, beardless face, I looked like I belonged here. I wore black jeans with shredded knees from my multiple tumbles at the skatepark and a simple black T-shirt. The only thing that suggested I didn't belong here was the complete lack of acne.

Yet I could pretend for just a moment that one of those lockers I was staring at was mine and that I was someone looking forward to college or—more likely—someone hoping there was a party this weekend. Someone whose parents were still alive but were *so annoying*, and someone who dreamed about an apartment in New York City or a fraternity that would welcome me next year. It was kind of a nice fantasy.

But I was just feeling sorry for myself. I was a powerful being, after all, not a fragile human child. There was pleasure and fun to be had all over the planet, so I tucked my dark, sad thoughts away and stood from the bench, ready to find some mischief.

I walked back the way I came, taking my time and letting my board dangle from my hand. I turned a corner around

FALLEN WOES

a row of lockers and a sudden exclamation followed by the clap of a textbook hitting the smooth cement ground startled me from my thoughts.

CHAPTER 6

"**S**hit!" she said in a hiss as the book hit the ground.

Following the book was a small metallic *clink* against pavement and then the distinct scent of blood reached my nostrils.

Her long honey-colored hair fell forward over her shoulder like a curtain as the girl knelt to retrieve her things from the ground. She grabbed her book and nestled it into the crook of her left arm and grabbed something else from the ground: a razor blade. A small trail of blood was dripping from her thumb down to her wrist.

I almost started to take a step toward her, but before I could move, another person approached her. She shoved her book into the bag on her shoulder and shot to her feet, her face fierce. But she pressed herself back against the lockers, away from the newcomer.

"Awe, I'm sorry. Have I interrupted another failed attempt?" He was tall and buff—but since I could still hear practice happening across campus, I assumed he wasn't a football player. He wore expensive high-tops and clean, stylish clothes. His light brown hair swirled around his ears and was gelled to tame its waviness.

"Clever joke, and original, too," the girl said, her voice dripping with sarcasm and disgust. She shoved the razor blade into the piece of paper in her hand and carefully curled her fist over it. "You realize this is clear evidence of bullying and bringing a *weapon* to school. I can get you expelled for this."

"Yeah, if you can prove it. Which you can't," he said with a confident smirk. He pulled the balled paper from her hand and shoved it into his jacket pocket.

Weirdly, my stomach was roiling with anger, watching this.

"I thought I was doing you a favor. I just thought you needed a little encouragement. And means."

"You're an idiot," she protested, her hands curling at her sides.

"I do love it when you're mean," he cooed derisively, his face changing from mocking to interested.

I knew *that* look well, but I did it better.

He stepped forward, crowding her and leaning an arm against the lockers, above her head. He took her hand in his and brought it to caress his crotch.

My feet were in motion, but she reacted quicker. She jerked her hand from his and slapped him across his cheek. He stepped back, startled but laughing. She stormed away blindly and gracelessly collided with me. The skateboard dropped from my hand with a loud clatter as I caught her elbows to stabilize her. She fixed me with the briefest of glares and resumed her retreat.

Now without a target, the jock closed the distance between us and stared down at me. His expression went through all the confused, straight cis-boy emotions at the sight of my attractive face, landing—as the fragile ones often did when they suddenly question their sexuality—on aggression.

Recovering from his *Pause*, his eyes moved to take in the rest of me: my stocky height, wide shoulders, and slim waist. His expression changed to mocking as he eyed my plain clothes: the holes in both of my knees, and my tattered skate shoes. Skateboarding was rough on shoes; it had nothing to do with being poor.

"What the fuck are you looking at, queer?" he snapped at me.

The homophobic slur barely phased me, but I'd killed men twice this guy's size for far less. He was just lucky I wasn't in the mood to kill a loathsome kid. And the exchange with the girl had me distracted.

I gave him the silent command to *leave*, and he retreated wordlessly, shaking his head in confusion over *why* he'd backed down from a twink half his size.

I retrieved my skateboard and walked up to the girl's locker. It was still wide open, and her padlock rested just inside, in front of her stack of books. On a notebook that was sticking out, I read her name scrawled on the cover: Jaimie. Not wanting to pry any further, I locked up her locker and turned away.

But I didn't move immediately. Instead, my eyes drifted to the side, in the direction she'd fled. Something about that whole exchange irked me and kept me rooted to the spot, intrigued. I couldn't figure out what, but it had something to do with *her*.

I followed the scent of her blood in the air—it was minute but still detectable—until it disappeared inside a classroom. I could see her inside, but the door was locked and looked like it required a keycard. I shifted inside, reappearing in the center of the wide classroom, still a decent distance from her.

She stood at a sink across the room, her back to me, washing the cut on her thumb. The classroom was wide, with retractable partitions that could divide it into two spaces. Easels were set up on one side of the room and potters' wheels on the other. The counters and sinks along the wall were spattered with decades of paint and pottery glaze drippings.

From my spot across the room, I silently watched her, taking in the details I hadn't had a chance to earlier. She wore light-washed jeans that were tattered at the hems and a dusty rose-colored cardigan with suede patches at the elbows. The sweater also looked worn and dingy—like it was several years old. Her long light brown hair was loosely wavy and pushed back behind her ears as she washed her hands.

She shut off the water and tore off a length of paper towel to dry her hands. I approached silently and was just placing my skateboard down on a chair as quietly as I could when she turned and saw me. She jumped backward against the sink in her surprise, letting out a string of swear words and fixing me with an annoyed and defensive glare.

"What are you doing here?" she demanded as she quickly pulled her cardigan sleeves down over her wrists and knuckles. "You can't be in here without a keycard."

"I—I have a keycard," I lied automatically, holding my hands up innocently. "I'm new and just wanted to scope the place out."

Her eyes narrowed even further in skeptical suspicion.

I realized now why I'd followed her, why I'd found her curious. She didn't *Pause*, like everyone else. Lesbians, asexuals, and even the aggressively straight men do some flavor of *The Pause*, but she hadn't. I could chalk it up to her being in an angry fluster when she bumped into me, but she hadn't this second time either.

It was refreshing. I hate *The Pause*. Yes, I use it to my advantage. Yes, I've grown used to it. But it's always a reminder that everything was a consequence of *my face*. If genetics hadn't made me beautiful, I would've lived out my life as a plain man, found a wife, had half a dozen children, and died. All well over a hundred years ago.

"And do you make a point of sneaking up on people while you're scoping places out?" she demanded.

"I just...wanted to make sure you're okay," I told her, putting my hands into the pockets of my jeans. "That was kind of intense."

"Yeah, I'm fine," she said with a shrug. She picked up a ceramic mug and filled it with water from the sink. The sleeves of her cardigan were heavily stained with paint, as were her knuckles and fingernails. "It's just, you know, your standard Thursday, right?"

I must have made a face of some sort because she hesitated as she passed by me.

"Not, you know, for you, probably," she said quickly. I didn't understand what she meant at first, but then I remembered I'd lied and said I was starting here soon. She was worried that I feared bullies. I almost laughed. "I just mean it's par for the course for *me*."

"Why?"

Her first impression hadn't painted her as a particularly easy target in my eyes. While she was dreadfully thin, I wouldn't have called her weak. Now that her face wasn't twisted into a defensive scowl, she was notably pretty. She had a honey-colored eyes that matched her hair, a small nose, and lips I'd taste in an instant. She seemed entirely normal, just...threadbare.

"Because I'm the loner girl that everyone's deemed a suicide risk." She shrugged, rolling her eyes. She stepped over to an easel and set her cup down on the table beside it.

"You'd think they'd want to help the suicide risk, not *encourage* her by planting blades in her locker," I pointed out, turning to keep watching her, perplexed by how calm she was over it.

"Yeah, you'd think," she huffed, letting out a bark of laughter. "But teenagers suck. And it's easier to be mean." She gave me a sharp look, as if deciding whether to tell me something. "I'm *not*, by the way."

At first I thought she meant she wasn't mean, because I already knew she wasn't a suicide risk. I'd seen enough in my time, and—while I couldn't admit it at that point—I'd been one for decades. This had just been one instance, with one guy, but she was implying *everyone* here saw her this way. It was baffling.

"But why do they think you are?" I asked, sauntering in a wide arc around her. I leaned back against the whiteboard of the classroom studio.

She looked at me skeptically. To her, I was a complete stranger who'd snuck up on her twice now. I held my hands up disarmingly and gave her an innocent grin.

"Hey, this is your big chance, right? To tell a fresh, doe-eyed face, someone with no predetermined assumptions."

She hesitated, staring at me like she'd heard those words before and been burned. I kept my face relatively neutral, adopting an expression that I hoped communicated *fuck those assholes, tell* me *what really happened.*

After a beat, her face mimicked my *fuck it* attitude. I could almost hear her telling herself *What do I have to lose? One more person not believing me? Big deal.*

Fuck, I like this girl, I thought, already respecting her far more than I was ready to admit. But I swallowed my amusement to ensure she wouldn't clam up.

"I was mauled by a stray dog when I was twelve," she explained after another moment. "My little brother got too close to it, and the dog lashed out. I got there just in time to shield him. The dog grabbed my wrist, but that was all it bit because I didn't fight it."

"You didn't fight it?" I repeated, confused.

"I'd seen it in a movie once." She shrugged. She was fiddling with the frayed edge of her sleeve cuff. "The idea was that you shouldn't retaliate violently and instead show it there's no reason for it to be afraid, and it backs down.

Anyway, it let go, but its teeth had torn through crucial veins. I was taken to the hospital."

"And somehow it spread that it was a suicide attempt," I said knowingly. "You're marked forever as a mental case."

She nodded and looked at me levelly, as if waiting for me to reject her story and return her trust with malice. She was so used to it apparently that she expected it. Like me and *The Pause.*

Admittedly, it *did* sound like a fantastical coverup, thought up by a twelve-year-old, yet I had no reason not to believe her. But whether I believed her or not wasn't exactly the point. She'd almost died, and the fact that her classmates *mocked* her for this was horrifying.

"And your brother's okay?" I asked after a moment, deciding to push past the topic. I had a soft spot for little siblings.

"Yeah, not a scratch on him—from that encounter, I mean. He's a kid, so scratches happen." She shrugged and started fiddling with a paint-crusted palette.

"And you adopted the dog, right?" I asked, assuming there was something happy to come out of the story.

"No. That's the most fucked up part. The apartment superintendent killed it," she said, clenching her jaw. "It was frightened. It was just doing what animals do. It released me and backed off, but they killed it anyway."

The compassion in her eyes for a stray dog that attacked her was surprising. And it seemed to cause her more pain than her cruel classmates who undermined her self-worth every day. I believed her without question.

"Thank you, by the way," she said after a few seconds, her voice softened. I'd dropped my eyes to the floor as I struggled to think of words, but I glanced up at her now, confused. "For not asking to see the scars. Everyone always does. And no one ever asks about the dog. No one cares."

"Yeah, well, they're all assholes, apparently," I said, rolling my eyes. The bitterness that she refused to feel roiled in my gut. "Fuck them."

She snorted and nodded in agreement. She sat down heavily in a chair in front of her easel, crossing her arms over her chest.

"Fortunately, I don't give a shit," she said shrugging. "I have bigger things to worry about than what people here think about me."

"Bigger things like what?" I asked, smirking. I liked her callous humor at what would be traumatizing for a normal teenage girl. I wanted her to keep talking.

She shut her mouth and pursed her lips ever so slightly. She tilted her head and regarded me with a similar suspicion as before, when I'd snuck up on her.

"That's some upper-level trust you're requesting there," she chided me. "Not first-meeting conversation. You still haven't even told me who you are."

Oh, right. I wasn't certain if I should make up a name or tell her my real one. I wasn't coming back here, and I wasn't going to see her again, so why should I worry about giving her my real name?

"My name's Grayson," I said before I'd fully planned on lying. The name just rolled off my tongue, resembling my real name enough that I'd respond to it. "Yours?"

"Jaimie," she said simply. She held my eyes for one more second and then dropped them to her hands, which were fiddling with her sleeve cuffs again.

"So, what bigger things do you have to worry about?" I asked again, genuinely curious.

She sighed and rolled her neck around to stretch it, while deciding whether to trust me with whatever she had to say. Finally, she stilled her head and looked up at me.

"Evil stepmother" was all she said, looking levelly at me.

"Okay, Cinderella," I said automatically after snorting slightly.

I meant it as an innocent tease, and while her smile stayed in place on her face, her eyes made it clear that she wasn't amused. I immediately wanted to suck the words back into my mouth.

"I'm sorry, I—I don't know why that was my first thought..." The words felt weird on my tongue, really weird. When was the last time I'd apologized to anyone? When was the last time I'd genuinely talked to a human more than just to seduce them? I couldn't remember. "Parents can be the *worst*. But I'm assuming you're a senior...you're almost free, right?"

She gave me an almost pitying look, which shut my mouth and made me want to smack myself in the forehead. I'd *just* been having this same thought minutes ago: that freedom wasn't quite what these near-adults thought it was. Yet here I was spewing that useless platitude I'd mocked earlier. Her sharp, reproachful look rattled me: this girl somehow already knew the harsh truth of the reality that waited after high school. What could possibly be going on in her life that she was already so resigned?

"All right, well, I'll...I'm going to go," I said after the awkward silence stretched for too long. It was past time for me to leave. This conversation was too weird and too jarring and even though I had more questions now than when I walked in here, it was stupid to stick around any longer.

I picked up my skateboard and backed away from her, toward the door of the studio. She turned to her paint brushes and pulled one out. She paused and glanced my way again.

"Wait," she said after me, and I obeyed, curious. She looked like she was waffling on what she wanted to ask. When she did speak, I could tell it wasn't what she'd really meant to ask. "You got an Instagram to follow or a phone number or something?"

I had neither, actually. I didn't carry a phone, and I didn't do any social media. I only had a TV and an old laptop. My one email address was purely tied to streaming services and my bank accounts.

"That's some upper-level trust you're requesting there," I said easily, teasing her with her words from earlier. "Not for a first meeting. See you tomorrow."

She nodded and turned away from me. I waited until I was outside the studio before shifting away.

CHAPTER 7

The interior of the club was cool, shiny, porcelain-white and lit with blue rope lights. It reminded me of the end of *The Abyss*, when—spoilers—the huge alien craft surfaces from the bottom of the ocean. The walls were white, the light was blue, yet everything seemed to be *dark* inside the club.

I spun and spun on the dance floor, loving the feeling of the base vibrating up through my feet. My mood had lifted significantly from the deep despondency of earlier that day. Enough that I could drink deeply of the night and dance as merrily as any of the other miserable fucks out tonight.

Most of the time I chose women for my flirt, fuck, and feed. Their beauty is more delicate, often they had more hair to tug on, and I loved the wetness between their legs and their ability to orgasm almost endlessly, like myself. But I'm hardly straight. I love bodies, any bodies. Any age, any race, and any gender—chosen or assigned at birth—it doesn't matter. All was beautiful, all was arousing, and in two centuries, there wasn't much I hadn't stuck my dick into.

Tonight, I craved a man. Probably from my attraction to that mixed-race witch earlier, holding his newborn baby, and probably because of the encounter with Malcolm. Then there was that weightlifting jock and his cruel prank, sticking a razor blade in Jaimie's locker. Everything from the day had left me agitated and wanting to put my dick in something a little *tighter* than a pussy.

After dancing for a song or two on my own, I sought out my target. The man I chose was a rugged, beefy man with darkly tanned Mediterranean skin, a killer chest, and a close-cropped beard. Beards send me absolutely feral. I envy them, I'm attracted to them, and I want to dominate them—purely because I'll never have one.

I approached the Mediterranean beauty on the dance floor and pressed myself against the front of him, putting my hands to his muscular chest and sliding them up to his neck. The man was startled at first, but after his *Pause* his hands were on my narrow hips.

Our hips moved in sync as we bounced back and forth to the beat of the trendy song. He ran his hands through my hair. I pulled on his neck to bring his face down to mine, and I kissed him, briefly, but roughly.

The song ended, and I pulled his face to mine again. I pressed myself against him, and he planted his hands on my ass, squeezing hard. I laughed into his mouth and reached behind me to extract his hands, then I pulled him from the dance floor.

I contemplated a quick fuck in the bathroom, but the man suggested his place, and that sounded too appealing to resist.

In the cab ride to his apartment, I leaned my head back against the seat and thought over the whole day so far. I'd spent so much of it brooding, and I hated to brood. Rosaline was back and wanted to *talk*. Which would undoubtedly end in hot, intense, manipulative sex and me trapped in her clutches again. I'd once again be powerless to fight her cruelty or say no to her demands. I'd been a good kid, on my way to being a good man, before Rosaline got her hooks in and twisted me.

My soul disintegrates in her hands, and when I crawl away, all I manage to do is stick the pieces of it back together with something flimsy, like hair gel. Sorry. I'm shitty at metaphors.

I've never been good at repairing my soul. Not alone. And I was always alone. The Lapsi curse no longer prevented companionship, yet I'd never wanted companionship outside of pleasurable, relatively anonymous sex.

The man leaned over to me in the back seat of the cab and kissed my lips, just to make sure I was still interested and to make sure the steam between us didn't settle too much before we made it to his place. I kissed him back and nipped at his bottom lip to show I was still very much into it, but then I pulled back, still smiling. When I sank back into my thoughts, it wasn't Rosaline's face I saw, but Jaimie's.

It'd been such a simple, brief conversation, yet it had made me feel alive, and she interested me in ways no one ever had. She had everyone wanting her to fail, everyone teasing her and encouraging her to kill herself. And why? Lapsi could be cruel, to each other and to humans. I'm not saying it's *good*, but it's more understandable. Lapsi are predators, territorial and beastly. But mortal humans? Aren't they supposed to be kind? Isn't that what their religions preach?

Yet Jaimie, in the face of all of that traumatic cruelty and the assault on her self-esteem...brushes it off? I wondered if it was all just a front. Whatever it was hiding, I felt this weird urge to help her, which confused me. I'd never felt like helping humans before, aside from pleasuring them and aside from making sure they were comfortably home again after feeding on them—when I wasn't Rosaline's puppet, that is.

What if I leaned into this desire to help her. What if I let that blossom and flower? Would helping her or simply being—what do you call it? A friend?— glue a piece of my soul back into place?

And she hadn't done *The Pause*. Twice, she didn't do it. Her gaze cut through me, like she wanted to find the *truth*. It perplexed me and it terrified me. If I let her look too close, would she cut deep and see right into the ugly that's within me? But if she tore me open, it wouldn't be like Rosaline, who reveled in cruelty. Maybe Jaimie'd tear me apart to find the good pieces and save them. Or was this just foolish whimsy?

The cab arrived at the man's place, thankfully drawing a curtain on my thoughts.

We were barely inside his apartment before I had his shirt unbuttoned. We both kicked off our shoes as soon as the door was closed.

"You're too young to be this eager," he said breathlessly as I pushed him over onto his bed.

"That's what *you* think," I teased him, as I straddled his lap. I pulled my shirt over my head and tossed it aside.

"Besides, aren't guys my age supposed to be full of life and *virulent energy*?"

"Sure, yeah, but mostly I'd expect curiosity," he said running his hands up my legs and looping his fingers through my beltloops. "Oh, the things I could show you..."

"Mmmm, and I, you," I purred, chuckling silently as I lowered myself on top of him until our chests met.

I brought my lips roughly to his and kissed him deep and hard, rocking my hips against his as he moaned into my mouth. He dragged his nails roughly down my back, not enough to hurt, but enough to send a rippling wave of tingles through my whole body and make my back tense and my shoulders tip skyward. I groaned and propped myself back up on all fours, sliding down his body until my feet found the floor again. I unfastened his jeans in one motion and, with a quick tug, pulled them off, boxers and all.

I knelt between his legs and lowered my mouth onto his hard, thick length. He sat straight up and tangled one hand in my hair while his other gripped a fistful of his bedspread.

"Oh, fuck yeah, baby," he crooned, rocking his hips and thrusting deeper into my throat. "Oh, you're so good at that..."

It helped that I didn't need to breathe so I could take him as deep in my throat and for as long as I desired. And don't get me started on what else I could do with my throat that a human could never. I kept going until I felt he was almost there and then moved off of it and rocked back on my heels into a crouch.

"That's not the only thing I'm good at, gorgeous," I murmured, standing up and leaning over him.

Breathlessly, he said, "Baby, if your ass can take me half as well as your throat can—"

I cut him off with a kiss. "I was thinking the other way around, *sweetie pie*," I purred when our lips parted, returning his pejorative pet name with an equally obnoxious one. I put my hands roughly to his bare hips, digging my fingers into his firm ass cheeks.

"Wait, what..." he said, his words coming sluggishly as he processed what I'd said.

I wrapped one hand around his dick while my other hand slid lower on his backside, edging toward his hole. His breath hitched in a half-gasp and his eyebrows knitted together in arousal-muddled confusion. His hands gripped my hips, threading again in my beltloops.

"Trust me, babe, you'll enjoy every second," I told him honestly, peering into his eyes and biting my bottom lip. "But I'm top."

The confusion left his face, but his brow furrowed even more. One side of his mouth quirked upward into a cocky smirk.

"Are you, now?" he said after a moment. His smirk became more of an arrogant grin, and he huffed out a light scoff.

My eyes narrowed in annoyance at his scoff, slight as it was. *Oh, now, don't be arrogant*, I silently chided him, forcing my face not to twist into a sneer and instead running my tongue over my bottom lip.

Truly, I could understand his bewilderment. He looked older than me, and he was bigger and more masculine, and I was, by all appearances, a *twink*. Under those circumstances,

I understood his assumption that he would top me. But I didn't appreciate the *arrogance* that'd creeped into his expression. *Serves me right for going for someone older.*

His eyes lost their mockery for a second as they tracked my tongue's movement across my lip. I put my hand to his throat, my thumb and forefinger finding the edges of his jaw and turning his head upward to look at me. His expression darkened in a mix of arousal and bemusement at my nerve.

"Yes, I am," I said, my thumb moving in a caressing circle on his jaw, just below his ear. "And you're a *switch*, aren't you?"

He swallowed back whatever thought had been forming on his lips and shut his mouth. His eyes returned to mine, and he gave a slow nod into my hand. I'd sensed switch energy from him in the club, which was why I'd chosen him.

"So why not let me give you the best fuck of your life," I mused. With my hand still on his throat, I pushed him back down onto the bed. I lifted his leg and kissed a line up his thigh toward his still very erect dick. He moaned, despite himself, and then louder again when I traced my tongue slowly up his shaft and swirled it around his tip.

I stood, again, and swept my hand down his raised thigh. I cupped his ass and prodded one finger just at his entrance. He gasped in barely contained pleasure while his back arched and he grabbed two fistfuls of the bedspread. His toes curled by my thigh.

"Oh, fuck," he blurted as his writhing caused him to take my finger just a little deeper. I laughed and pulled my hand back, returning to stroking his thick, muscular thigh.

"It's either that or spend your whole life wondering what I'd feel like..."

He huffed out a laugh that was half-nervous and still—infuriatingly—half-scoff, and he pushed himself up on an elbow. He looped his other arm around my shoulders and pulled me forward so I hovered above him. He was *hungry* for me, but the gleam in his eye also held an arrogant challenge.

"All right, baby," he said, biting his lip and staring at mine. "Only because you're so pretty. Then we switch and I can show *you* some things."

I kept the annoyance from my face at his continued arrogance, even when he couldn't deny how his body was reacting to me, and at his suggestion that he was only humoring me and would fuck me afterward. Instead, I grinned graciously and instructed him to turn over.

It wasn't that bottoming couldn't be pleasurable—it can be, with a touch like mine. But because it reminded me too much of the times when Rosaline would force me to be bent over by others, I required a certain level of *trust* in my partner before I'm comfortable bottoming. And it isn't a level that's achieved during one or even the occasional two-night-stands. I certainly didn't trust this man near enough for it.

Yet despite all of it rankling me more than usual, I wasn't going to hurt him. No, instead, I was truly going to give him the best fuck of his life: one he would always compare other experiences to and would never come close to achieving again.

FALLEN WOES

I left him immediately after we both came. Normally that would have been the time that I fed on him: after the first orgasm and then following up with at least one more round of sex. Instead, I left while he practically begged me to stay for a shower and a second round. He wasn't even suggesting we switch the dynamic anymore. I'd fucked the arrogance out of him, fully satisfied him, yet I left after one round so he would forever be wanting.

That was hardly the satisfying experience I'd hoped for after the weird day I'd had. I was strung tighter than I was used to. Boarding earlier had been a mild relief, but not enough. What I really wanted now was a rollercoaster, but unfortunately, all the parks in the country were closed by now.

My teeth twinged with the first pulse of bloodlust, and I groaned in frustration. I'd fed plenty just yesterday, I shouldn't be hungry. *Stupid tantrum at the skatepark.* I'd mesmerred ten or more people after it, and my blood surplus was diminished. I was irritated enough that I almost returned to the man's bed for a feed after all.

Instead, I chose one of my typical feed haunts: quick in, quick out. *No flirting, no fucking*, I told myself. I shifted just outside the venue, to stash my skateboard in yet another hiding place. But when I turned from the alley and stepped onto the sidewalk in front of the building, I froze.

Parked at the curb was a custom Harley that I recognized. *Malcolm's* Harley. I'd already told him off once today, so what was he doing outside one of the places he swore he and his men would avoid out of respect for me? I was squaring my shoulders and preparing to storm into the bar and kick him out when a familiar blond emerged from the entrance.

Fuck.

As panicked as I was at seeing her, I was torn between running away to save myself and curiosity. So instead of putting as much distance as possible between us, I shifted to the roof of a building down the block, my eyes fixed on the entrance of the club.

Rosaline stepped out onto the sidewalk, followed closely by Malcolm. I expected her eyes to immediately find mine, but she kept looking straight ahead, impatient and frustrated. Malcolm pressed against her from behind, his gray-streaked long hair falling around his shoulders in glorious waves. He seemed more aware of my presence than her, but since he hadn't sired me, he wasn't feeling *me* specifically, just my Lapsiness. He glanced around with narrowed eyes, searching, and I ducked down, sitting on the roof with my back against its retaining wall. I didn't dare move, and a moment later I heard the roar of his motorcycle peeling away, away from my position.

What the hell were they doing here? And why hadn't Rosaline sensed me? Clearly they were looking for me, and she should have been on high alert.

The ring.

I couldn't believe I'd gotten so used to its irritating presence on my finger that I'd already forgotten about the protection I'd purchased.

Holy shit, it actually works. With an amused huff, I dragged my hand down my face. I was safe from her at last.

Feeling satisfied, and no longer interested in feeding, I shifted back to my apartment. I walked to my bedroom, already stripping off my shirt and unbuttoning my jeans in preparation for a shower. But when I tossed my shirt onto the pile in the corner, something dark red on my bed caught my eye.

A bouquet of the most blood-red roses lay on my pillow. I dove for them and snatched them up, my panic rising again. Affixed to the packaging was a card with a fancy calligraphied "R" scribed in red ink.

With a savage growl, I stormed to my kitchen and shredded the roses in the kitchen sink. I narrowly resisted plunging the thorned stems into my face and, instead, shoved everything into the garbage disposal. As it ran, I gripped the edge of the counter, my shoulders tense and my forehead pressing into the cool marble lip.

Rosaline couldn't find me anymore and couldn't track me. But she had Malcolm, who knew all my haunts and my habits. They'd scour the earth for me, but Rosaline'd just shown me that she already knew where I *lived*. Damn it. It was bad enough that I had to abandon my routines, lie low, and hide like the coward I was, but now I also had to *move*. Otherwise, my ring did jack-shit to protect my sorry ass.

What am I supposed to do? I silently asked the ether as I stood there, gripping the counter like it was withholding all the answers.

Again, Jaimie, the girl from earlier, and the open hallways of that California high school campus floated through my mind. I'd been kidding when I told her I was a new student. I hadn't intended on returning to those halls or ever seeing her again. But the idea grew more appealing by the moment.

I didn't have to hide from the world, burying myself in seclusion, away from people and from fun. I just had to hide from *her*, and a high school was the *last* place Rosaline would ever expect to find me.

Hell, I could do high school for a bit, until Rosaline gave up on me—as relentless as she was, she'd get frustrated and quit, right? I didn't know. I'd never actively hidden from her whenever she reappeared; I just fought her and lost.

And I'd get to see Jaimie again. Talking with her had done something to me: it had *calmed* me in a way I'd never experienced—or, rather, I hadn't experienced since I was mortal, surrounded by family and *peace*. I was having trouble pinning down what it was about her that had my mind coming back to her over and over.

Perhaps I was gravitating toward her because I knew she was an artist, and maybe I was unconsciously wondering if she was my next Great for my wall of fame—many of whom I'd spent weeks with, fascinated by their energy. Maybe she was an unrecognized talent that I'd get to say I knew before.

She had my thoughts spinning. From the weird calm she gave me, to the refreshing fact that she didn't do *The Pause*, and to the nervous fidgeting of her hands, which contrasted the fierceness of her honey-colored eyes.

I sighed and stood up straight, running my hand through my hair while I rolled my neck as if it were stiff. I needed to get a grip and focus on my circumstances, not on a quiet, fascinating human. At least until I saw her again tomorrow.

I needed a hot shower. I needed to move. And I needed to finally put up wards on the new home. Wards always made me feel like even more of a coward, but if I wanted to hide from Rosaline, I'd finally need them.

And unfortunately, I was going to need a cell phone. I'd prided myself on resisting them this whole time. There's no thrill in technology, unless it's used in accelerating bodies to extremes, up and down slopes or into space, so cell phones and video games never held any appeal for me. But if I was going to blend with twenty-first–century teenagers, I needed one.

CHAPTER 8

"I've been here for less than four hours and I've already been asked to something called 'Homecoming' by four girls and two guys," I said exasperatedly as I approached the spot on the grass where Jaimie was sitting with a sketchpad on her knee and plopped down onto my back in front of her, as gracelessly as I could muster.

It was after fourth period and I'd been dying for it to be lunchtime. Obviously not because I was hungry, but because I wanted to *talk* and to *move*. I couldn't remember the last time I'd sat so still for so long.

High school was awful. It was both mind-numbingly, *stupidly* boring and exhausting. I tried to follow along with the teachers at first. But apparently math is completely different from when I learned it, and after realizing this, I gave up and daydreamed through the whole class. But *finally*, it was lunchtime and I could stretch out on this lawn and finally talk to the object of my curiosity.

She looked at me, startled at first. It wasn't *The Pause* but rather like she couldn't believe that *anyone* was giving her the time of day or that I hadn't changed my tune about her after talking to other classmates.

"Yeah, well, you're a babe," she said with a shrug, her surprise melting into casual skepticism. "You didn't know this?"

So she does find me attractive. So much for that theory.

"You're supposed to keep me humble," I mumbled before I realized I was speaking aloud.

"I'm what?" she asked, her brows coming together even more.

"Nothing," I said, waving my hand. I rested my head on my other hand, on the grass. "Is high school always this stupid and exhausting?"

"Did someone tell you it was a picnic?" she said sarcastically. "'Cause someone lied."

"Picnic, no. But fun? Kind of." I shrugged. I looked up at her face, so naturally but not arrestingly pretty, without any makeup at all. Her long, wavy hair was tucked behind her ears and pulled over one shoulder. She wore a gray T-shirt over frayed jeans and the same worn cardigan from the day before. "So, what is this Homecoming thing?"

"First, it's a big football game. Then the next night, there's a big formal dance. Girls dress either like bridesmaids or in the smallest, tightest dresses that can legally be called *decent*, and they grind to trendy music." As she spoke, she flipped her sketchbook to a new page and selected a new marker.

So, a combination of the ball I'd lost my virginity at and my typical night at clubs. *And* from the sound of it from other students, it was the highlight of the school year, apparently, until Prom for the older students.

"It sounds atrocious," I admitted aloud. She snorted and nodded. "You go to that kind of thing?"

"Never have, no." Her hand paused only slightly at my question. "How have you never heard of Homecoming?"

"I don't watch a lot of high school teledramas, I guess," I explained with a shrug, hoping I'd named the type of show correctly, but from her brief, incredulous glance, I guessed I hadn't.

"Your old school didn't have it?" she prodded skeptically. *Fuck*.

"Oh, I'm...homeschooled. Was homeschooled." Technically, not a lie. "I decided to change it up though. For the sake of...some normalcy." Also not a lie.

"And why did you start on a Friday?"

"I don't *technically* start until Monday. I just needed to get out of the house. So sick of moving, and boxes," I said, holding my hand up to block the sun in my eyes. This also wasn't a lie. I'd been packing all night.

"You've just been...hanging around?" she asked, putting her marker down and looking at me incredulously. "You know that's technically trespassing, right?"

"Shhhh...technically, yes," I said, putting a finger to my lips. I grinned mischievously at her. "But I'm very good at blending and hiding in plain sight."

"Oh, are you?"

"I was in your last class, and you didn't even see me," I pointed out, causing her to frown. Technically I'd been in *all* of her classes so far, just watching and observing. If I came back on Monday, though, I'd make sure I limited it to just two classes with her. I didn't want to *stalk* her.

She glanced up from her notebook, startled but also skeptical. I grinned and sat up, moving closer to her only so I wasn't blocking the walkway anymore. We were up against a locker pavilion—an enclosed space for underclassmen lockers that looked as claustrophobic as an airplane.

Jaimie kept her sketchbook on her knee, but she shifted her weight and pulled out a plastic bag that had a sad-looking peanut butter and jelly sandwich in it. She tore it and offered me half. I shook my head. It was such a meager lunch. No wonder she was so skinny. She took a bite of her sandwich and picked up another marker. I'd thought they were artist-brand markers, but now I realized they were just Crayola.

"So...evil stepmother, huh?" I asked casually after a minute, hoping to hear more about these *bigger things* of hers. She didn't look up and just shook her head and kept chewing. She wasn't going to open up that easily to me. That was fine.

"There's static everywhere." She shrugged. "What are your parents like?"

"Uh..." *Crap. Yeah, I should have parents, right?* "I don't know. Normal? A little absent. Kind of old-fashioned."

"You have any siblings?"

I froze at the question. So far I hadn't lied to her. Just half truths. My parents *were* old-fashioned, because they'd lived two centuries ago. But my siblings? I didn't want to admit they were dead, because then she'd feel sorry for me. But I couldn't call them "absent."

She glanced up when I didn't answer. I pressed my lips together and hoped it wasn't noticeable and shook my head in answer.

"How old is your brother now?" I asked, to get the conversation off of me.

"He's eleven," she said, with a small smile. The kind of smile I would have if my little brothers were alive.

Hell, he's around Henry's age, I thought, my smile wavering. I glanced down at the sketchbook in her lap, but she angled it away from me.

"So, I tried to find you on Instagram," I admitted after a moment. "I'm kind of a newbie at it, though. And I only had your first name, so..."

I'd gone out and bought a phone last night, after my shower. Everything about it was exhausting. Every app required an account, and *curating*—whatever the hell *that* meant. In Instagram, I'd created the damn account, inserted a few pictures of Ben Barnes—an actor who looked enough like me in his teens and who'd played Dorian Gray in an adaptation. But after the grueling steps of setting up the account, I was stuck. I didn't know how to wade through every Jaimie on the planet.

"Oh, so *now* you want to trade 'grams?" she teased with a smirk, capping her marker and selecting another. She pulled out her phone and opened her app, then handed it to me. "My name's not attached to it, because, you know...classmates will just troll it."

I memorized her profile name so I could find it later. I didn't know how to connect to the school's wi-fi, so while she doodled and ate, I held onto her phone and scrolled through her posts.

She was damn talented, working mostly in markers or paints. Her marker art was colorful and bold. She liked to do faces and large, whimsical scenes with lots of color. She didn't shy away from fan art and cartoon characters from pop culture, but she also created her own characters. Her paintings were more textured and lifelike, alternating between abstract and highly rendered details.

I stopped on one image and couldn't move past it. It looked like it was a square acrylic painting of a broken mirror. In each of the fragments of the mirror was a different image. One held a sliver of a very attractive face, just the eye and cheekbone. Another contained a vibrant-looking octopus tentacle, curling out of frame, and bloodied knuckles in another. In one empty fragment, where the wood behind the mirror would show, was a burst of colors, like a rainbow cloud from the seventies. Other parts showed more of the features of the man reflected in the mirror: an attractive man of her own creation, but, biting my lip, I could see some influence in it from the lovely Ben Barnes and maybe a little Andrew Garfield. It was a weird, semi-macabre, semi-whimsical blend of styles, and it showed the ugly parts that often weren't reflected in such gorgeous exteriors.

She was incredible. She might be a *Great*. I'd never found a Great this young.

Unable to put my awe into words without gushing, I handed the phone back to her. With a small smirk, she handed the sketchbook over to show me what she'd been working on.

Apparently as I was scrolling through her posts, she'd been sketching *me*. I wouldn't call it sketching, though. It was more like she'd been scribbling aimlessly, but somehow the scribbles all connected into the details of my face: my jawline, the shadows in my nose, the lines of my eyes and eyebrows.

"Hot, damn," I said automatically, genuinely awed. "This is amazing. You're good. Can I?" I motioned to the sketchbook and the other pages in front of this one. She shrugged and leaned back and picked at her sandwich.

I thumbed through a few of the pages to find more marker art of cartoon characters and one of a complex maze that was unfinished. Several of them seemed to show similar images, like she was drafting a concept and figuring out what worked best. It was what she'd been working on before I sat down.

"Are you working on a bigger project or something?" I asked, looking up from the sketchbook at her.

She finished her sandwich and balled up the plastic bag in her hand, pulling her sleeves back over her knuckles.

"There's this—"

Before she could finish her thought, expensive high-tops stomped into my peripheral and a hand grabbed the sketchbook roughly. I leapt to my feet instantly.

"Awe, baby, you never show *me* your stuff!" the guy teased, stepping back and keeping the book out of our reach. It was the buff bully from yesterday.

"Tristan, give it back, asshole!" Jaimie snapped, on her feet, too. Her fists clenched at her sides, but she didn't make a grab for it.

Tristan was surrounded by a posse of other mean-faced teenagers. I counted three boys and two girls. To his left was a skinny brunette, also in expensive-looking clothes. She could be his sister or his girlfriend.

"Aww, baby's gonna cry," the girl teased, pursing her lips in a fake sympathetic pout. Tristan laughed.

"Have I ever cried in front of any of you?" Jaimie challenged icily, glaring at the girl and then at Tristan as he started turning pages in the sketchbook.

"No, you're right. See, Jaimie doesn't cry, she just *cuts*," one of the boys jeered, miming drawing a blade of some sort across his inner wrist. "But you don't know how to do it right, Jaimie baby. You always forget, you have to go down the road, not across the street."

As horrifying as the teasing was, my focus was on Tristan, as he thumbed roughly through the book.

"This stuff is far too bright and colorful for our little emo here," Tristan mused playfully. "Do you paint rainbows to distract yourself from the *sads*, honey?"

I moved forward, putting myself between Jaimie and the others at the same time.

"She said give it back, asshole," I growled.

"Oh my!" Tristan said, after an exaggerated gasp as he turned a page in the sketchbook and reached the scribble-sketch of my face. He tore the page out and held the picture up in front of me, as if to compare it to the real thing. "How precious. The dark broody ones always find each other, don't they?"

The group behind him jeered and laughed derisively.

"Is that why you've left your precious studio to mingle with the commoners? Because of Steve McQueer, here?"

"Last chance, ass-hat," I threatened, unfazed by the unoriginal jab.

"You look far better in scribble-form, pretty boy." He grinned at me and tore the piece of paper in half.

My temper broke then—not because it was of me, but because it was *art*. It stirred up a fraction of the rage I'd felt when my family's portrait was destroyed.

I lunged at him, and he jerked backward, surprised by my speed—I hadn't tempered it to appear human like I should have. I savored the shock in his face at being thrown off balance by someone half his size, and grabbed the sketchbook out of his hand. The pieces of the torn paper fell to the ground, but I ignored them.

Tristan recovered and lunged, but I met him halfway. We squared off, our faces inches from each other's like vicious dogs in a ring, staring the other down.

"Is there a *problem* here, boys?" a deep, older voice sounded from behind me.

I continued to glare at Tristan, reading the risk-calculation grinding away behind his eyes, weighing the consequences of decking me in front of administration or backing down.

The boy was a solid muscular specimen. I could see the veins popping out of the muscles in his arms and practically smell the testosterone secreting from his pores. This boy was a juicer if there ever was one, and the wrong word would send his roids into overdrive. *At least my dick is undoubtedly bigger*, I thought saucily.

I fixed him with a grinning sneer. Because my back was to the authority figure, I could be cocky. Actually, I could be cocky anyway. I was older and stronger than everyone here, and I didn't have to abide by any rules. Tristan did though. His precious *future* was at stake. I communicated to him with my cocky sneer that he should try it if he dared. *I* had nothing to lose, but he did.

Finally, the tension left Tristan's posture. He settled his weight back into his heels, though he leaned forward to deliver a last cutting remark.

"You watch your back, pretty boy," he snarled quietly into my ear. Then he turned his back on me.

"You watch yours," I mumbled quietly as I hooked my foot around his right shin, pulling his leg from under him as he took a step.

He went down, face first into the grass, to the sounds of derisive laughter from his peers. He was just starting to push himself up when a pair of hands grabbed my shoulders from behind.

"Office, *now*," the authoritative voice said tensely, steering me away toward the office.

I turned in his grip and handed the sketchbook back to Jaimie. The expression she fixed me with mingled between perplexed and awed as she took the sketchbook back and hugged it. I threw her a devious grin and a wink as I let myself be steered to the office.

CHAPTER 9

I was happy to go to the office, but not to be reprimanded for violence on school property. I needed to sign up for classes. The teacher planted me in a chair outside the principal's office, but before he could walk into the office to explain what happened, I mesmerred him to forget why he was there in the first place. He left the office, looking like someone who'd lost his keys.

Twenty minutes later I was ready for classes on Monday and no one was the wiser. I selected my schedule so I had only two classes with Jaimie and two with the prick Tristan. I chose classes with him purely so I could mess with him. I hated the juicer in ways I'd never hated a human.

I didn't go to any classes after lunch and skateboarded around the town to kill time until school was out. I trailed Jaimie to the art studio, not to talk to her again, but to keep an eye out for creeps that might mess with her. This went beyond curiosity now. I *cared*.

Once she was safely inside the locked studio, I left the school and selected a new place to live: a simple apartment on the edge of town. Then I called up the witch from the day before and asked if she had any special deals for "repeat customers" or "upgrade" packages available. I could've asked for her to refer me to someone who lived closer, which would've been more logical. But I'd *liked* them, even if they hadn't been my biggest fans.

I was fascinated, envious, and appreciative of their little family. Because they were beautiful, and because they represented what I would never have: love, a child, a family, careers, stability...it was a long list.

The witch—Libby—at first was wary of doing a job so far from home, but when I told her it was in sunny California, close to a beach, she agreed if she could bring her family.

The move and the warding took all weekend, the three of us getting separate rooms in the same hotel on the beach. During the day, they worked on warding my apartment and I worked on packing up my old one. I'd moved everything essential into the new place before they started constructing the wards. All I had left to pack was the stuff going to storage.

In the evenings, Libby and Colt took the baby to the beach—or rather, *I* took them, and then wandered away because we weren't friends and we weren't traveling partners. It was just a business exchange.

I climbed up on the pier and watched them from a distance. They held the baby between them and kissed in the sunset. They lay on the sand, just at the tide line, with the baby on the sand between them. The baby squealed in confused delight as the cold water washed over her feet.

They were beautiful in ways I could never be. And they seemed so happy, so normally perfect. It wasn't envy or jealousy: I just admired things I couldn't have in a harmless, sad, broody way. Like their normalcy: I didn't *want* it, but I achingly admired theirs. My life hadn't been normal since my family died.

The shock and the tidal wave of events that had followed the destruction of my home kept me from fully understanding my drastic *change*. The funerals and trying to set everything back into some semblance of order kept me from exploring the nuances of my condition, even as I was starving.

My teeth itched the evening after the fire. Even as it grew worse, I barely noticed it over the pain in my heart. I signed the papers transferring everything to myself and ignored that I could hear the lawyer's pulse from across the conference table. When I shook his hand at the end of the meeting, the lively warmth of his hand caused my fangs to sprout forth and scare the shit out of me. Thankfully, the lawyer hadn't seen.

The next day I was feverish. I thought I was hearing voices, but really I was just hearing *pulses*. Everyone around me in the inn was thrumming with blood. It was deafening. How had I never noticed how loud people's blood was before? I felt both heated and chilled at different intervals of the day, but I didn't seem to sweat. I thought I was just getting sick. I welcomed it, if it killed me.

That evening, Edward, my closest childhood friend, visited me at the inn to commiserate and drink with me. I was wildly thirsty by this point, but the drink did nothing to satisfy it. It was the same with food. Nothing helped.

I'm sure I looked drunk, but I wasn't. I was just craving *something*, and I had no idea what it meant yet.

I blacked out when Edward helped me to my room, and when I woke, he was in my arms, my lips at his throat and my fangs retracting. I'd drained him dry, unaware of what I was doing and unaware that it had sated my madness. I could think again, and by God, I was horrified.

But then *she* was there. To applaud me for my first kill.

She didn't wait for the fire of my anger and despair to cool before she came into my life and bent me to her will. She used my anger to fuel other fires, and she consoled my despair with her body.

That's how it started. With sex over a corpse—a *second* corpse, if you counted my baby brother's.

She released me long enough to get the rest of my affairs in order with moving. But she was with me when I picked up my painting. She mewed and cooed in fake sympathy as I cried over the artist's rendering of my now-dead family. And she was with me when I left the countryside for Bath.

Being with her that first time was practically endless emotional sex. She consoled every stage of my grief by having me bed her. When the despair and the sadness wore off, and the anger and rage took its place, I would fuck her in my anger, pouring all my hatred into demeaning her. She let me *think* I was fucking her. But she was fucking me. Always. Whether she was doing it herself, or having someone else do it, I was the one used, and I didn't always know it.

Sex was her ultimate weapon: toxic pleasure. Every time I got angry or every time we fought, she would make it end in sex. Eventually, I grew *hard* every time I got angry—something that took *years* to undo once I finally left her. She used sex to turn me into a monster, and I was a good little lapdog at the promise of a treat. I buried my guilt—and my conscience—in sex, mostly with her in the early years, but then with others. Many, *many* others, and most didn't live to talk about it.

When I wasn't a good enough lapdog or—more often—when Rosaline just wanted to see me punished, she'd have others fuck me. Demeaningly, humiliatingly, violently: whatever her mood, she was the final say. It didn't matter that I would get to kill the fucker afterward—the humiliation was already achieved. I'd savor those kills the most: killing them in the slowest, worse ways, even if—in many ways—they were Rosaline's victims too and often forced to do what she said.

I wouldn't always get to kill them, though. Other times—*especially* if it was someone who'd been more willing to do her bidding—Rosaline would lock me away afterward, alone in a room for days with no stimuli whatsoever, feeding me vile, cold blood with a straw through a hole in the wall. And she'd spend those days of my captivity fucking the man she'd had rape me. When she finally released me, she'd tie me to a chair with silver chains and make me watch while she killed my attacker, further denying me any power in our vile, toxic enterprise.

The first time I was in the throes of Rosaline was for fifteen years—unheard of for Lapsi back then, thanks to our curse. But I hadn't known about the little caveat of the Lapsi curse back then. If I felt any physical pain caused by the curse's anti-community clause, I attributed it all to my hatred of Rosaline and my self-loathing. I've been with her a few times over the past two centuries, and I can't remember the exact tipping points that made me finally quit her each time, but I remember the first.

The painting.

When we moved to Bath and set up our house, I couldn't bear to look at it, but I refused to get rid of it. Rosaline promised to put it away and take care of it, and I forgot about it for years.

When I finally remembered and got up the nerve to look at it, I couldn't find it. I thought it would be in the attic, but it wasn't. I found it in the cellar, where moisture had caused it to slowly rot.

I took the painting and left Bath and Rosaline behind, moving instead to London. There, I worked to undo some of the damage to my soul and explored the depravity of the city, experiencing its pleasures and its violence, often in the same night. I met a lovely playwright one evening and sparked an obsession in him, inspiring his timeless character Dorian Gray. I can't be offended: of all the penny dreadfuls to inspire, he's the best.

Theecondd time Rosaline got her hooks into me was in America, in the aftermath of the stock market crash of 1929, when humans' life savings disappeared into nothing overnight. Mine took a hit as well, but I had *lifetimes* to rebuild my estate.

Rosaline enjoyed large, world-altering, cataclysmic events and their aftermath. To her, they were a playground. And with me tied to her again, hooked on her in a loathsome addictive stupor, her playground was twice as fun. I was like a heroin addict on a bender: lost to the world and unaware of what I was truly doing—of the impact I was having. Until finally, I, like a junkie, hit rock bottom and dug myself back out of it. Each time swearing *never again*.

Yeah, I was an addict—and Rosaline was the drug and the dealer. And I was *mostly* unaware of what I was doing. I'd make the excuse that I wasn't in control of my own actions, but when someone kills someone while on heroin, he's still a murderer, right?

I resurfaced around the time that the economy finally started to recover, thanks to the war that seemed to involve every damn country. I refused to return to Europe, but I wanted to be far away from Rosaline, so I continued west. I watched the world evolve around me and slowly pull itself out of the despondency, and I tried to do the same.

The first time recovering from Rosaline, it took thirty years to undo any of the psychological damage. This time, I tried harder.

In the late sixties, I went to the jungles of Vietnam. I wasn't there looking for Rosaline, but I kept expecting to see her behind every tree. The fighting, brutality, and death surrounding the war was exactly the kind of lawless carnage she craved. I didn't see her though; I was still free to act the way I wanted in the guerrilla-filled jungle.

I wasn't there to fight on any side or to further any cause. I was there for atonement and self-punishment. I "fell" into a lot of booby-trapped spike pits, savoring the pain as the spikes penetrated my torso or my legs, and the pain of having to pull myself off of them. I dove on grenades to shield men on either side.

I was okay with damaging my body because it always healed. I deserved the pain. I deserved to be broken, over and over, because I'd broken so many lives. Those people didn't get to walk away after it, but I did.

While I was there, I learned a lot about people, and humans by watching and observing them. There were decent men there: men who didn't want to fight. Through them, I learned *anyone* can be fucked up and changed by carnage. Most of these men had been thrown into the fire, like me. And it made a lot of them into monsters.

I did what I could to stop the worst of them. I killed any that I came across who were just there to rape and pillage. It didn't matter the side: there were monsters on both. But I couldn't be everywhere, so I didn't make much impact.

The third and final time I relapsed and found myself back with Rosaline was in the 1980s, once again in New York City. The AIDS epidemic and Reaganomics made it into a playground for Rosaline once again. The city was a mess, homeless were everywhere, monsters ran amuck, but at the same time, people weren't afraid.

The world had changed so much in those fifty years. People kept better track of each other, everything was recorded medically. People couldn't just disappear as easily. Yes, people disappeared and cases went cold, but it was *different*. And there was so much more love in the world. AIDS was killing millions, yet the queer community was thriving more than ever before. They weren't hiding: they were *loving*.

It bled into my tattered soul, making it easier to quit Rosaline this time. That bender only lasted three years. And once clear of her, I fled to San Francisco, and while I enjoyed many women, I also began exploring more of my queer side.

I learned the ropes of sex with men that wasn't rape or dominance but was love making. It was freeing, healing, and transformative.

I didn't do much as far as atoning this time, though—not like I had in Vietnam. I couldn't see a point since I'd just relapse again in a few years. Instead, I found skateboarding and focused on existing, constantly striving to be the neutral worm.

In the late 1990s and into the early aughts, I fell in with a gang of Lapsi, run by Malcolm. This biker gang mostly just liked to fight and fuck. It was another lawless order, but it wasn't like it was with Rosaline. With them, I had control.

It wore on me, though, like Rosaline had. Sure there was less sexual assault, and *less* death and murder, but it was still violence. I missed just skateboarding and riding roller coasters and fucking around for pleasure only. So I quit the gang, and until this week, I hadn't seen Malcolm in years.

I spent years being fucked and controlled by my dick. Now that I was free of her—and planned to stay free of her—sex will always be on *my* terms. My decision. My control. My pleasure—to give and to receive. And anyone who ignores that boundary, or anyone else's boundaries in my presence, forfeits their right to live.

And now? Now I was sitting with my feet dangling from a California coastal pier, watching a happy little family enjoy the tide on their feet, craving their calm and their normalcy and looking forward to my first official day of high school.

I was warding my place, and my body, so that my backdoor was no longer open to relapses. I was hiding from Rosaline so I could hold onto my little piece of neutrality, normalcy, and *possibly* redemption: all of which I saw in a young girl named Jaimie.

CHAPTER 10

"**Y**ou're both stronger than you look," the man remarks as Rosaline finally manages to secure the second silver-cored cuff around my struggling wrist and straightens to her full height.

"Yes, but don't worry, he won't fight anymore," Rosaline purrs. I watch her as she circles behind me and presses into his side, sliding a hand up his bare torso. "Will you, my love?"

I say nothing and clench my jaw to hold in the growl building in my throat. I'd fought hard against being restrained like this, bent over the leather spanking bench in our New York penthouse, but it seems gratuitous to growl and spit now that I was caught. Much as I don't want to show my submission, I crawl the rest of the way onto the bench, into the proper prone position to relieve the pain of the edge pressing into my pelvis.

I glare at the two of them: Rosaline looking cool and almost bored, despite her disheveled hair and torn dress, and the mortal man looking hungrily—yet warily—at my clothed body. My ass is perfectly presented for them.

"There's a good boy, Mason," Rosaline purrs from beside me, slipping something into the waistband of my trousers.

She tugs and the fabric at my hip sheers away, cut by the razor-sharp knife she held. I seethe while she makes short work *of cutting away my trousers, and stifle a groan when she pulls the fabric from beneath me and my semi-erect dick. She fastens my ankles into the cuffs. These also have a silver core—specially designed for us and our games. As she locks me into them now, however, I wish they better secured my ankles directly to the bench. If I strain too much, I could break my ankles. Broken wrists I can deal with, but broken ankles mean not being able to walk for weeks. What were we thinking?*

"There now. He's all yours," she says cheerfully, backing away and circling around to my head.

The man approaches behind me and grips my bare hips roughly, but then, as if thinking better of it, he grabs handfuls of the back of my expensive, delicate shirt. I stare at Rosaline, pouring all my disdain into that look, and my expression barely flickers as the man pulls roughly, rending my shirt down the back. Despite me wanting to stay silent, a groan escapes my lips as my dick hardens further, painfully pressed between me and the padded bench I'm strapped to. Damn it. *I have little doubt that Rosaline mesmerred the man to do that, knowing what it'd do to me.*

"Blindfold" is the only word I utter through my clenched jaw as my destroyed shirt falls around my elbows. My tone is gruff, but Rosaline knew it for what it was: a plea.

Because if I can't see, I can pretend it isn't a man driving into me. I can pretend that it's Rosaline railing me with something phallic and that this was even marginally consensual. With a blindfold, I could dissociate just enough to preserve my fractured sanity.

She rakes her hand through my now-tangled hair and delivers a sharp slap across my cheek as her only response to my plea. She retreats backward and pulls a chair into a position in my eyeline, taking a seat and crossing her legs.

Not even a bit to protect my teeth, *I think, glaring at her as she takes a seat.* Bitch.

"Go ahead now, whoever you are. And don't bother being gentle. He likes it when it hurts," she purrs, looking bored again.

"But he's just a kid," the man murmurs behind me. His knees brush the pads of my feet, but he isn't leaning into me or prepping his cock against my ass. He places a hand to my hip, and his touch is gentle—protective even. "He can't know—"

He doesn't finish his sentence, though. His words cut off as if someone clamped a hand around his mouth.

"Believe me. He knows what he likes," Rosaline tells him firmly, and the man's grip on my hip tightens. "Now. Fuck him."

The man makes a strangled grunt, and with a rough tug, he pulls my hips toward him, positioning me better to take him. I grit my teeth as the leather padding clings to my dick and releases it with an unpleasant smack. The man's tip prods my hole, and I tense my shoulders, bracing as well as I can against the bench.

He hesitates for a second, his grip on my hips spasming, and he splays a hand on my back, his thumb caressing one of my vertebrae. The touch is gentle: loving. *Completely at odds with his rough movements and the promise of violent sex.*

It confuses me for a second, but then its meaning snaps into sharp focus. He doesn't want to do this. His protests are real but wiped from his lips—from his mind—by Rosaline. He is as much a victim here as I am, bound by Rosaline's mesmerism. But still, he fought against it and broke through to give me this one affectionate touch, despite Rosaline wanting him to be savage.

This out-of-place touch was an apology. Simple. Minuscule. All he could manage through Rosaline's grip on his mind.

In this moment, I love him. I pity him. I wish I could free him, more than I wish I could free myself. I mourn him, too, because while I'll survive this, he won't.

I'm merely his last meal. His prize before he's torn apart. I'd never even bothered to get his name.

He's a puppet, an extension of Rosaline's malice. He isn't doing this to me, Rosaline *is. And in some sick, twisted way, this makes it easier to accept and dissociate.*

The man shifts, and both hands return to my hips.

I clamp my mouth shut, locking my tongue to the roof of my mouth so I don't chance biting it off—this isn't my first time being fucked without something to bite down on. I grip the edge of the bench tight enough that the metal frame creaks. I let nothing show on my face as I glare at Rosaline's smug, cold expression. I intend to stare her down the whole time I'm getting railed.

But as soon as the man plunges into me, dry and violently, I cave. I shut my eyes tight and dig my teeth into my forearm to keep from shrieking from the pain.

I will survive this. He won't.

Usually in this moment, I'd be imagining all the ways I'd get back at Rosaline and the ways I'd fuck her for revenge. Even though part of me always knew that I was never truly getting back any of the dignity she stole: she was always the winner. Always.

This time, as my mind retreats into the same place that I buried my conscience, the mind-prison fissures. It's only been three years with her this time around, but already the mental prison is cracking. And a single thought escapes those cracks as the man continues to plough into me, with staggering, rough thrusts.

I need to get out.

I caught up with Jaimie before fourth period on Monday, outside our shared class in a hallway that surprisingly wasn't crowded.

She glanced at me sharply as I hopped off my board, and shook her head, silencing me before I even spoke. She had her phone pressed to her ear.

"Look, I know you don't give a shit about me, but he's a kid, and he's sick. You need to go and pick him up!"

I assumed she was talking about her brother.

"No, *I* can't. I can't just leave school," she snapped, running a hand through her hair in frustration. "Yes, I know I'm eighteen now, but that doesn't mean I can just *leave*. And even if I could, I can't make him walk home with me if he's sick! *You* have a car." She paused again to let the other person talk. "No. You should—look, as much as I wish I was, I'm not his legal guardian: *you* are—since you married my dad. So why don't you do something with that title you so desperately wanted, by getting off your lazy ass and bring him home from school!?" She paused as the other person talked. "Well, all right then. I guess he has to stay there and be miserable. What else is new?"

I don't know who hung up on who, but Jaimie pulled the phone from her ear with a hiss and stared off in front of her for a few seconds before closing her eyes.

"I'm going to pay for that later," she mumbled, half to herself. She turned to me. "But it was satisfying."

"You okay?" I asked lamely, for lack of anything better to say. Obviously she wasn't okay. "What's up?"

"My brother's sick at school, and they want to send him home. But dad's asleep, my stepmother won't wake him, and she won't get off her ass to pick him up," she explained quickly, her face still flushed with irritation. She paused as several students passed us and filed into the classroom. The bell would ring in a minute. "I can't go get him. I can't leave, and I don't have a damn car, anyways."

"What if we had a car?" I asked automatically, before realizing I was offering to help. I didn't own a car, but I could get us one easily if that was the only thing stopping her. "I can take you to go get him."

She looked at me skeptically, surprised again that I cared enough to offer help.

"I've never had to do it, but I think they'll let me check him out of class," she admitted, hesitantly. "But you don't have to. Besides we have class in a minute..."

"Fuck school," I said with a shrug, then I grinned. "This seems a little more important."

I glanced past her, quickly calculating my next move. Down the hall was the pretty brunette in expensive clothes who'd been standing next to Tristan on Friday. I'd since learned her name was Laura, and *not* related to Tristan. She undoubtedly had a car I could borrow.

"Meet me at the back lot in a few minutes," I said, winking at Jaimie. She frowned but nodded after a beat.

It didn't take much mesmerism to coax Laura into handing over the keys to her car. I didn't own a car, but I knew how to drive. Do you think a boy who grew up in a time with just horse-drawn buggies and carriages wasn't going to learn to drive every new iteration of automobile?

If Jaimie recognized the dainty, posh sedan as Laura's car, she didn't give any sign. We got in and pulled out of the parking lot.

"There's something you should know about my brother before you meet him," Jaimie said after she pointed me the correct way toward the elementary school. "He's smart. Like, *really* smart."

"Like a prodigy?"

"Kind of, but not really. A prodigy is like...they're born with knowledge or skills...the right term is gifted, really. He learns things super-fast and he's lightyears ahead of his classmates—and almost passing me," she explained, both with a mix of pride and apprehension. "It makes him chatty and just...not what you expect from an eleven-year-old. Just so you're prepared."

He sounded like my sister, Clara, who'd been surprisingly good at sums at a young age. The fact that I was about to meet a kid my brother's age with a mind like my sister's had me suddenly uneasy.

We pulled up to the school and Jaimie got out. While I waited for her to come back with her brother, I contemplated fleeing. I didn't *have* to do this. I didn't have to subject myself to the discomfort of meeting this kid. But I'd done this as a favor to Jaimie. Even though I didn't owe her anything, and I could just leave, I didn't want to.

Just please, please *don't look like any of my siblings. I won't be able to handle that,* I pleaded silently to the air.

About five minutes passed before the office doors opened again and Jaimie stepped out, accompanied by a skinny kid. The two were definitely related, with the same light brown, almost blond wavy hair. His was wilder and almost to his shoulders. He was skinny, but not rail-thin like Jaimie, as if he had a marginally heartier diet than her. Jaimie carried his backpack by her side, and he shouldered a gym bag. His eyes were downcast, and he looked positively miserable but not necessarily sick.

Jaimie opened the back door for him, and the kid crawled onto the backseat. I turned halfway around so I could look at him and greet him. He lifted his eyes to mine and narrowed them in guarded confusion.

"Who are you?" The defensive tone was probably unintentional.

"Grayson, meet Mikey," Jaimie said as she climbed into the front seat and closed the car door. She turned and looked back at Mikey over the center console. "Mikey, this is Grayson. He's a friend, doing us a favor in picking you up."

"We don't have friends," Mikey said quietly. The defensive look and tone had left him, and now he seemed almost bored, or tired.

"He's new. He hasn't learned to hate the damaged girl like everyone else yet," she explained to him with a small, sad smirk.

I'm not like everyone else, though, I wanted to say aloud but didn't. I wasn't cruel like her classmates. I have cruelty in my past, but I wouldn't call myself cruel anymore.

Mikey turned his eyes to me with a grave expression, too serious for a kid of eleven.

"Are you going to save her?" he asked me suddenly.

That was an odd, seemingly loaded question. I was doing a favor for Jaimie, yeah, but saving her? Jaimie was guarded and not very talkative, so I still didn't know much about her, but I saw the strength in her. I'd heard how she talked to her stepmother. She didn't take bullshit from her classmates, and she stood up for herself.

"Your sister doesn't need saving," I answered after waiting to see if anyone would elaborate what he meant. An odd silence hung in the air after I spoke, and after a moment I assumed we were done talking and turned back to the wheel.

"Can we get ice cream?" Mikey asked suddenly as I turned the key in the ignition.

"Mikey!" Jaimie chided in surprised reproach. "First of all, you're sick, remember? You don't get ice cream when you're throwing up."

"I'm not that sick..." he mumbled quietly, dropping his eyes to his hands. "I could do ice cream...or frozen yogurt..."

I hid my grin behind my hand before Jaimie could see it. Mikey had faked sick to get out of class. I couldn't blame him. What kid hadn't faked ill to miss lessons or something unpleasant?

"Where did this come from? When have we *ever* gotten ice cream?" she continued to reprimand. There was something in her tone, like she was embarrassed to have to explain this. It slowly dawned on me that the discomfort was because of *money*. Trips to get ice cream or frozen yogurt were a luxury.

"I just thought I would try," the boy said with a tired shrug. His sad resignation pulled at heartstrings I didn't know were still intact. "I thought that maybe since you have a boyfriend now that he might treat."

"That's not...he's not—that's not what this is," Jaimie sputtered. She wasn't flustered in the shy, teenage, embarrassed way. It was more like when a parent is panicking because a kid is being embarrassingly but innocently rude. "Mikey-Man, don't you think if I had a boyfriend, I would've told you about it before now?"

Laughter was bubbling dangerously close to the surface in my chest. I liked this kid more than I'd expected to. He seemed so sullen and miserable, but he was still just a kid. Sweets were the forbidden fruit: the ever-motivating vices that are monumental to childhood, before the harsh realities of adulthood steals the joy away. I'd often stolen measures of clotted cream and other confections from the larder to share with my youngest brothers as part of my burning desire to keep their childhood bright for as long as possible.

"That's not the point, Jaimie, don't you see?" I said, allowing the laughter to vibrate through my words. I eyed Mikey in the rear-view mirror with mirth. "The boy wants ice cream, and he's gotta try every angle. Lucky for you, though, I'm exactly the person to be swayed by such tactics. I'll treat. Point the way, Mikey-Man."

CHAPTER 11

As Mikey directed me to the frozen yogurt place of his choosing, I watched him in the rear-view mirror as often as I could. He'd brightened significantly since entering the car, but his eyes were still sad as he stared out the window. It was like he was alternating between the joyful anticipation of a rare treat and some harrowing sorrow. He wasn't the chatty happy-go-lucky kid that Jaimie had prepped me for.

Jaimie sat quietly in the passenger seat, trying to keep her own emotions from her face yet I could see a battle raging behind her eyes. A battle between annoyance at being overridden, and her continued awe at my unexpected kindness. It pained me to consider what could be going on in her life to be so unused to simple affirmation or favors.

When we walked in, Mikey explained the concept of the place to me: you fill a cup with your flavor of choice from the soft-serve machines and then add what toppings you want. At the end it's weighed, and that's how they charge.

I handed him and Jaimie a cup and then stood back to observe them. I quietly told Jaimie not to worry about cost, but I wasn't going to step on her toes any further. She directed Mikey to the multitude of soft-serve machines where he couldn't decide on a flavor, so he chose both Blue Raspberry Tart and Cake Batter.

Jaimie told him he could only add toppings in amounts that corresponded with some math equation that I didn't pretend to understand. Somehow it limited his ability to overindulge but also made it something that interested him. He chose jellied candies shaped like fish that he told me were oddly named "Swedish fish," some kind of sour candies, and yogurt chips. Jaimie went simpler with her cup, with cheesecake flavor, graham cracker crumbs, and a tiny portion of raspberry sauce.

"I'm going to give you so much crap if you end up throwing that up, kid," Jaimie teased him as we took a seat outside, her voice still a little reproachful of his brazenness. "And don't forget to thank Grayson for his generosity and for putting up with you."

"I won't throw it up, I promise. I'm...not actually that sick..." he mumbled as he stuck his spoon into his colorful art sculpture. He was still sullen, yet he was simultaneously thrumming with awe at the treat in front of him. He raised big eyes to me. "Thank you, Grayson. I've never been able to do this."

"Least I can do for a kid that got me out of class," I said, giving him an encouraging smile. I felt bad intruding on Jaimie's oddly parental territory, but I didn't regret giving him this little happiness.

Mikey spooned yogurt into his mouth, and the look of childish pleasure in his eyes pulled painfully at more of my heartstrings. It hurt to watch, but I also didn't want to look away.

"So you know that if you go home sick, you can't go to practice, right?" she said after they were eating for a few minutes. "Your *faking* sick not only inconvenienced everyone, but it sacrificed going to practice and playing with your teammates."

"That's okay. I don't want to go anyway," Mikey said, staring at his bowl and shrugging. "How was math class today? How far into this chapter did your teacher get?"

"You don't want to go to practice? You love soccer," Jaimie said, not willing to change the subject so fast.

Mikey shrugged again. "I don't want to do soccer anymore," he mumbled, playing with the remains of his dessert.

"What?" she asked, startled and concerned. "What do you mean you don't want to do it anymore?"

"I don't want to go anymore. I just don't." He shrugged. His skinny shoulders had to be getting tired from shrugging so much. He fiddled with his spoon, his appetite for frozen yogurt practically dried up.

"Mikey, we have a deal, remember?" Jaimie said softly, a small note of desperation in her voice. "You do soccer so I can use the studio after school until I have to come get you. On other days you have math club—"

"I don't want to do math club anymore, either. It's lame and I'm the only one that likes it..."

"What?" she demanded again. "But...Mikey, what about me? We have a system. It's the only time I have to work on my stuff. This is literally the only thing I ever ask from you."

"It's not the only thing," he said softly, spooning in another mouthful. "You also have me do your homework. Because I'm 'gifted.'"

"*Mikey*," she said in horrified reproach. She flashed her eyes toward me for a second, embarrassed.

"What? He's not mom. You only said I shouldn't tell her," he said calmly, shrugging.

"Deb is *not* your mom," she snapped, losing a bit of her temper. It wasn't harsh, but it was enough to make Mikey look guilty and backpedal.

"Sorry, I'm tired," he said, deflating. He dropped his spoon and rubbed his palms into his eyes. "It slipped out."

"He doesn't do my homework *for me*," Jaimie clarified, turning to me. As if this mattered to me. "I let him read my math lessons and do the assignments. It keeps him quiet and out from underfoot while I cook dinner and clean up. *Then* I do my assignments, and he checks it. It's to keep his mind occupied since he's far ahead of his own grade level."

"And she gets a built-in tutor. Because she isn't that great at math," Mikey said, trying for brotherly teasing, but the delivery was off because of his dark mood.

"Well, I get twice the lessons, and it saves my grades," she teased back, but irritation still flavored her tone. "But you're changing the subject, Mikey. You can't quit soccer or math club. I need you to—"

"I'm not going," he snapped sharply, his face looking pained but adamant.

A meltdown was coming, but I wasn't sure from *who*. Mikey looked close to lashing out if pushed further, and Jaimie...she looked so suddenly sad. She still wanted to protest, but I somehow knew she wouldn't. She'd sacrifice everything that made her happy if it meant he was safe and happy, but I hated to think of her having to sacrifice anything.

But there was something *else* going on with Mikey, something he was guarding with his defensiveness. Surely this fake sickness was tied to this sudden urge to give up his interests.

His eyes were red and inflamed, and I realized he'd been sniffling a bit. I'd thought it was to emphasize that he was sick, but now I wasn't sure. And I could smell something on him that I somehow hadn't noticed in the car: the subtle, primal scent of fear-induced sweat.

"Mikey-Man," I said, gently but firmly. He turned his eyes reluctantly toward me. "Your sister and I have cut class to come get you. I bought you frozen yogurt and let you eat to your heart's content. I wouldn't usually ask to be repaid in any way, but I feel like you owe us *something* here."

I was using a tone I hadn't heard myself use in two hundred years. The last time was probably when I had to get Henry and Michael to admit that they'd been hiding a kitten in Henry's bedroom. Mikey's eyes looked like he wanted to stay clammed up, but they changed to almost resigned. Playing on a kid's internal moral compass was always a better tool to use than anger.

"So, I'm going to ask you something, and you have to answer, okay? Because it's only fair," I said, resting my forearms on the table in front of us and eyeing him levelly. He looked wary but caught. "Did something happen today? Something that made you afraid?"

Jaimie glanced at me, surprised, but I kept my eyes on Mikey, staying calm and trustworthy. His guard immediately went up when I asked the hard question, but he was a scared, tired eleven-year-old kid, and he couldn't keep the guard up for long. His eyes dropped to the cup in front of him. After a minute he spoke, and it was exactly what I feared.

Mikey was being bullied by a kid in his class.

He explained to us, carefully and deadpanned, that his bully was on his soccer team and in his math class, where Mikey excels and others don't. Mostly it'd been mean comments from the insecure classmate, who felt threatened by Mikey's giftedness. He saw Mikey as undeserving of being so smart because he was so small and so poor.

Lately, however, it'd started involving more of his classmates, and things tended to escalate. Until today, the worst of the bullying had been pantsing him in the locker room both before and after practice, and Mikey was able to stomach and brush most of it off, like Jaimie did with her own ridicule. But today, things took a turn. Before school, the bully and his friends cornered him in the bathroom. They pantsed him like usual, but then they held him down on the bathroom floor. They slapped his face, hard enough to hurt but not hard enough to leave any mark. They spit in his hair and dipped his shoes in the toilet and finally left when the bell rang.

After the boys left, he stayed in the bathroom, curled up in one of the stalls until someone found him. He claimed he was throwing up, and they took him to the nurse. He spent the morning in the bathroom of the nurse's office, pretending to be sick until we came to pick him up.

FALLEN WOES

As he told us all of this, Mikey was clearly trying not to cry, but as he got further into explaining the horrors, his words came haltingly, as his throat constricted. His jaw trembled and I glanced at Jaimie for the briefest of seconds. Her eyes were tearing up, and she hugged her arms so tight her fingers were white.

"We have to get the school involved," she said, finding her voice at last. "They can protect you. We can tell Dad, and he'll get in touch with the school."

"You said we shouldn't ask Dad for anything," he pointed out, pushing his cup around on the table.

"I meant for *trivial* things," she corrected him adamantly. "This isn't trivial. This is about protecting you and making sure you're safe where you should be safe. You tell Dad when someone makes you feel unsafe."

"*You* don't tell him about Deb," he countered, looking at her with eyes far older than an eleven-year-old.

I slid my gaze to Jaimie without turning my head. She had her mouth clamped tightly shut, and she refused to turn toward me. She stared hard at Mikey, looking betrayed. Finally, she worked her tongue and unglued her lips.

"You let me worry about *me*, okay?" she said firmly. "We're talking about *you*. This is important. We tell Dad. He tells the school. This kid and his friends get delt with."

"I don't want to tell the school. If they get in trouble, everyone will just hate me more," he said miserably, dropping his eyes to the table.

This poor kid, I thought, baffled by how helpless we *all* were here. He was being bullied because he was smart and poor, and Jaimie too, because she was artistic and poor, as if no one was allowed to be both. This stupid classist bullshit was ridiculous to see in kids so young.

I wanted to find this kid, whoever he was, and teach him a good lesson. I don't kill kids, and violence against kids has never had any appeal for me. But for Mikey, I was considering harming a child.

I glanced at Jaimie, and my anger fizzled out a little bit. She looked heartbroken. This girl was fine being bullied because she was focused only on her brother's happiness. She'd do anything to protect him, but she couldn't protect him from the monsters at his school.

It was almost funny how ridiculous our little group was. Two troubled but empirically good kids, just trying to get by while being bullied. Then me. Damaged, fucked up me. I fit with these people far more than I'd initially realized.

"You know, Mikey, believe it or not, I was bullied too," I admitted to him gently, before fully thinking through what I was going to say. "For a long time."

I wouldn't technically call Rosaline a bully. She was an instigator, an abuser, and a groomer who'd broken me so she could build me up in her image, and she had turned me into a killer. The abuse I'd endured made bullying seem like a paper cut, but still, it was close.

"What did you do?" he asked, looking at me with doleful eyes.

I hadn't thought this conversation through. Nothing I did would apply in Mikey's situation, but I couldn't exactly lie to him and say that I overcame it or that I stood up to my bully. I hadn't. I'd just run away. I was still running away.

"I endured for a while. Then I became self destructive...thinking I didn't deserve better. Then I convinced my parents to pull me out of school and homeschool me." That part was obviously a lie, but I'd told Jaimie I was homeschooled, so I had to stick with the lie. "Until they moved us to a new town, and I thought I would try real school again. I thought maybe it would be different, and people would be nicer. But they aren't..."

"No, they aren't," Jaimie agreed, both wryly and sympathetically.

"I'm not saying I'm the example to follow—I really don't recommend it," I told him honestly. "I'm just saying...I've been there. You're not alone. People suck, and kids can be awful. But you can fight for yourself or ask for help. Don't be afraid to talk about it."

It wasn't real advice or anything. It was all just words, but maybe I helped him feel less alone at least. I had no idea what they were going to do or what was the right way to deal with it. It sounded like their parents were useless, which was concerning. And it sounded like Mikey was going to do everything he could to just fly under the radar, which would dim his giftedness and would screw Jaimie over.

"We can talk more about this later, just you and me, Mikey, okay?" Jaimie said softly. She reached across the table and put a hand on his shoulder. "We've involved Grayson here in too much of our crap already, I think. He's ready to run for the hills."

She was kidding, but I knew she was expressing genuine fear. Stuff this heavy would scare off anyone who had known someone for only three or so days. But I wasn't anyone. I was invested.

"You think we can take you home now, Mikey-Man?" I asked him, with a small smile. "Or do you have any more requests? You want to try your luck and ask for a new bicycle or something?"

I meant it as an innocent tease, but it didn't land like that. Jaimie glanced at me, cringing, and Mikey looked suddenly regretful and guilty. *Ooof. My bad.* I tried hard to apologize to Jaimie for the bad joke with just my eyes.

"We can go home," he said miserably. "Thank you, by the way. This was my first frozen yogurt."

"Anytime, kid," I said, giving him a genuine compassionate smile and trying to make up for my misstep.

They threw their empty yogurt cups away, and we climbed back into the borrowed car. Jaimie directed me to an apartment complex, walking distance from both the elementary school and the high school. She pointed me to their building, and I parked outside of it.

"Now, remember, you're supposed to be sick. So just go to our room and lie down for the rest of the day, okay? Don't bother Dad or Deb," Jaimie advised him, turning in her seat to face him.

"I know. I was going to do that anyway," he said calmly. Despite the sugar he'd just consumed, he still looked exhausted. "Sorry for being a nuisance."

"You're not, Mikey-Man. You're not," Jaimie assured him, but he didn't seem like he believed her.

Before he left the car, I asked him for the main bully's name. I didn't yet know what I would do with his name, but

I wanted it just in case. Mikey told me, saying the name like it burned his tongue. He left the car and walked to the outer door of their apartment.

"He's a good kid," I commented as he disappeared behind the door.

"I would do anything for that kid," she admitted softly, leaning her head back on the headrest and giving me a sad but proud smile. She was too young to look so parental, but I probably had the same look when my siblings were alive.

"I would too," I admitted before realizing I was speaking aloud. I didn't regret saying the words though, because they were true: I would die for that kid in a heartbeat.

CHAPTER 12

We got back to school just as lunch was ending. I dropped Jaimie off so she wasn't late to fifth period and found somewhere to park Laura's car. As expected, the same parking spot was no longer available, so I parked somewhere farther away, and far less convenient. Yeah, I'm petty.

I didn't return to school, though. I had something to do first.

I shifted to the elementary school and entered the school's office. I mesmerred my way into the office computers, much like I had when selecting my high school classes. Only I wasn't singing up for classes this time. I was looking up the address of one of their students so I could pay them a house call later. *Then* I returned to school.

I'd arranged to have two classes with Jaimie, to just be near her. And I'd chosen an art class so it would make sense for me to have a keycard to let me into the studio, even though I could get in without needing to open the door. I hadn't intended for my art class to be at the same time as hers, but as luck had it, drawing class was in the same huge room as her painting class.

Her class was working with watercolor, each practicing a technique the teacher had shown them. In mine, we were sketching the most basic still life of wax fruit.

I hadn't drawn much over the years besides casual doodles on scraps of paper or in margins of books. I'd never been properly taught, and since the teacher wasn't teaching technique today, I was just winging it. And it turned out I wasn't awful. Once the teacher suggested I gauge measurements by holding my pencil up and measuring with my thumb, it became easier. I wasn't going to pursue drawing professionally, but I could hold my own apparently, and this was one class I didn't find boring as hell.

After school, I once again followed Jaimie to the studio from a distance, to make sure she wasn't harassed. I waited a few minutes before scanning into the room. She didn't hear me enter, so as I approached the middle of the room, I rapped my knuckles on one of the desks to get her attention. She was pulling a large canvas out of one of the tall, narrow storage cubbies in the wall. She stopped when she saw me there, her expression guarded but not necessarily displeased.

"Hey," I said, giving her a half smile.

"Hey." She played with the stained cuffs of her sweater. "I didn't think you'd still be talking to me after everything today."

"Don't get so used to unkindness from others," I said, my voice taking on a compassionate note that I had never heard in it before. "I swear, not everyone is a shithead and a monster. They're still out there, but I'm not one of them." *Anymore.*

By all accounts I've been a monster before. I don't deny that. And I don't delude myself into believing my soul is clean, even after years of self-punishment. But I wasn't a monster in *this* moment. Not to her at least.

"Thank you, again, for everything today," she said, pulling the canvas the rest of the way out of the cubby.

"It was nothing." I stepped forward to help her.

The canvas wasn't heavy, but it was about five feet wide and three feet tall. Though unfinished, I could tell it was a whimsical, busy piece with details covering every inch. A curved piano keyboard stretched across it, a heavy theatre curtain was draped in the corner, with hundreds of smaller details in between.

"This is from your sketchbook," I observed as I took in everything on the canvas. "Is this for school?"

"It isn't." She'd moved away as I looked it over and grabbed her brushes and tackle box of paint. "It's for a contest. The local theatre is planning on covering its largest outer wall with a mural representing the arts. They're doing an art contest to determine the design. The prize is five thousand dollars, and you get to work on making it into a mural. Like, employed to paint it, I mean."

"Wow," I said, taking another look at the work in progress. I could easily picture it on the side of a building. "That's why you've been working on it after school."

"Yeah, and it delays going home," she mumbled with a shrug. I looked at her, but she wasn't going to elaborate. I could already glean from details over the past several days that her home life was rough, so I understood not wanting to spend more time there than necessary. "I'm already employed to work on painting the mural, whichever one is picked. The art teacher here set it up. It's just a job for the summer, but it'll be more of a something if it's *my* art up there..."

"It will be," I agreed, touching her upper arm gently before entirely meaning to. I withdrew my hand before either of us could linger on its meaning for long. "Your stuff is great. And this is going to be great."

"Thanks," she said softly. I could tell she was unused to praise that didn't come from her teacher or her brother.

Before silence stretched out too long between us, I pulled out my phone and opened Instagram. I scrolled quickly through her posts until I found the one that had intrigued me.

"I was wondering...you don't happen to have this one here, do you? Can I see it if you do?" I tilted the phone in her direction so she could see which piece I meant.

She went to her storage cubby again and pulled out a canvas wrapped in protective fabric. The canvas was smaller than her current work in progress, but it was still somewhat large at three feet tall by two feet wide. She unwrapped the canvas and tilted it against the cupboards so she could step back from it.

It was even better in person than it had been on the screen of my phone. So many details had been lost in the photographing process. The dark, uglier parts were heavily textured with thick, crude paint. I hadn't quite noticed that it was a framed mirror in the painting, but the images depicted in the fragments of mirror spilled out beyond the mirror frame. The tentacles reaching out of the mirror curled and crawled up the frame. The colorful cloud stained and mottled the wood finish. The eyes in one of the fragments were gorgeous, lifelike and wet.

"How much?" I asked without thinking.

"What?" She looked at me incredulously.

Oh, right, I thought, realizing my blunder. Teenage skater boys don't just buy paintings at the drop of a hat. If anything, such a kid would buy a print maybe, but even that would be odd.

"I, uh, showed your Instagram to my uncle," I lied after thinking for a minute. "He wanted me to take a look at it and ask you how much you wanted for it. He loves it."

"Oh" was all she managed to say. I was surprised by how baffled she was: surely this wasn't the first time anyone had expressed interest in buying her work. But maybe it was. I don't pretend to know how the art world works these days, especially for younger artists. "I honestly haven't thought about it..."

"You don't have to answer right away. Think on it, and let me know," I said with a shrug. "And don't you dare lowball yourself. My uncle is *rich*, and he loves art. Even if you ask three thousand—hell, four—he'll pay it."

"He'd pay three grand for *that*?" she repeated.

At my nod, she looked away and stared into the distance. She was probably thinking about what she could do with as much as four grand on top of the contest winnings. By the awe on her face, I imagined it would be life-changing for whatever plans she had for herself in the future.

I *really* wanted to know her plans and to help with them, but even if I had the best, most genuine intentions, she wouldn't be receptive to handouts. And I hadn't thrown out three or four grand as an arbitrary number. Based on the size of the painting, the skill behind it, and the hours of work that undoubtedly went into it, the amount sounded almost *too* fair. I'd pay more if she asked.

"I'll think about it, I guess," she said. Her tone still sounded awed and disbelieving, though. She wrapped the painting in its protective fabric and slid it back into its cubby, being even more careful with it now that it was apparently worth so much.

I figured I should leave her alone. I didn't know when the contest entries were due, but I didn't want to cut into the coveted little time she had to work on it before heading home. From the sound of it, her stepmother was so lazy that Jaimie was expected to cook to keep her and her brother from starving. So she had to be home by probably five or six, but I really didn't know.

She stepped up to her work in progress and looked at it, as if assessing where to begin working. I picked up my skateboard from where I'd rested it on a chair and was opening my mouth to excuse myself, but she stopped me by speaking first.

"What do you think I should do about Mikey?"

She was so guarded and apprehensive about trusting anyone that I'd never expected her to bring up the thing with Mikey to me again.

"I don't know," I said honestly. I didn't know what anyone should do in this situation: school affairs and how involved teachers could be was a complete mystery to me.

"You seem to strongly believe your dad would get involved. How much can teachers help?"

"I don't know. Mikey doesn't want me to say anything at all. He's worried it'll only make it worse, and—who knows—he could be right." She ran her hands through her wavy hair in her frustration. I tried not to let the movement distract me, but it was hard. Her hair falling loose around her face made me want to touch it with a startling urgency. "And I don't want to make him keep going to soccer if he doesn't feel safe. But I need..."

Now knowing how much she needed this time in the studio and how much she depended on Mikey having after-school activities so she could work, I wanted to help her and Mikey even more.

"It might not last, you know," I said with a shrug. "Kids can change their minds on a dime. Tomorrow, it could turn out that he wants to be friends—"

"Or tomorrow could be even worse. And Mikey can't always fake sick," she countered, not sharing my feigned optimism. It wasn't optimism for me, though. I had an idea about what I was going to do to help Mikey, but there was no way I could tell her. "You said you were bullied, too? Do you think I should encourage him to fight back? Do you know of any self-defense tactics I could teach him?"

"I don't know if fighting back is the best idea," I said, faking dismay. An idea struck me. "Think about the dog. You didn't fight back, even though it bit you and held on. You showed it there was nothing to fear, and it backed off. That could apply here."

"If Mikey turns the other cheek, the kid is just going to slap that one too," she protested flatly. "The dog logic doesn't work with people."

No, it doesn't, I guess. People aren't animals: they don't follow a set form of survival logic. They're cunning and aggressive. It hurt to realize that someone as young as Jaimie had already figured this out. But still, for my plan, I had to stand by the idea of the dog incident.

"I don't know, he might surprise you." I shrugged. "Tell Mikey to stay strong, okay? Don't fight back, but don't turn the other cheek, either. And if I'm wrong, I'll bludgeon the kid to death with my skateboard, and I'll buy Mikey frozen yogurt every day for a month."

She only offered me a small half smile for my humor. She nodded in acceptance of my advice but still looked doubtful.

"I'll leave you to work. I'll see you tomorrow, okay?" I said, backing away.

She nodded and gave me a small wave, before placing her tackle box of paint on her chair and opening it.

I shifted to outside Tony Spencer's house—Mikey's bully—and lingered only long enough to ascertain where the kid's bedroom was in the house. I could see a Spiderman poster on a wall from where I stood in the backyard. I concentrated on that room and shifted inside the house.

Tony was seated on his bed, with his notebook on his knees and a textbook open in front of him. He jumped at my sudden appearance, but before he could yell out for his parents, I pressed into his mind and put him to sleep.

I don't kill kids. I've never stooped to *that* horrifying level. And even if this kid was a little shit who hurt Mikey, I wasn't about to make him an exception to my principles. Instead, I intended to change his mind.

I'd never influenced a child before. With adults, it was complex, but I could suggest, I could coax, I could make them do something they wouldn't normally do, and I could erase parts of a *recent* memory. But a kid's brain was apparently much simpler. A kid doesn't bury things as deep, and they feel so much because they haven't learned to temper it all yet.

In Tony's head, I found an overwhelming amount of anxiety surrounding the idea of failing, of bad grades, and of disappointing his parents. His parents stressed grades and college when the kid just wanted to play soccer.

I saw his resentment for Mikey stemming from all of this. Things Tony struggled with seemed to come innately to Mikey, who seemed to excel despite being small, weak, and poor. It made Tony want to feel loftier than Mikey, and he chose violence and cruelty as his weapon.

I didn't quite know if my idea would work, but if Mikey stayed strong and didn't cower or back down, this kid wouldn't see him as weak anymore. Instead, he would see in Mikey something that could potentially be friendship. I planted the suggestion into Tony's mind that Mikey might help him in areas he struggled, if only Tony would show kindness and *ask for help*.

FALLEN WOES

As I worked, an image formed in his mind, and I realized he was dreaming as I planted my suggestions. I saw his subconscious starting to realize how befriending Mikey instead of bullying him could change his life. His grades might improve with Mikey's help. His parents would be prouder of him. Some of the anxiety he felt would release if he could get Mikey to forgive him.

The dream playing out in his mind was so full of hope, and all from just a simple suggestion. I pulled out of his mind, feeling hopeful myself. If this idea took, things would improve for Mikey, and it would take pressure off Jaimie, which was all I wanted.

I shifted away from the kid's house. Influencing him had taken a lot of energy and I needed to feed to keep my strength up. I shifted to the strip in Las Vegas, for once not interested in a flirt, fuck, and feed. I only wanted a euphoric dance on a dance floor and a quick snack from a stranger.

CHAPTER 13

On my first Friday night as a high school student, I went to the school's football game. I didn't go because I thought Jaimie would be there—I knew for a fact she wouldn't be—but because I just wanted to check it out. It was a hyped-up game called Homecoming. Apparently, it was the peak fall event, featuring a dance show at halftime, and alumni attended this game the most out of all of the games.

Football wasn't in my top three sports to watch if I had the inclination. So instead of watching the game, I floated among my classmates, observing their mannerisms and figuring out the best ways to blend. Several girls flirted with me, and several guys gave me the eye—a mix of territorial glares and appraising glances. I flirted back only enough to establish myself as friendly and to get close enough to bite them. I fed on a handful of the students but took no more than a mouthful from each.

As I wandered away from the game, I spotted my fellow boarding classmates in the courtyard, doing half-assed tricks off the planters and landscaping. They greeted me and called me over by name, and I was surprised at the glow I felt in my chest at their casual acceptance.

It was weird. I'd spent so much time alone over the years. Apart from my stints with Rosaline, and then much later with Malcolm, I never sought out companionship. Not just because I was physically prevented from community and acceptance but because I hadn't wanted to. It was hilarious that now that I could finally socialize with people, and *wanted* to socialize with people, I found companionship among skater kids, a lonely bullied girl, and her gifted kid brother.

While skateboarding, I felt the presence of a witch. Instantly alert, thanks to my recent run-in with a huntress, I looked around sharply. My eyes landed on a young witch sitting on a retaining wall, passively observing me and the other skaters. She couldn't have been more than fifteen. I approached her and took a seat next to her.

"Do you know what I am?" I asked her quietly so no one overheard.

"Of course," she said with a passive shrug. Her voice had a slight Irish lilt.

Yeah, of course she knew. She could sense me as much as I could sense her. But what was curious was her ambivalence. I was somewhere I didn't belong, and she didn't care?

I asked her why she hadn't exposed me or chased me off, and she just shrugged again. She said she had no prejudices, that she was the daughter of a healer, and claimed her aunt was Lapsi. She didn't want to stop me because I hadn't done any harm, and she had no reason to spoil my fun. She also admitted that she respected that I'd tripped Tristan at lunch.

Amused by her laissez-faire attitude, I asked if I could have a small sip from her. She obliged after recovering from giggling at the thrill of being flirted with. She was a naïve, young fool, but I didn't take advantage of her or take more than the sip I asked for.

Look, if anyone from the witch community in Southern California is reading this, please check in on Illiana Flynn, okay? Not to, like, reprimand her or punish her, but maybe give her a good lecture on who to trust? I'm just concerned and looking out.

The little sip of her blood was like a human taking a shot, but far more delicious. Witch blood is sweeter and more sustaining, but it's also intoxicating. When I walked away from her, I was tipsy and in a wonderful mood. I went back to skateboarding with the others.

As I was talking with a younger student, I caught sight of a familiar silhouette in the distance crossing the parking lot toward the main campus. Her arms were crossed over her chest, and she stared at the ground as she made her way to the campus. Jaimie.

What are you doing here this late? It had to be nine thirty by now. I knew where she was headed, but not the *why*.

Before I could decide whether to follow her, a younger student boldly dared me to do a tre-flip, thinking I couldn't do it. Little did he know that I mastered the super complicated tre-flip *and* the laser kickback in the nineties.

I started on the retaining wall, did the trick he'd dared me to do, landed smoothly, and added two other hard moves on top of it. I was laughing as I finished the last trick and turned back to look at the flabbergasted student.

Someone walked into my skateboard's path and stuck his foot out to catch the skateboard. It sent me gracelessly sprawling. My hands hit the ground first, then my knee, scraping the flesh deeply. As I ground to a halt, I heard derisive laughter and a voice. *Tristan*.

"Careful, pal, why don't you watch where you're going?" he said down to me, his foot still on my board.

"Yeah, sorry about that, *pal*," I shot back as I got to my feet. Still a little tipsy from witch blood, I stumbled as I straightened up, but I made sure to hide the palms of my hands as they healed. "I must have missed the sign that said '*parvenu* crossing.'"

"What the fuck did you call me, pretty boy?" he demanded. He leaned closer and invaded my personal space with all the cliché machismo that the idiot could muster. Once again, I could smell the testosterone surrounding him like a cloud.

I sighed and rolled my eyes. "*Parvenu*," I repeated, slowly. "An old-world slur for 'new money,' you dense jackass."

I missed old-world slurs. They sound so harmless now, but, man, we had some good ones.

"How about I punch that smart mouth off your face, wuss?"

Oh, wuss? That's the best he's got? I mused, smirking at him. I would have liked to see him try to punch or tackle me. He had a right to think he was stronger than me because he was more than six inches taller and twice my girth. But he had no idea what I was or how puny *he* was in comparison. It'd be hilarious to see his face as he tried to tackle me and realize I was a brick wall coiled into a hundred-and-sixty-five-pound body.

"Or perhaps a more accurate one for you would be 'plutocrat,' which is a slur for someone that thinks he's powerful *just* because he has money."

Tristan growled and lunged at me, but I danced away a few steps. His fingers brushed my shirt as he reached for me, but that was all. His foot was still on my skateboard, and he took another step toward me, pushing the skateboard along with him.

"Careful, pretty boy, your foot's so far in your mouth, you might choke on it," he said.

"Yeah, I'm sure you'd rather me choke on your dick instead, right?" I glanced down at his crotch, pursing my lips like it displeased me. "I think you may be overestimating just how much you've got there."

"I didn't hear your girlfriend complaining any," he countered easily, looking at me darkly. My eyes narrowed at him involuntarily. "Where is our little mental patient, anyway? I'd love to give her one more good time before she offs herself."

I briefly pondered how it might humble him to have the little man walk away rather than rise to the bait. But really, I'm a petty bitch.

I kept my face passive to hide my intentions, then kicked the skateboard that held half of his weight. It skittered out from under him, and he stumbled forward. Laughing, I dodged his stumbling frame and skirted around him. I picked my board up from the ground and took off running.

I heard him coming after me and the other kids laughing and cheering me on. I cackled as I ran, leading him in the opposite direction from where Jaimie'd been headed. I wasn't running to be a coward, I was running purely to mock him and to get a rise out of him.

I felt like an adolescent kid for the first time in so long. *This* was living. This was innocent fuck-it foolery that makes adolescence worthwhile, and I loved it.

Once I was far enough away from him though, I stopped and shifted to a different part of the school.

CHAPTER 14

I reappeared outside the art studio and peered into the window. It was dark inside, but she'd closed the partition that split the large classroom so no one would see the light from outside. A seam of light came from the folds and the outer edges of the partition. Though it wouldn't be audible to human ears, I could make out the distinctive sound of Metallica from deep within the classroom.

I'd forgotten my keycard at home, so I shifted just inside and made my way to the partitioned part of the classroom. The music was loud, and I knew she wouldn't hear me approach, so I did my best not to startle her. Her back was to me as she filled a ceramic cup with water for her brushes. I was just about to knock on a desk to announce myself when she turned from the sink and saw me. She shrieked but managed to keep her grip on the water cup as she bumped backward into the counter.

"Stop doing that!" she snapped, rightfully irritated. She quickly fixed her sleeves so the cuffs covered her whole wrists again.

"I don't do it on purpose, I swear," I assured her, holding my hands up in defense. In hindsight, I should have texted her, but I was still new to phone etiquette.

She rolled her eyes and picked her phone off a nearby desk and shut the music off.

"What are you doing here?" she demanded, looking at me fiercely.

"I was...watching the game of...football," I said slowly. I took a step forward and stumbled a bit. "Or as we call it in my homeland....no, *wait*, it's football there too. Dummy." I chided myself with a snort, tapping the heel of my hand against my forehead. I straightened and faced her again. "What are *you* doing?"

"Working," she said in a clipped tone, nodding to the large canvas with her work in progress on it. She looked at me incredulously as I tripped and knocked a tissue box off the teachers' desk. "Are you drunk?"

"Maybe a bit, yeah," I said, still slowly, starting to moonwalk around her canvas. I wasn't *that* drunk, but I figured it would lighten the mood if I acted silly. She'd looked about ready to kill me when I walked in. "Some kids were sharing..."

"You have any more?" she asked, surprising me. I paused mid-moonwalk and looked at her, trying not to show how alarmed I was. She seemed so straight-laced, it was weird for her to ask for booze now.

"I didn't think you drank or...whatnot." I peered a little closer at her face to gauge her expression. She was in a bad mood, definitely, but it wasn't aimed at me. "Did something happen?"

"Just a bad night. Bad, bad night," she said, shaking her head. She shoved her hands into her jean's pockets. "I don't want to talk about it."

"Well, since I don't have alcohol to provide, I'll have to endeavor to cheer you up purely with my charm," I said with a grin. I took a few steps toward her and dropped into a low bow. As I stood up straight again, I held out a hand to her. "I know the dance isn't until tomorrow, but would you join me in a dance now?"

"What?" she demanded, looking at me like I was nuts.

"Not this sorry excuse for dancing we have today," I explained. I couldn't help myself. I was in an exceedingly good mood, and for once I didn't want sex to entertain me. "I mean a *proper* dance, like I grew up with. What do you say?"

"No...no thank you," she said, shaking her head. She still looked like she thought I was nuts, but at least a small smile tilted the side of her mouth.

I wish I could play with that mouth, I mused as I looked at her lips. I withdrew my offered hand and shook myself before I could take a step closer to her.

"Very well." I stuck my hands into my pockets and leaned back against the teacher's desk. "How are you here so late? I thought our keycards don't work after six on school days."

"I have an arrangement with the teacher," she explained, playing with a stray thread on her frayed cuff. "She erases the keycard records over the weekend. I have a similar arrangement with the school library too so Mikey can amuse himself on the weekends when I'm here. After his soccer games every Saturday, I mean."

"You hang here every weekend too?" I asked, tilting my head as I peered at her. I knew about artist dedication and the number of hours involved in painting, but *still*. She was only a kid. I'd have thought she had family things or just...other things to do on weekends besides hanging in a school art studio...and with her brother underfoot no less.

"It's better than, you know—"she shrugged uncomfortably" —being at home. Besides, I need to get in all the time on this bad boy as I can. The entry deadline is coming up in a week."

I glanced at the large canvas, surprised at the progress she'd made in less than a week. It was an incredible piece with so much detail and vibrant color, but not too detailed that it wouldn't make sense on a larger wall. I could see it perfectly as a mural.

"It's incredible," I breathed as I held back from touching part of it. For some reason, I wanted to touch the part where a trumpet player was climbing out of one of the black keys of the keyboard or where children danced along it like it was a bridge. "How did you gain such trust from your teachers? Aren't they supposed to all be wicked and suspicious?"

"They just want to help." She shrugged and averted her eyes. "Mrs. Gillmore even lets me keep all my supplies here. They're all hand-me-downs, but more than I can keep at home. And I store all my finished pieces here...as you've seen."

I nodded and glanced toward her cubby of finished pieces and new canvases.

"That reminds me," I said, looking back over at her and smiling. "I spoke with my uncle, and he agrees on the asking price for your painting. As soon as we can get it to him, he's ready for it."

Her hands went to her heart in her mix of surprise and relief, as if her chest couldn't contain it. Then she pressed them over her mouth as if to keep some embarrassing sound from escaping. Her eyes looked wet, like they were threatening tears.

"Oh my god," she said, her voice sounding weird and distorted through her hands. She dropped them a fraction so she could be heard better. "You have no idea...how great this is...how this changes things—How much I—" She clamped her hands back over her mouth to stop the stunted trail of gibberish until she could form a complete sentence.

She and I had figured out an appropriate asking price for the large painting that I—not my uncle—wanted to buy from her. She'd balked at the idea of asking three grand for it, but I'd done the math. If she charged by square inch, which many artists do, three grand was too low. Factoring in the size of the piece and the retail cost of the materials—pretending they weren't bought secondhand like they were—I managed to talk her *up* to four grand, which I still thought was low, especially in this economy.

She needed this as much as I needed the painting for my collection. If she knew it was me buying it, she'd feel betrayed, but this wasn't a handout. I was paying for a skill and the time put into it, because I loved the product.

As she struggled to get a handle on her sudden elation, I moved closer to her, opening my arms to see if she would accept a hug. She surprised me by folding herself into them with barely a thought, wrapping her arms tightly around me.

"Thank you," she said as she turned her head to the side against my shoulder. I put a hand to the side of her face to keep her head there for a moment longer. She didn't seem to mind. "For so much. Thank you."

I knew she didn't mean just setting up this business transaction. Her brother Mikey was doing better in his situation at school. The bully had stopped teasing him and was even protecting him from others now, and a friendship was blooming between the two kids. She equated it to the advice I'd given her that day, and she was grateful. All I'd really done was unlocked an idea the bully might have come to in his thirties, when it was too late.

"You have nothing to thank me for. This is all because of your talent," I told her, resting my chin on her head. "But if you feel the need to show thanks, I'll take it in the form of that dance I asked for earlier?"

She pulled out of the hug, and I reluctantly released her. She stared at me like she couldn't tell if I was serious. Or maybe she was trying to figure a way *out* of dancing with me. Finally, she rolled her eyes and feigned disdain. "Fine."

I queued up a jaunty instrumental song that used to be popular in my youth and pulled her into a part of the studio where there was more room. It took several times through it to teach her the steps of the dance. She stopped rolling her eyes and followed along with me. All the while she couldn't stop laughing and complaining that I was nuts for knowing the steps.

Eventually, she grew winded and shut off the music. She replaced it with a softer, slower song from this century. Then she held out her hands so we could just sway to the music, like teenagers do these days. She was still laughing, though.

"I think you've seen too much Bridgerton," she chided me as our footsteps slowed.

"Oh, *Bridgerton*," I repeated, drawing the word out exasperatedly. "That complete farse of a drama. *Trust me*, there was not that much sex in high society London."

"Oh, are you an Austen enthusiast, then?" she teased.

"*Austen* lived a whole generation before the *fictional* Bridgerton family," I teased back.

"So how did you learn to do such a dance, then?"

"I told you, my parents are rather on the old-fashioned side." I lifted her arm for her to spin under it. She obliged and only stumbled a little bit, snorting softly as she regained her footing. "Oh, if only they could see me now, they'd be appalled," I found myself saying without thinking. "A skater boy in ripped jeans and not a cultured thought in my head. How will I find a wife now?"

"Find a *wife*?" she snorted. "Damn, they *do* sound old-fashioned. But screw parental expectations. The ripped jeans suit you. More than a wife does, anyway."

I liked this side of her. So calm and so open. She should get good news more often.

"You're so refreshing," I heard myself say softly, before my brain caught up with my mouth.

"Refreshing?" she repeated, tilting her head slightly. "How so?"

"Realer. I feel like you look at me and you see me. Even if you don't know you see me, you do," I explained, trying hard to commit to what I was saying and not backpedal like I wanted to. We'd stopped swaying. "You don't see just my attractive face and react to that. You don't do *The Pause* and then reboot your brain to allow room for other opinions of me besides my face."

"Maybe I *do* do *The Pause*," she said, her mouth twitching up into a smirk. "And I just keep it from showing on my face."

"No, no...don't tell me that." I shook my head and drew my eyebrows together. My hand was on the side of her face, one finger toiling with a strand of her hair. I didn't remember moving my hand to her face. "I don't want to be that to you..."

"What...do you...what?" she asked slowly. She looked like she was trying to keep some worry out of her face.

We were moving closer, or it might have just been me. But I was suddenly drawn to her, tilting my face to hers.

She pulled back suddenly, breaking our mutual trance. As she stepped away from me, she stumbled. I gripped her arm to steady her, but when my fingers closed on her forearm, she let out a cry of pain and recoiled from me. She threw a hand over her mouth too late to stifle the cry.

"What?" I asked, stupefied momentarily. Had I grabbed her too hard, forgetting my strength? No. No, I knew I hadn't. I'd barely touched her. Unless I'd touched a part of her that was already hurt. "What's wrong? How are you hurt?"

"I'm not. I'm fine," she said, a little too quickly. She pulled her arms close to her chest and hugged herself.

"Jaimie—" I said, almost pleading.

"Leave it alone, Grayson," she said sharply. She'd been so open and unguarded earlier, but now her guard was back up with a vengeance.

"No. Tell me what's wrong." I spoke softly, but I wouldn't be swayed. Ice lined the pit of my stomach.

"Nothing's wrong. I hurt my arm when I was sneaking out," she said, backing away toward her painting.

I shook my head, pleading with my eyes for her not to lie to me.

"I'm not talking about it," she said firmly. "You should go."

"Jaimie, no." I didn't take a step toward her, but I wasn't about to just leave.

"Please, leave me alone," she said, her voice getting high in her desperation.

"I'm not going anywhere until you show me," I told her, staring at her imploringly. *Please don't make me force you to show me. I don't want to do that to you.* "Jaimie, please..."

She stared me down for another moment, as if calculating how to get out of showing me and calculating what would happen if she *did* show me. But my unwavering stare wore her down. Finally, she took a steadying breath, as if about to say goodbye to a precious secret, and uncoiled her arms from her chest. She pulled up her sleeves and held her arms out for me to see.

There were the infamous scars around her left wrist that were undoubtedly caused by the tearing teeth of a dog, not a blade. But that wasn't the concerning sight. Neither were the bruises up and down her arms in varying stages of healing. Across her forearms were red, angry stripes, undeniably caused by a belt. The belt had broken layers of skin, causing it to weep, but hadn't quite made her bleed. Instead, dark bruises were forming beneath the angry skin that she should probably clean.

"What...who did this?" I asked, my voice surprisingly steady. I wanted to reach out and close my hands gently over the wounds and bruises, as if that would make them go away.

"Evil stepmother, remember?" she said simply, not meeting my eyes.

CHAPTER 15

I wanted nothing more than to shift to her apartment and tear her stepmother's head off. And the only thing that kept me from doing this was my simultaneous desire to take Jaimie into my arms and hide her from everything shitty in this world.

Instead, as each desire fought for dominance, I hovered somewhere between the two and stayed glued to the spot.

This was the "bigger problem" she'd joked about? I'd assumed her bigger problems—bigger than teasing and bullying—were that her family was struggling with money or that she couldn't go to college. Not *this*. I never fathomed that her evil stepmother was actually monstrous.

Could we really have just been dancing? That felt like an eternity ago. Had we really just almost kissed? Why did it feel like there was a fifty-foot chasm between us?

"Are you going to go run and tell people now?" she demanded, speaking for the first time in a long moment. She pulled her sleeves back down and stared at me, trying to keep her face from showing anything but defiance.

"Why haven't *you* yet?" I asked, trying to keep my voice in check.

"Because I don't need to. I'm handling it." She grabbed a chair and pulled it over to her canvas.

"Jaimie, this isn't something you just 'handle,'" I protested, following behind her. I grabbed a chair too and took a seat feet from her. "You can't hide this. You should tell someone."

"And if I do? What do you think will happen, Grayson?" She looked at me challengingly. I'd never wanted her to call me by my *real* name more than in that moment. More than anything, I wanted to drop the human façade. "Honestly, what will it do?"

I couldn't pretend to have an idea about what would happen. The only thing I thought of originally was that the stepmother would be arrested and all Jaimie's problems would be over. But the challenge in her eyes now made me question whether I was being too naïve.

"I don't keep quiet because I think it's pointless, like nothing will change. No, it will do so many things to my already precarious, fragile family," she said, pulling on the thumb knuckle of her left hand roughly. "You think I haven't thought of what I should do or what I can do? You think I don't know that life isn't supposed to be like this? There are options and support services for kids like Mikey and me, but they will destroy more than they fix.

"We'll be separated. Mikey will be put in a group home probably, where he'll have even less support, and even fewer people looking out for his future. I'm eighteen, so I would just be set loose on the world, with *nothing*."

"Okay, point taken," I said, taking her hand in mine just to stop her from tearing her knuckles open. I put my other hand to her face and turned it to look at me again. I didn't know where this softness in me came from, but I knew it was her doing this to me. "Then talk to *me*. No secrets, okay? Tell me what's going on."

"What's going on is my stepmother is a bitch. She's always been a bitch." She didn't pull her face away from my touch.

"And your dad doesn't know this?" I asked, finding it strange that a spouse couldn't see something this obvious.

"He doesn't see her at her worst. He doesn't see what she shows to us. She was nice at first, to win us over, but she only cares about my dad," she explained calmly but bitterly. "She loved him in high school, but they didn't get together until after my mom died—when I was nine. She's sweet as pie around him, when he's home and awake. But us..."

I waited patiently for her to continue.

"Mikey and I are a constant reminder that he loved someone else before he loved her. She has to take care of us because Dad works nights and sleeps during the day, but she hasn't put in any effort since the day they got married. She won him, so she didn't need to try with *us* anymore. So *I* take care of Mikey. I always have. I never let her punish him for any reason. I step in and take it instead."

"Tonight?" I asked carefully.

She hesitated a moment. "Tonight Mikey broke a plate." She sighed and pulled her face away from my hand finally. "We don't have that many dishes...not that she uses any anyway. She doesn't eat what I cook for the two of us. She lives off frozen dinners she buys for herself. But Mikey broke one of our few plates, and she was angry at the thought of having to buy more dishes. She yelled and demanded that Mikey face her, but..."

But Jaimie took it instead. I wanted so badly to kiss her, but I knew that wasn't the appropriate reaction. Instead, I held my forehead to this beautiful, selfless, amazing girl's forehead. She was too young to have to deal with this. Too young to be so maternal. She shouldn't have had to find out how selfless she could be until years from now, when—if ever—she was a mother.

I loved her for this selflessness. She protected her little brother from harm. She protected that precious, uncanny child that I too would do anything for, even after meeting him only once. She did what I couldn't do for my siblings.

"You have to tell your dad, at least though," I said after a moment. She pulled her forehead from mine at the suggestion. "He's your dad, and you haven't said anything bad about him this whole time. Which means you love him; you don't resent *him*. So why not tell him?"

"Because I'm afraid," she admitted quietly, her eyes suddenly fearful. But it wasn't a fear of harm or violence, more like a fear of heartache. "He loves Deb. He's stupid for loving her, but he does. It'll either destroy him to realize the woman he loves is a monster—"she paused and looked away, the fear growing in her eyes "—or he might choose her over me. If I don't tell him, I can at least be spared finding out."

"You could leave. Like you said, you're eighteen," I suggested softly. I already knew the argument she'd come back with.

"Yeah, yeah, I could," she agreed with me without sounding like she agreed with me. "I could leave before I'm kicked out. But I'd be leaving Mikey in my place, with no one to step between him and my stepmother's temper. I won't do that."

I nodded, unsurprised by her argument.

"I won't leave without Mikey, but *legally*, I can't take him with me anywhere. If family services intervenes, I still won't be able to take him with me," she explained, staring away from me again, thinking about the options. "It's only a matter of time before she forces me to leave. I know she will. I'll have to find a place, try to stay near Mikey, but I could never afford anything...I'd have to try living in a different state, probably."

I understood how impossible it was. Rent in Southern Californian is atrocious, and she didn't even have a job yet. I didn't need to ask why she didn't already work because I could piece it together easily. The kids in her class already made her life at school hell. I could only imagine what hell they could put her through if she was forced to serve them at In-N-Out or at a coffee place.

"It's why this contest is so important. And why your uncle's purchasing that painting is so...phenomenal. Everything goes toward possible rent so I can keep helping Mikey," she said, giving me a weak smile. "I've had a plan, and it just got little less farfetched. The contest, if I win, combined with the painting, will be a few months of rent. I have a job set up working on the mural all summer. If I coast, and don't piss Deb off, until graduation, I'm set. After summer, my asshole classmates will go away to school, and I'll be comfortable getting a job somewhere here. I can continue taking care of Mikey as much as I always have, and I might even have enough to register him for college classes when he turns twelve so he's challenged and doesn't get emotional problems... "

She was facing a reality that kids her age typically don't. Kids today are told the fundamental lie from birth that college is the way. So most kids her age are only thinking about college after graduation and about kicking the reality of brutal adulthood down the line a little further. But Jaimie, though she wasn't necessarily eager to face adulthood this suddenly and though she wasn't financially ready for the hard slap of adulthood, knew it was coming for her sooner than others, and she was trying to brace. All while being battered by cruelty from every side.

There was more of myself in her than I'd realized. She longed for her sibling's happiness more than her own. Hadn't that been my biggest concern as I approached adulthood—before it was brutally snapped away?

I'd worried about my twin siblings, who might never have found contentment in a world that wasn't built for them. And I'd just wanted my kid brothers to be kids for as long as possible. Here Jaimie was sacrificing everything for her brother when she shouldn't have to.

"You're doing everything for him, and he doesn't even realize it," I said softly, smirking a little to show her I was teasing. "Putting your own future on hold for his."

"Oh, he realizes it. Trust me, I don't let him forget it," she said, one side of her mouth turning up into a half-grin. "And after he's an engineer or a quantum physicist, I'll cash all this karma in. I'll be the deadbeat older sister that lives in his attic and paints all the time. And I'm looking forward to it. I just have to get him to that point with his sanity and his beautiful brain intact."

"By staying with the hag and putting up with her abuse." It wasn't a question.

"It's not that bad most days. We have a system in place. It isn't ideal, but it works most days." She pulled her hands from mine and crossed her arms over her chest as she sat back in her chair. "She gets away with not doing any housework or having a job because she has 'chronic migraines.' I don't think it's as chronic as she lets on, but she receives some disability benefits for them. Her temper comes from her migraines, so it's easiest to just fly under the radar. Both here and at home. We find any excuse to be away from home for as long as possible, to avoid her. We don't ask her to do anything; we just do it ourselves. Can it all come toppling down any day? Yeah, but we're just about ready for when it does."

I hated that she had to be so ready. I hated the universe for handing her this shitty hand of cards to play. I hated her father for being blind to what was happening. And I hated her stepmother most of all. Just thinking about her made my blood boil in my stagnant veins. I understood Jaimie's logic, and I was floored by her survival tactics, but it didn't mean I accepted them as easily as she did. In fact, I refused to accept them.

"So can we drop it?" she asked after I didn't respond or protest for a moment. "Can we just go back to being casual, new friends who don't talk about this shit?"

"I'll drop it, if that's what you want," I said. "But the next time something happens, you text me, okay? I'll be over immediately. Okay?"

"Okay. I will," she agreed. But she was lying.

I knew she had no intention of texting me the next time. But this lie was okay. Because there wasn't ever going to be a next time.

I kept her company into the small hours of the morning, lying on the floor, my head on my skateboard as she painted. She put her music back on, but at a lower volume this time. I watched her without fully meaning to. She grew so focused when she painted, shutting the world out completely as she blended her bright colors and applied them onto the canvas.

She was beautiful, and she wasn't even aware of it. Or she was aware and just didn't care. And she was so strong. *This* she was aware of undoubtedly, but no one else seemed to be, except me. It was our little secret—ours and Mikey's.

We didn't talk about much during those hours, yet I felt the bond between us solidifying. Maybe I was just imagining it, or hoping. But *what* was I even hoping for? Surely not love. I didn't need love. Salvation maybe. Yeah, maybe I was hoping for salvation. Not love.

Looking back on it all, these hours were my favorite and my most cherished. I felt alive, even though we weren't doing anything. It was a night with no sex. With no action. No seeking of thrills. And yet I felt alive because we simply *were*.

After two in the morning, she packed up her stuff and I walked her home. I boosted her up on my knee so she could climb back through her bedroom window to the room she shared with Mikey. I promised her I'd get the money from my uncle in the morning and get it to her.

When the window shut, I didn't leave the area. I waited around for an hour, until it was a more reasonable time on the East Coast so I could make a call.

"Okay, Mason, you're really abusing the repeat customer privilege here," Libby said when she answered the phone. "It's only six a.m., and I haven't even had any coffee yet."

"I'm sorry. This is a less exhaustive favor, I promise," I assured her, after wincing at her reproach. I'd assumed, with a baby, she would've been up for a while already. "I was wondering if you could work some research magic and find me a healer out in my neck of the woods? And quickly, if you can. I'm vastly ill-equipped to find one myself."

She paused, and when she spoke next, her voice was full of hesitant, wary concern. "Mason, seriously, how much trouble are you in?"

"I'm not in trouble. And this isn't for me," I assured her calmly. It was extremely weird to have a witch concerned about *me*.

"This is the third time in as many weeks you've come to me with vague but urgent concerns," she reminded me, still with that wary concern in her voice that weirded me out.

"I'm just working on expanding my network," I explained, adopting a blasé no-big-deal tone, even though I knew she wouldn't buy it. "I'll pay you whatever you want for the information."

"You don't have to pay me for looking a name up in the witchy-phonebook," she chided, as if rolling her eyes. "What is it with you Lapsi and always insisting on shoving more money at me than I ask for?"

"What else are we going to spend our money on?" I mused absently. "Thank you, Libby, really." I paused, wanting to have a little bit of fun. I changed my tone to a flirtatious one. "And tell your husband I said *hey*."

She paused on the other end, startled. I almost laughed.

"Are you...into my husband?" she asked, and I could hear the surprised amusement in her voice.

"I'm merely an admirer of beautiful things. You're gorgeous too, Libby," I added, so she didn't feel left out. I wasn't lying or flattering; they both were attractive, and they'd made a beautiful baby.

"Jeez, I already said you don't have to pay me for this favor. You don't have to pay me in flattery either, Mason," she said, still amused. "I'll text you what I find in a few minutes."

I idled around Jaimie's apartment complex while I waited for Libby's text. I moved to the communal quad area, away from any bedroom windows, and skateboarded around for a while. A security agent came by once, but I sent him away with mesmerism. Finally, Libby got back to me with the name, address, and phone number of a healing witch in this same town. I couldn't guess how to pronounce the Irish first name, but the last name was Flynn. Possibly Illiana's mother.

Next, I shifted directly into Jaimie's apartment to pay her slumbering stepmother a visit.

I wasn't there to kill her, much as I wanted to. That would disrupt Jaimie's life too much, and I didn't want to tear anything up anymore. I wanted to help build something better.

Much as I didn't want to, I pressed into her mind and dove through the waves of this vicious woman's psyche. It wasn't hard to find the emotions I was searching for: they were pretty close to the surface. The resentment for her stepchildren simmered like a hot spring that ran *deep*, feeding into and poisoning so many other parts of her mind. I reached for its source, and closing my metaphysical fist tightly around it, I squeezed hard until it crumbled into cinders. She wouldn't miss this part of her mind, so I didn't feel bad about viciously destroying it.

Before withdrawing, I left behind the nagging reminder that she had an afternoon appointment with someone who specialized in keeping periodic migraines away for good. I wasn't just destroying the toxic part of her mind, I was helping to heal the rest of it too.

I wrote the address of the witch on a paper and left it by her bed. Then I shifted away without looking back.

CHAPTER 16

"I come bearing caffeine and decadence for my favorite people," I announced as I pulled open the studio door and stepped inside, balancing the drink carrier on my skateboard. Mikey was on the floor, coloring a complex 3D maze that Jaimie had sketched for him, and he glanced up with huge eyes and thanked me profusely when I handed him an iced un-caffeinated beverage, topped with whipped cream and candy pieces.

I set my skateboard down on a desk and pulled Jaimie's hot drink out of the holder. Our knuckles brushed as she wrapped her hand around the cup, just above mine. I didn't want to let go, but I didn't want to make it weird, so I retracted my hand from hers and stepped back.

"As requested," I said. "You just said coffee...but espresso has more of a kick to it, so I got you a latte." Not only was it stronger, it had far more calories in it, which she desperately needed.

"Oh, god, it's not a pumpkin spice latte, is it?" She paused with the cup to her lips.

"No, it's caramel. Why, do you like those?" I asked, wondering if I should have gotten that instead.

She shrugged. "I have no idea. I've never had one." Her mouth twitched slightly into a smirk. "It's just fall, and PSLs are notoriously loved by teenage girls. I bet I'd hate it though."

She took a sip and closed her eyes for a long moment while she appreciated the richly sweet taste on her tongue. I already knew they didn't get sweets or dessert-like things very often, so this was a magical moment for her.

"You're spoiling me," she said as she recovered from her first taste. "This is sinfully delicious, and I can't really afford to acquire a latte addiction." She took another sip, closing her eyes again. "But thank you so much. I need this today."

It was only the day after we'd been in the studio so late. She'd been up past two in the morning and had been up early to get Mikey to his soccer game at the recreation fields. She'd met me at the side of the field, away from her dad, so I could deliver the check for the painting. I didn't stick around long but did give Mikey a good cheer, making him turn and wave. I'd gone straight to the studio after that to retrieve the painting.

I immediately hung it in the best spot on the wall of fame in my living room. It wasn't visible from the door, but when you stepped farther into the apartment, it was perfectly hung and lit: the focal point of the room. I could have stared at it for hours—and maybe I did, texting Jaimie while I did so.

It was now mid-afternoon. Mikey's game was over, and he and Jaimie had retreated from family time to be in the studio on campus, as they usually did on Saturdays. Her dad worked nights during the week, but rather than going straight to sleep Saturday morning, he stayed up for Mikey's games, lunch afterward, and then quality time with his wife. Jaimie had a long-standing, unspoken agreement with her stepmother that she would make Mikey and herself scarce during that time. I hoped that wouldn't be necessary much longer, but Jaimie didn't know that yet.

"How's your day been, other than tiring?" I asked.

"Uh, it's been okay, just...weird," she said, her brow furrowing slightly. "It's been very weird."

"How so?" I asked, leaning in as my curiosity piqued. Had she seen the difference already?

"Deb actually went to the game today," she said, her eyebrows drawing closer together. "She's never done that before. She usually claims a migraine or an asthma flareup or something to cover up her disinterest in Mikey. But she came and..." She looked even more confused. "She wasn't unpleasant. She didn't come to lunch, though. She had some vague doctor's appointment to run off to."

"Did she apologize for last night?" I asked, lowering my voice, in case Mikey was eavesdropping.

"No, but..." She looked away, shaking her head. "She mentioned a desire to go back to church. I didn't even know she ever went to church in the first place. It's like she woke up a different person."

I guess it's too much to expect an apology, after all, I thought pessimistically. She was returning to faith and seeking forgiveness from a deity rather than from the people she'd harmed. Not exactly what I was hoping for, but it was a start.

"That does sound weird," I agreed sympathetically. "Maybe she's turning over a new leaf."

She snorted softly. "Yeah, right," she said and took another sip from her coffee. "More likely, she's trying out a new level of passive aggression, and I just haven't spotted it yet. I'm not letting my guard down."

"I wouldn't either." I turned and glanced at the painting, deciding it was time to change the subject. "How's the painting going?"

"Just touching it up, really. It should be finished in a day or two. Then I'll photograph it for submission."

I hadn't looked at it much last night as we were hanging out. I'd allowed her privacy while she painted rather than watching the progress and the art unfold. It was truly a glorious piece, with something happening no matter where you looked. *God, if this doesn't win, the judges have no taste at all, and I'll buy it for triple the prize money.*

"When it's finished, you should paint him next," Mikey said from behind me. He was sitting up and watching us, the straw from his drink in his mouth.

"She already has." I looked to Jaimie and gave her a quick, knowing wink.

I knew she thought I meant the sketch she did of me on my first day of school, but I was talking about the mirror painting now hanging in my living room.

"Can I go to the library and browse?" Mikey asked, getting to his feet. He was still in his soccer uniform, and his knobby, thin knees peeked out under his shorts, covered in grass stains. "I feel like reading."

"I'll take you, Mikey-Man," I offered. "We'll leave your sister and her finishing touches in peace for a bit."

"You don't have to," she protested softly. At first I thought she was asking me to stay, but then she continued. "I can take him."

"I don't mind, really," I assured her, touching her elbow automatically before realizing I'd done it.

"Do you like Jaimie?" Mikey asked after my eyes adjusted to the painfully bright California sunlight. He still had his iced drink in hand, more than half finished with it. "Tony says you like her."

"Oh, definitely," I agreed, giving him a wink to imply that my meaning was innocent enough. I didn't really know how to define my feelings toward Jaimie, but I knew they were too complicated to try to explain to an eleven-year-old. "But I'm okay being friends. She doesn't want more than that, I think."

"I think she likes you," he said, shrugging. He was looking straight ahead, sipping his iced drink.

"What makes you think that?" I asked with laughter beneath the surface of my voice. "I feel nothing more than tolerance from her."

"She's never given her number to anyone before. She doesn't text anyone else."

"Because I'm her friend, Mikey," I said, amused by his reasoning. "Her only one, basically. That's why she texts just me."

"And she lets you watch her paint." He shrugged. "She doesn't do that."

"I don't watch her paint though."

"You watch *her* paint. You don't watch *what* she paints or how she paints. You don't analyze her, you just see her."

"Jeez, Mikey, have you been spying on us?" I asked him, in mild bewilderment but amused by his bluntness.

"No, she told me, dummy," he said, jumping up onto a cement retaining wall, his straw in his mouth. "You may be friends. But I'm her *best* friend."

"I promise not to encroach on that territory," I assured him as he eyed me with slightly narrowed eyes.

"How long does it take to learn to skateboard?" he asked, suddenly changing the subject.

I let out a small bark of laughter at the sudden switch. "Years. Years and years," I teased. "I can teach you some time. But, be warned, it is not a cheap sport."

"Why not?"

"Well, there's the board itself...then the shoes. It *ruins* shoes. Then there's the trips to the emergency room for broken bones. All the sprains. All the stitches..." I watched his face change from doubting to wary then to annoyed.

He rolled his eyes. "Yeah, yeah, I get the idea. It's not for me anyway."

"Hey, Mikey, you're pretty good at secrets, aren't you?" I asked, trying my hand at the sudden subject change. On a whim, I wanted to see something. "Can I tell you something that you can't tell anyone? Not Jaimie, and not Tony either?"

He nodded, tossing his cup into a nearby trash can. "Shoot," he directed me.

"I'm not a normal teenager," I told him. "I have special powers that make me stronger and faster than anyone else."

"Oh, really?" He arched an eyebrow in the air. He probably didn't believe me, and why would he? But he was at that age between belief and nonbelief: too old to believe in impossible things but still *wanting* to believe.

"Yeah, really. I'm old, too. I don't age, I don't get hurt easily. If I do get hurt, I heal very fast. I can show you if you want."

He looked like he still didn't believe but kind of wanted to. "So, are you a super hero, then? Are you here to save Jaimie?" This was the second time he'd asked me that. I already kind of was saving her, but that's not why I was doing the things I was doing.

"I don't have to do that, Mikey. She doesn't need saving. But I think she's saving me."

"If you're superhuman, how is she saving *you*?"

"I'll let you know when I find out, Mikey-Man." I shrugged. "So, do you believe me?"

"If you want me to, fine," he said in a tone that only an eleven-year-old can achieve: half reluctant acceptance and half mocking. "If that's what you want to be."

"And what do you want to be, Mikey?" I asked. "A mathematician? A doctor?"

"Something helpful," he said after a moment. He shrugged again. "Something brave, and noble. Something that protects people. Or designs things that help or protect people."

"Ah, so you want to be a *knight*?" I grinned. "A noble knight with a sword, protecting the countryside?"

"Or a Jedi Knight?" he said, grinning widely.

"Even better! Kylo, Obi Wan, or Luke?"

"Luke, definitely!" He fell back into a fighting stance, holding out an invisible lightsaber.

"Well, then, Luke, I implore you to join me on the dark side or fight me to the death," I goaded him, jumping up onto the wall to be on the same level ground as him and activating my own invisible lightsaber.

We never made it to the library. Instead, we waged a lengthy, exhaustive lightsaber battle across the campus. He would jump onto and then off of tables to attack me with his imaginary sword. I caught him easily, to make sure he didn't hurt himself, and surprised him each time with how easily I took his weight. In the end, he lobbed both of my arms off with his lightsaber, and I collapsed to the ground on a patch of grass. He collapsed on top of me, breathing heavily and laughing. I was laughing too, in a way I hadn't in two centuries.

Our play-fight reminded me of sword fighting with my little brothers and of roughhousing with them to the chagrin of our parents. Acting this way with Mikey brought a pain to my chest, but it wasn't a bad, harrowing pain. It felt *good*, actually. It was the kind of pain where you're still grieving a loss but something is starting to fill in part of that hole. Where you're starting to feel alive again for the first time since the loss. I liked this feeling, because I never thought I would feel it.

"So much for feeling like reading, huh?" Jaimie's voice came from above us. We opened our eyes and found her staring down at us. She looked amused but was trying to fake reproach. "Having fun?"

"Absolutely we are. I was showing the young padawan the ways of the force, and of the dark side," I explained as I sat up. Mikey got off me and stood up.

"Oh, well, in that case," she teased, rolling her eyes. She handed a backpack to Mikey and held out my skateboard for me. I took it as I stood up. "We should get going. Homecoming is tonight, and teachers and students will be arriving soon to prepare and finish decorating or whatever. I don't want us to get caught here."

We walked off campus but not necessarily in the direction of her apartment complex. Mikey wanted to try out the skateboard, just for kicks. I instructed him on how to stand on it and told him to just focus on balancing while I pushed him. After a bit of walking and talking and pushing him while holding him steady by his hips, I loosened my grip and had him push himself forward with one foot.

He slipped, and though I caught him from falling, the skateboard went skittering several yards forward. Laughing, he ran after it before it got into the street.

"Thank you, by the way," Jaimie said, pausing on the sidewalk and turning to me. "For being so good with him. You don't have to."

"I don't do it because I feel I have to," I assured her. "He's a good kid. And he reminds me of my brother." I refrained from saying brothers plural or siblings, but she tilted her head sharply in surprise.

"I thought you said you didn't have any siblings."

"I don't. But I did," I said with a shrug.

Her face changed instantly to sympathy. Her jaw didn't exactly drop in her surprise, but her mouth opened to say words that hadn't quite formed in her brain yet.

"But aside from that, I like him. Like I like you." I said this without thinking, only to stop whatever sympathetic comment she was conjuring up, but as the words escaped my lips, a terror I'd never experienced formed in the pit of my stomach.

It was laughable. I'd always been confident in my prowess, performance, or ability to bed anyone. But to ask a woman if she could see herself *loving* me? I'd never done that before, and it terrified me.

I knew I'd opened a can of worms, and I could see Jaimie's face changing from sympathetic to...I don't even know. It wasn't hope, but it wasn't horror. Maybe she just hadn't thought as deeply into the words "I like you" as I had in the two seconds since uttering them.

Maybe spending so much time around teenagers has transferred some of their hormonal feelings and tendencies to overthink onto me...

"I like you too, Grayson," she admitted quietly, but in a friendly way, with no meaning behind it. "I haven't had a friend in a long time."

"Oh, hell, don't let Mikey hear you say that," I said, a grin forming on my lips as I gently tucked all those weird, undefinable feelings back into the tiny box where they belonged. They nestled into the box beside the wish that she would call me by my real name. "I promised Mikey that I wouldn't encroach on his 'best friend' territory."

"Wow, boosting yourself up to 'best friend' status already? Presumptuous of you," she teased, swatting at my chest.

"You have no idea," I mumbled, as I looked away toward Mikey.

He'd reached the end of the block and traveled into the street. It wasn't concerning, though, because we were in a suburban area, with little car traffic. He was standing on the skateboard in the street, pretending to shift his balance and maneuver the stationary skateboard. The board moved under his weight, shifting him into the adjoining street.

"Mikey, out of the street!" Jaimie called to him, but not with any note of worry in her voice.

Mikey glanced back at us. But as he did so, he shifted his weight too much and lost his balance. The board shot out from under him, and he fell heavily onto his right side and arm.

We started his way but weren't running. It was just a mild topple; he'd be fine. But a car came around a bend in the road, heading straight for Mikey, who was getting up on all fours in the middle of the lane, unaware.

The car was coming *fast*.

CHAPTER 17

I wasn't thinking about *blending* at that moment. All I processed was a car approaching Mikey and the need to act. Without even a "secrets be damned" thought, I shifted to him and, wrapping myself around him, shielded him from the speeding car with my body.

The car started to swerve, but too late. I heard Jaimie scream, but only distantly as the car's right fender struck my back. I yelled in pain and gritted my teeth against it as my spine and shoulder blade shattered. The metal of the car's frame bent around me, and the headlight broke, its pieces shredding part of my back. My left humerus snapped with a startlingly loud crack.

The impact sent the car spinning out of control, and its momentum carried it across the other lane until it hit a fire hydrant and stopped.

I groaned as I released Mikey and crumpled to the ground, a broken mess. It took a moment for my spine to reassemble itself and everything to go back to normal. When I opened my eyes, Mikey was staring down at me, still sitting in the street.

"You weren't kidding," he said, awed. "You are a superhero."

I sat up and looked around, assessing everything. The car had uprooted the fire hydrant, which was aggressively spraying water into the air and over the car. The driver wouldn't be able to get out until they turned the water off.

"We gotta move," I told Mikey, getting quickly to my feet. I still wasn't thinking about anything but getting Mikey to safety, but it was dawning on me that Jaimie had seen *everything*. I wouldn't be able to deny anything without mesmerism.

I took Mikey's hand and led him quickly back to Jaimie, who hugged him fiercely, but she kept her eyes on me the whole time. She didn't exactly look scared, but she looked wary and serious.

"We need to get out of here. Now," I told her, biting back my need to pour everything out to her in that instant. I held my hand out to her.

"That's Tristan's car," she said tonelessly, her eyes suddenly blank. She was in shock.

"Jaimie, we have to go," I repeated. "Take my hand."

Slowly, she complied. The second her fingers brushed mine, I shifted us away.

I brought us to right outside the perimeter of my wards and herded them toward the door of my apartment.

"Did we just—did we just teleport!?" Mikey exclaimed. He'd be skipping into my apartment, but Jaimie still held him protectively in her arms. "We did, didn't we?"

"Mikey, not now," Jaimie said softly to him.

I unlocked the door to my apartment and held it open for them to walk through, but they didn't. Jaimie's shock was wearing off, and she was starting to process what she'd seen happen to me. The wariness and passivity were giving way to suspicion and incredulity. She'd followed me to the door, but now she really didn't want to follow me through it.

"I'll tell you anything you want to know," I promised her. "Just not out here where people can hear. Okay?"

I didn't influence her, when I easily could have. And I didn't lay it on thick with an imploring gaze or with pleading. My secret was blown, and though I wanted Jaimie to know everything—to finally know my real name and say it—I wasn't going to force it or plead for it. If I had to pick up and leave again, I would.

Jaimie hesitated for a moment, but Mikey was practically vibrating in his awe and excitement, so she finally gave in and walked inside with him.

She didn't advance farther into the room, though. She stayed close to the front door, her back to the wall, keeping Mikey pressed against her, her arms around his chest.

"What the hell are you?" she demanded.

I knew that would be the first question. The trust I'd built was gone and I was now just a "what." I tried not to let this sting.

"He's a superhero, duh!" Mikey said. The kid looked like he was meeting Santa Claus. *Oh, poor kid*, I thought. *I'm going to disappoint you so much if you keep thinking I am a hero.* "Is Grayson your 'alter ego'? What's your power? You can be hurt, but heal? Like Wolverine? Or Deadpool?"

"Mikey, for the love of God," Jaimie reproached, gritting her teeth.

"Deadpool is more accurate," I mumbled under my breath with a little huff.

Jaimie looked at me sharply, narrowing her eyes. "You said you would explain," she said. "So start explaining. What are you?"

"It has a lot of names. The *preferred* term is Lapsus, or lapsus ventus, which means Fallen One or Fallen Favorite. Or a Descendant of Cain. But the most banal term is Vampire." I ran a hand through my hair. I'd never had to explain what I was to anyone, let alone someone who wouldn't be receptive. She'd had hard proof, but she still wasn't going to let herself believe me.

"I liked the 'superhero' idea better," she said, her frown deepening.

"Yeah, so do I," I agreed, rolling my eyes. "But unfortunately, I am no fucking hero. I'm nowhere close."

"You saved me though!" Mikey added. His eyes had grown even bigger. "That makes you a superhero!"

"I'm not, Mikey. Please don't call me that. I'm just a guy who happens to care about you. But it's not enough to make me a hero." I shook my head, suddenly not sure what to do with my hands. "But I care. I care about both of you more than I have since—" My voice caught, surprising me. It was my first time uttering this in a long time. I didn't ever tell other Lapsi about my past. The only person who knew my past was Rosaline. And, well, you know how that went. "Since my family died."

I didn't pull the "dead family" card because I wanted her sympathy or because I wanted to manipulate her. I merely wanted her to know me finally. I've never wanted anyone to know more than I wanted *her* to know.

"I was born in 1852, in England to a wealthy family. I had four siblings—a set of fraternal twins that were sixteen, and two younger brothers that were ten and nine. The night I was changed, my family and entire household were slaughtered by the Lapsus that changed me. And she burned my house down." I paused, dropping my eyes as the images flashed through my mind, images I tried to always block out. "I loved my family. My siblings and I were so close—like you guys are close—and I haven't been close to anyone since then."

"So, what, you've adopted us as your replacement family?" Jaimie demanded. Her eyes had softened a little, but she still was resentful.

"That's not what I've been trying to do. I don't know what I wanted. I don't think I wanted anything, I just...was curious. I was lonely. And now—I don't know."

"And you're a vampire," she said flatly. "A lonely vampire."

"Lapsus, yes," I said with a tired shrug. I chuckled softly. "And lonely—apparently—yes. See, up until recently, part of our 'curse' was to be denied community, denied love, friendship, and companionship. And that never bothered me before. Because I—" *Because I felt I didn't deserve it anyway. Because I didn't want to get close to anyone. Because I was made into a toxic monster.* "I never wanted it before. But I wasn't living. And you've made me feel alive—not even just you guys, but others at school, too. I know masquerading as a high school student is wrong, and weird, and you have every right to judge me for that. But...for the first time in a hundred and eighty years, I've gotten to feel like a *kid*. I don't expect you to understand."

"Yeah, you're damn right I don't understand," she said, snorting and rolling her eyes. Her face hardened, like she hadn't intended to agree with me or show humor. "I don't know why in the world you would choose to be in high school, when you're free to...not."

"Because I could be a *kid*," I repeated, with a shrug. "I've been stuck looking like an attractive, yet *young* eighteen-year-old for almost two centuries, and I've been forced to deal with things *way* more mature than an eighteen-year-old should. Yet everyone still looks at me like I'm a kid. They underestimate me. But in school, no one expects me to be anything more or anything less than a stupid kid. And it feels *good*.

"And *you*, you've made me feel alive in different ways. You and your brother feel like *kin*. You're forced to be more mature than your years—like me. You're looking out for him, and only him, like I was for my..." I trailed off, not wanting it to seem like I was using my dead family for pity. "You've brought out emotions I thought were dead. I didn't like lying to you, but honestly, would you ever have believed me?"

"I'm still not sure that I do believe you," she said, shaking her head. But she'd dropped her arms from around Mikey.

"Are you kidding?" Mikey said, stepping away from her and farther into the room. "How can you not believe him? You *saw* a car wrap around him! He broke, but he healed immediately! What else can a Lapsus do?"

"Everything about us is meant for survival. So we heal quickly, and it's very hard to kill us—but not impossible.

We're very strong, we don't age, and we can shift—what you call teleport—to escape our enemies. And we can...influence mortals' minds: we can mesmerize them into changing their minds or into doing something they wouldn't normally do. It's all intended for survival."

My eyes moved automatically to Jaimie when I mentioned the mesmerism. I watched her face and saw her piecing things together, like I knew she would. She closed her eyes for a long moment while she took a steadying breath and tried to process her thoughts.

"This is beyond cool!" Mikey said, grinning. "And you have to drink blood? What is that like?"

"Yeah, that's the caveat, kid," I said, suddenly uncomfortable. "Feeding is necessary, and we make it enjoyable for both involved parties. But it is like an addiction to a junkie. An uncomfortable, intimate, shameful, necessary evil." I looked at him soberly. I felt the need to sugarcoat it because he was a kid, but I also didn't want to lie to him anymore. "There are bad Lapsi out there. And I...have been bad before. Very, very bad. But not for a while, and hopefully never again."

"Were you bad because your family was murdered?" he asked with the bluntness of a child. I would have been amused if it were anyone else's family besides my own.

"Yes, yes, I was," I said, grimacing. "It's why I don't want to be called a hero."

"Did you get revenge? Did you kill the Lapsus that killed you?" The kid still wanted to paint me as Deadpool, and I wished he wouldn't.

"Not yet, Mikey. Someday, I hope," I admitted, lowering my gaze from his. "I need to clean up my soul a little more first."

"I'm sorry about your family, Grayson," Mikey said, sobering finally from his excitement.

"My name isn't actually Grayson. It's Mason. Mason Gravesdale."

Jaimie's eyes had unnarrowed and softened, but at me admitting my actual name, her eyes became sharp and hard again. She recognized the name as my supposed uncle's name, from the check I'd given her earlier that day. She stormed farther into the apartment, scanning the walls. As she reached the living room, it was impossible to miss it. She found her painting hanging in pride of place on the wall and froze. Her face displayed the hurt, anger, and betrayal I'd braced for, but I still didn't know how to defend myself from it.

"Unbelievable," she said after a moment. She backed away from the painting, shaking her head until her eyes locked on mine angrily. "Un-fucking-believable. I was so happy because it was my first real sale, and it was to someone who just saw it and wanted it. But it was *you*. You and your need to *save me*—no, that's not it. So you can save your goddamned soul."

"No, Jaimie, that's not what *this* was," I protested adamantly, shaking my head. "I've wanted to help you, yes. But this—" I pointed back at the painting on the wall "—this was something more. This was just for me. Because—"

"I don't need a *benefactor*, *Mason*!" she snapped, her eyes flashing. She said my name like she was spitting venom. "I won't be your *pity project*. I don't need your help, I don't need fixing, and I don't need handouts!"

She pulled the folded-up check from her pocket and held it in front of her, prepared to rip it in half. I moved forward quickly—resisting the urge to shift to her—and wrapped my hands around hers before she could tear it.

"*Please, please* don't do that," I said quickly. "Because if you do that, I'll have to give the painting back. And I don't *want* to give it back. I love it. I swear it, Jaimie, I need it, because that painting depicts *me*. I was changed because I'm fucking pretty. It has been my bane, my punishment, my shame. I wish I wasn't, but if I weren't, people would see the darkness instead. I am *broken*. I'm a monster. Even though I still *want* to do good, I still *want* to care, but I can't change what I am.

"Your painting shows the dark and the light, the beautiful and the ugly, the brutal and the gentle, the scarred and the monstrous. You painted me before even knowing me. There's no way I can make you understand, but I mean it."

I don't know if I got through to her. I don't even know if the meaning I interpreted from her painting was her intended meaning. But it seemed my gushing about her art softened her anger a little—but only a little. I'd ruined her trust, like I ruined everything. I didn't move my hands from hers, and she didn't recoil from my touch, so I counted that as a small victory. A *small* one.

"I'll stay out of your life from now on, if that's what you want," I told her after giving her a moment to reply. "But please, keep the money. I *swear*, it isn't kindness, it isn't a handout. It is payment for your craft. You are talented, and you deserve to be paid for your art."

We stared at each other for a long moment—me pleading with my eyes and her refusing to show anything but her resentment.

I knew I deserved her ire, but I wasn't sorry for how I'd meddled. Yes, I'd overstepped and forcibly changed someone's brain chemistry—two people's brain chemistry—but I'd done it with good intentions, and I'd improved them. So it was wrong, but it wasn't wrong. And it hadn't been out of pity, it'd been to help.

"You're not a pity project, Jaimie," I said quietly. "I don't pity you. I admire you."

I removed one of my hands from hers and reached up to touch the side of her face, but she pulled back and extracted her hands from mine. She begrudgingly shoved the check back into her pocket.

"Don't ever fuck with my life again," she said, finally finding her voice. She backed away and took Mikey's arm. "Or Mikey's. Or my family's. My family isn't for you to *fix*."

She backed away to the door, pulling Mikey with her. He looked at me with regret and like he didn't understand why Jaimie was so pissed, but he didn't resist. She opened the door to the outside, and they walked out of the apartment, slamming the door.

CHAPTER 18

Against better judgment, I still went to school the following Monday. I knew I shouldn't and that I should've left well enough alone, but part of me held a tiny, vain hope that she didn't hate me.

She had, after all, only said not to mess with her life anymore. She didn't say "Go to hell, and never speak to me again," so maybe she could forgive me. It was only a small hope, but hope enough to delay disappearing from her life until I knew.

I got to school early on Monday, not because I was expecting to see Jaimie there early, but because I had a group presentation in first period and the group wanted to meet early to practice—not that I did any *actual* work on the project.

I'd left my favorite board in the street after the car crash, so I rode my longboard through the halls. I was less practiced on it, and though the acquired reflexes were returning quickly, my eyes were on my feet and the sidewalk in front of me while I boarded rather than straight ahead.

I was almost to the quad when a shoulder connected with my chest, body-checking me off my board and into the lockers. My flailing arms sent locks rattling as I struggled to regain my footing.

"You're going to pay for what you did to my car," Tristan hissed as he grabbed a fistful of my shirt and pressed his forearm across my chest, pinning me to the lockers—or at least he *believed* he was pinning me.

"Yeah, well, your shitty driving nearly killed me, so I think we're pretty much squared," I returned easily, gritting my teeth in trying to restrain myself. This kid had the *gall* to be pissed about damage to his car, after almost killing me and a *child*. "I'm a little surprised that you drive that sleek little sedan. Aren't guys with tiny dicks and roid rage supposed to drive big trucks to compensate?"

"Tall talk for a pretty boy who's probably never even seen a vagina."

God, if you only knew, I thought, my smirk breaking into a wide, unhinged grin. "Do you really think that, with a face like this, I don't have free range of *all* the women, *all* ages, *all* the time? Tell me, how much action does that tiny dick get you, huh?"

"You talking about my dick so much is making you sound like a *queer*," he snarled, leering cruelly at me.

"Careful, now," I warned him, still amused and not intimidated. "Us queers *own* that word now. And us so-called 'queers' aren't as timid and weak as you think we are."

"Doesn't look that way from where I'm standing, cocksucker," he scoffed. He leaned in closer, and the smell of testosterone and protein powder wafting off him turned my stomach. "You may have Jaimie fooled into thinking you're a big, strong hero, but all I see is a wimp."

Joke's on you, bro, she already knows I'm no hero. But my temper spiked at him mentioning Jaimie. I hated her name on his lips and the menace in his tone.

"I don't really know what you intend to win in this dick-waving contest, but you have *nothing* to wave," I chided him, my tone delivering a warning that was lost on him. He thought I was just making another jab at his steroid use shrinking his package, but really I was talking in terms of strength. He thought he could pummel me, but if he tried, he'd be humiliated. *You puny man. Compared to you, I am a Titan.*

"Maybe I'll wave it in Jaimie's direction, and we'll see what you can do about that," he warned, his voice reflecting all the menace I'd only gotten a sense of earlier. "I know you think you're protecting her. But one day you might not be here."

My patience evaporated, and I let just a fraction of my temper loose.

I pushed off from the lockers easily, forcing Tristan to take a step back. The surprise on his face was satisfying, but not satisfying enough. I grabbed handfuls of his shirt in both of my hands, and in one swift motion, I lifted him six inches off the ground and turned to slam him back against the lockers. It must have looked comical: me being so much shorter than him and half his size, lifting him like he was paper. Fleetingly, I wished someone was around with a camera.

It'd been amusing at first letting Tristan think he could push me around, but I was *done* playing. He'd shown no remorse at almost killing Mikey, and he was threatening Jaimie with sexual assault, which forfeited his right to live.

"Listen, prick, you *know* I was there when you crashed your car. So *you* know that *I* know that you swerved but didn't even touch your brakes." I growled the words but simultaneously pressed into his mind so he could feel the meaning and threat in every single one of my words. "How would it look if it came out that you didn't even try to stop? Near-child-killer doesn't sound too great on a college application, does it, Tristan?"

There was no way I could prove to authorities that Tristan hit us. I couldn't prove that I was even there since it would raise questions about how I walked away unscathed. But as I pressed into Tristan's mind, I made sure *he* believed with every fiber of his being that I could destroy him by sharing this information. I wanted him afraid of what I could do to his body *and* his future.

I left his mind and released my grip on his shirt, making him fall back to the ground. He stumbled and glared at me with hatred, but he kept his mouth closed against any more insults or threats.

"That's what I thought, *plutocrat*," I spat, though his silence was satisfying. "Stay away from Jaimie, and away from me, and there won't be any more problems."

I straightened my T-shirt, then retrieved my longboard and skated away.

I was surprised to find Jaimie eating lunch outside rather than being hard at work finishing her painting. I told her so, by way of greeting, as I handed her the paper coffee cup—my weak peace offering.

She took it, with a skeptical look of surprise, but didn't speak immediately, like she was sifting through which biting remark to say first. I took a seat by her, against the wall where we'd shared my first lunch period.

"The teacher's having a meeting in there today," she explained, instead of biting my head off. The expression she gave me was a mix of wariness and resentment. "Besides, the painting's basically done. I just need to varnish and photograph it."

"That's awesome!" I said, sitting up straighter. She didn't return my excited look, though.

Her face remained unwelcoming, but she took a tentative sip from the coffee cup. At first she looked grateful for the caffeine and rich espresso, but then she grimaced and held the cup in front of her, staring at it like it offended her more than I had.

"Ugh, what is this?"

"A PSL, because I thought you'd want to try it," I offered, cringing. "Not good?"

"No, not good."

"One sec, then." I shot to my feet and shifted away. I reappeared a second later holding a second cup that I'd stashed, just in case.

"Caramel this time, which I know you liked."

She huffed, like she resented me doing something nice for her, after everything, but set the PSL aside and took the second offered latte.

"I saw you nodding off in last period and figured you'd appreciate the boost," I explained as she took a slow, grateful sip, savoring it.

"You were in—" She shook her head and huffed again. She took another sip.

I'd been there, but I'd purposely cloaked myself so I wouldn't alarm her. Tristan's threat had left me even more protective of her. But when she was swaying in her seat toward the end of class, I made a quick coffee run.

"What are you still doing here, now that the jig is up?" she demanded, though not angrily. "Are you just here to grovel for my forgiveness?"

"Well, I had a presentation in first period, and I didn't want to leave my group hanging. Plus, I had a math test in third," I said with a smirk. But then I sobered. "And I can kiss the ground at your feet, if that's what you want. But you don't seem to be the type that wants groveling."

She sighed and set her cup aside after another sip. She ran her hands over her face and through her hair in exasperation.

"Deb did laundry yesterday," she said after a long moment. "Like...*everyone*'s laundry. She's never done that before. And I thought she was full of shit, but she *did* go to church like she said she would. She researched job listings. And..." She looked across the quad at nothing in particular. "And she says she won't have migraines anymore. She found some new 'magical' medication that will banish them for good." She looked at me sharply. "Was that you, too?"

"I can't cure migraines," I said, shaking my head. But before she could express any relief, I continued. "But I strongly recommended a witch that can."

"A witch—" She shut her mouth against the rest of her sentence and groaned into her palms, while her fingers massaged the bridge of her nose. "Christ, Mason. This is so wrong. What you did was so wrong..." She lowered her hands and looked at me with reproach. Horror and relief fought for control of her expression.

"I know I overstepped. I meant well, and it was the only way I could help without killing the bitch," I reasoned gently. She looked at me, unamused, so I continued, holding my hands up. "Look, you can say it was wrong, but look closer at what I did. I took away the thing that made her a monster. I couldn't erase the past, but I could make it less likely that she would be monstrous in the future. She won't hurt you, or Mikey, again."

She looked like she wanted to argue, but she hesitated, her expression cycling through a number of emotions. "She won't?" she said finally, like she needed to hear me say it for certain.

"You said her temper comes from her migraines." I held out one finger, then lifted a second finger. "And that her malice stems from her resentment of you two. Well, she won't have migraines anymore. And I removed that resentment from her mind. I'm mad she hasn't apologized or groveled, but maybe she will in smaller ways..."

Jaimie let out her breath slowly through her nose. She picked up her coffee and hugged it to her chest with both hands. I didn't blame her for being conflicted. I'd have been conflicted too, if I hadn't had my morals shredded and buried for the better part of two centuries.

"And did you coerce Tony as well?" she asked after another deep breath.

"I barely did anything to him," I told her honestly, though she had no reason to believe me. "The young are fluid and sponge-like. I just planted the idea that Mikey would help him if he apologized and *asked*."

She stared at me for another long moment, alternating between bafflement and irritation until her shoulders relaxed and she gave me a small nod. She surprised me by scooting closer to me so we were shoulder to shoulder. I froze when she leaned her head heavily onto my shoulder, shocked that she was initiating contact, but then I leaned into it, grateful. I rested my head on top of hers, breathing in the scent of her hair.

"I don't think I should thank you," she said after a moment, playing with her sleeves in her lap.

"I don't think you should, either." I shifted my weight so I could put my arm around her shoulders. Absently, I kissed the top of her head and rested my cheek against her hair again. "I'm sorry I meddled. I just wanted to help, and this was the easiest way, aside from just shoving money at you guys. You wouldn't have liked that."

"You're right, I wouldn't have," she agreed with a huff. "Although you kind of did, with the painting."

I lifted my head and cupped her chin so she could look at me.

"I meant everything I said about that. It was a *fair* price for a gorgeous piece. I swear," I told her, staring into her honey-colored eyes earnestly. My knuckle brushed her cheek, but I dropped my hand and slid it into hers, on her lap. "Other than my name, and when I said I didn't have any siblings, I tried not to lie to you. I had to bend some truths, but I've been honest."

She searched my face for a moment, her mouth twisting in indecision. "You haven't fully lied to me, but I know almost nothing about you." She shifted her hand so our fingers could interlace. "It's somehow been all about *me*."

"Because you're interesting. I want you to feel seen," I told her honestly with a shrug.

"Still though, it isn't fair, is it?" she asked. "Give me something about you."

"That's a big ask, Jaimie," I said, wincing. I started to pull my hand from hers, but she held on. "I've done things I don't like to think about and that I can't just wash away...I'm better now, but trust me..."

"Fine. Don't go into that," she argued with a shrug. "Tell me about your life *before*, or tell me about what you're like...this decade?"

I sighed and leaned my head against the wall behind us, thinking about safe things I could tell her.

"All right. I was the oldest of five kids and the heir to my dad's estate. My twin siblings, Clara and John, were my best friends. Clara was gifted, like Mikey. She could've been a mathematician or physicist if she were born in a different time. And John...John just wanted to play the piano." I tugged on a handful of my hair with my free hand. I'd never had the opportunity to tell these details to anyone. "I kind of threw my childhood to the wind so I could preserve my youngest siblings' childhoods, like *you*. But I was social and loved flirting with women at dinners or balls. Then a whole lot of bad happened. I lost them, I lost myself. I became a monster, crawled out of it, then was dragged back..."

I didn't continue for a moment. Jaime, bless her, remained silent, letting me decide whether to continue or not.

"But this decade..." I began again, after an exaggerated shrug. "I don't know...I like rollercoasters? And skateboarding. And I'm a filthy slut."

Her brow furrowed and her mouth curled upward on one side in a confused grimace, like she couldn't decide whether it was appropriate to be amused by my admission.

"No, wait, I take back the 'filthy' part. I'm a *proud* slut," I clarified, smirking. "But yeah, I have a lot of sex, and often."

"How much is a lot?" she asked, still looking like she didn't know what facial expression was right in this instance. It was adorable.

"At least one person a night, almost every night...for more than 180 year. I probably have the highest body count in the state," I admitted with a lopsided grin. It drooped a bit, and I looked at our hands. "And...this might be the first time I've ever held someone's hand."

"I see," she said, glancing down at our intwined hands, frowning. "And did you wash your hands since the last one?"

"Excuse me, I'm a slut, but I'm a *gentleman*," I said in fake reproach, nudging her with my elbow. I leaned my head back against the wall again. "Honestly, though, I haven't been with anyone in a bit..."

I racked my brain, trying to recall who had been my last. Was it the gorgeous Mediterranean man in New York? That'd been weeks ago. *Huh*.

"Yeah? What changed?" There was a wariness in her tone, and I could guess what she was thinking: *please don't say it was me.*

It wasn't. Not *entirely*.

"Eh, I just haven't been in the mood for once in my life." I shrugged. "I've had a lot on my mind."

"It can't be school. I've never seen you do, like, one assignment," she jabbed playfully.

"Hey, I like my drawing class," I defended with a smirk. But it slipped again, and I looked straight out at the green space in front of us and at the groups of kids scattered about.

Really, I *had* had a lot on my mind lately, distracting me from my usual antics. It wasn't just because I was trying to hide and keep a low profile, and it wasn't just because I was maybe falling for Jaimie. I'd been semi-absorbed into the group of skater kids at this school, and rather than going out to clubs, I'd been spending my evenings horsing around with them at the local parks. I'd almost call them friends. Almost.

Huh. Is this normalcy?

"Well, you may be a slut, but I...I'm not," she said after we were quiet for a bit.

"*What*?" I said in fake shock. I sat up straight and looked at her incredulously. "You mean the girl that uses every available minute to paint and that everyone either ignores or makes fun of *isn't* sleeping around?"

She smirked at my sarcasm and rolled her eyes. Then she bit her lip. "I just meant—"

"I know what you meant," I told her, sobering. "I assumed you're a virgin. But I'm not an incel. I don't care, and it's not what makes you desirable to me."

She looked surprised at my easy acceptance and casual dismissal, but my last words hung heavy between us. Her brow twitched upward and she looked like she wanted to pull on that thread and ask what about her I found *desirable*. But she didn't. Instead she swallowed almost uncomfortably and looked away, picking up her coffee again.

I glanced down at our hands, still locked together in her lap. I'd meant it when I said I'd never held anyone's hand before. Not unless I was leading them somewhere more intimate. In fact, this was the longest I'd been this close to someone and not kissed them. Weirdly, I didn't want to: I was content with just this much contact. *Who am I?*

"So," I said after a moment, squeezing her hand gently. "Are we good? We're friends again?"

A side of her mouth twitched upward, and she looked me in the eyes. "Yeah," she said soberly. "Just promise that you're done meddling. No more stepping in to make my life better."

I was about to agree without hesitation, but a familiar meathead with curly brown hair caught my eye. Tristan was seated at a metal picnic table across the quad with his rich groupies, and he'd just thrown a glance our way and paused, as if seeing us so close together caught his attention. His eyes flashed with fury.

"I...I can't promise that," I said honestly, still eyeing Tristan with disdain. I sent him a silent mesmer command. *Don't come over here.*

Jaimie followed my gaze and turned back to me, shaking her head. "No. Don't you dare," she protested.

"He...he wants to hurt you, Jaimie," I admitted to her, my jaw clenching, remembering his threat from this morning. He wanted to do worse than hurt her.

"I mean, yeah, he deserves to have his face bashed in. Hell, I want to kick him in the balls every time I see him," she said hurriedly, gesturing anxiously with her coffee as she spoke. "I'd rather you rough him up than have him have a sudden *change of heart.*"

"Oh, that's not what I had in mind at all," I said, my voice so low it was almost a growl. Tristan was still staring fixedly at us, his hand clenched into a fist on his thigh. I shot him my darkest glare, giving him just a peek at the Monster Mason. A noticeable shudder went through him, and he finally looked away, slouching forward to purposely turn his body away from us.

"Hey," Jaime said sharply, jerking away from me a little. "What was that?"

"What was what?" I asked, drawing my eyes back to her.

"You...you went away for a moment there," she said, her gaze darting over my face, searching for something. "What looked out of you just then wasn't you. I didn't like that."

"I...I'm sorry," I said quickly, horrified. I hadn't meant for her to see me slip my mask on for that brief second—or was *this* Mason the mask, and I'd let it slip? I brushed the thought away and wiped any residual anger from my face to give her my angel eyes again. "I won't do anything to him as long as he keeps his distance. He just bothers me so much."

"Yeah, me too," she admitted, relaxing a little but still eyeing me warily, as if waiting for the mask to slip again.

"Why is he so fixated on *you*? Of everyone here, why you?"

"He's always been an ass," she said with a shrug, shooting him another careful glance, then turning her body to block him from her sight completely. "We were thrown together a lot as kids, at work picnics and stuff like that, but we were never friends. My dad works for his dad's company, and as kids he acted like that meant he *owned* us."

"He still kinda does," I grumbled darkly.

She inclined her head in incredulous agreement. "He was there for the dog incident," she continued after a beat. "Mikey was only four, and Tristan started to step in to save him—and I'm *sure* he wanted to make a big show of it. But I got there first and I guess it hurt his *ego*. He spread the rumor in retaliation..."

"Fucking hell," I scoffed and rolled my eyes, hard. "What a fucking pig."

"Yeah, and now he nearly killed Mikey. So fuck him." She waved her hand absently, then pointed a finger at me. "But *don't* fuck with him."

"He's on his third strike," I told her honestly. "I won't promise to stand down when he makes his next move."

"That's...that's fine," she said hesitantly, like she didn't like the idea of what she was agreeing to. "But until then, don't poke the bear."

"I won't," I promised with a half smile, amused because I was more of a bear than Tristan.

We were silent for a moment, neither of us knowing what to say next. She looked at the ground for a moment, lost in thought.

"It's hard to imagine a life where the evil stepmother isn't evil," she said finally, shaking her head. "Where I don't have to do...everything. What do I do with myself now?"

"You can finally be a kid. Like me. Two kid-newbies, figuring out how to be kids," I joked.

"I don't even know where to begin," she said, grinning slightly. She tilted her head at me. "What do kids do, Mason?"

"Skip class, maybe? I can show you what I do for fun," I mused.

"What, sex?" she blurted with a teasing smirk but then pressed her lips together, like she hadn't meant to say that. "Or, what, teach me how to skateboard?"

"No, you know what? I have a better idea than either of those things," I said, my grin widening.

CHAPTER 19

"Where are we?" Jaimie asked, looking around at her new surroundings.

We were in a paved promenade, which on a Monday wasn't as densely populated as it would have been on Saturday but was still littered with people and families. She looked over at the stone monument to our right, which had several colorful images of coasters. Above the center window, the monument lauded "The Greatest Coasters Ever Built."

"We're still fairly close to home," I explained, grinning. I spread my arms wide and motioned to the whole park around us. "Welcome, Jaimie, to Six Flags Magic Mountain. One of my favorite amusement parks."

"I've never been here," she admitted, putting a hand up to shield her eyes from the bright sun as she stared up at the steel monstrosities reaching for the sky.

"Never?" I repeated, surprised. "How can you live so close and have never been?"

"Theme parks cost money for us mortals," she mocked. "And time, which my dad never has much of, and Deb could never be bothered."

"But you *have* been on a rollercoaster period, right? Like on a pier? Or at least a ride at a fair?"

Jaimie dropped her hand to her side and turned toward me, shaking her head in answer to my question.

"Okay, then, in that case," I said, pursing my lips as I planned what to do first, "you're either going to love them. Or hate them. There isn't really an in-between. But I absolutely love them. They're thrilling, and you get to feel scared and exhilarated in a controlled environment."

She looked wary at my description.

"Okay, we are going to start...not small necessarily, but *classic*. Come with me." I took her hand and led the way to Colossus.

Colossus *was* an old, classic, wooden rollercoaster, first built in 1978. But in 2014, they revamped it into Twisted Colossus: the longest hybrid of steel and wooden coaster. Where two tracks used to race each other, riders now looped through the coaster twice. Despite its revamp, it was still the most classic and basic of the coasters at the park. I explained all of this to Jaimie as we neared the coaster.

She moved toward the end of the line, which wasn't long, but it was unnecessary. I steered her to the fast-pass lane so I only had to mesmer the fast-pass ticket checker rather than jumping to the front of the line and having to mesmer a crowd.

Moments later we were seated, belted, and barred into the car, and we started the initial, clicking climb up the largest hill.

"What is that one?" She pointed to our right at the neighboring orange and green coaster, whose riders were currently climbing a hill twice as high as ours.

"That's Goliath. My favorite here." I spoke loudly over the clicking of the track below us.

"I want to go on that one next," she told me, eyeing the tall coaster.

"We haven't even tested this one to see if you like coasters," I said, laughing at her gung-ho tone.

"I already think I'm in love with them," she said, grinning. But the grin disappeared as we reached the top. She gripped the bar over her lap but gave me one last nervous smile as we tilted downward. Then we were released into the bowels of the coaster.

On a coaster, your heart goes into your throat, and you can't help but release a scream as your stomach constricts and sort of floats within your body. You pull your knees in tight, as if this alone will save you.

Riding a coaster gives you a sense of *controlled danger*, or terror with minimal risks. You get an adrenaline release without expending any energy to do so. It's thrilling: pure and simple.

We coasted around the turns and rocketed down the drops, and I listened for Jaimie's voice, but I couldn't distinguish her screams from the others. I turned to gauge her reaction when we reached the halfway point and restarted the long, slow, clicking climb up the big hill. Her hair was a mess and falling across her face, and she was still staring straight ahead, almost shell-shocked. But it melted into awe, and then a wide smile split her face.

"Now we do it all again!" I told her.

"Good!" She pumped a fist into the air and grinned at me, with the manic look of someone who has fallen in love with roller coasters. I'd never seen her calm, muted face smile so big, and I wanted to reach across and kiss her. "But first—"

She gathered her hair into a halfhearted bun and secured it with a tie. I'd also never seen her hair up and away from her face before, and combined with the giddy smile, it was like seeing a whole new side of her. She finished just as we crested the top of the hill, and then down we went through it all again.

"Holy shit, I've never felt alive until *right now!*" Jaimie exclaimed as we walked down the exit ramp of the ride, back to the main park. "That was amazing! That feeling in my stomach...do you feel that too on a ride?"

"I do," I agreed, laughing. "My heart doesn't *beat,* but I feel everything. Nothing makes you feel alive quite like rocketing toward the ground."

"It's funny, really," she said, suddenly looking thoughtful. "How we feel the most alive when we think we're about to die horrifically."

"Yeah, and what does it say about those of us that seek out that feeling?" I mused with a smirk. We'd stopped walking right as we reached the large fake-rock letters spelling out *Goliath.* "That we have a death wish?"

"No, we don't have a death wish. I know I don't," she said, shaking her head. The messy bun she'd arranged jostled, and part of it came loose. "But it sure as hell feels good to scream in the face of it. Doesn't it?"

I grinned at her through the glaring sunlight. Is that what I was doing? I'd been thinking lately that I had a death wish—and that I deserved it. But maybe I was laughing at it instead? Is that why I was always so reckless?

"Your hair's coming loose," I told her instead of agreeing with her.

"Right," she said, smirking. She reached up and redid the ramshackle knot on her head into a tighter bun, high enough for her to rest her head comfortably against a headrest. "On to the next one?"

We walked through the fast-track lane to the front of the line for Goliath. Once there, it was only a short wait for the ride.

"So, what kind of things did you do for fun before these existed?" she asked as we waited. "Or, growing up, what did you do for fun?"

"Well, believe it or not, life in Regency England was dull as hell," I told her honestly. "Teenage fun was horseback riding, reading, and fake sword fighting with little siblings. The occasional ball was the only highlight. And in adulthood? More horseback riding, but also hunting or shooting fowl. Topping it all off with an evening of brandy and cigars in the library with Father."

"It sounds only a *little* better than how it was with women," she offered as consolation. "It seems for them it was all just sitting, sewing, reading, and sketching. Which, I would like the sketching part, but still. *Boring.*"

She wasn't wrong. I'd thought the same thing as I watched Clara grow up. She was exceedingly pretty and would've had her choice of suitors, but she was condemned from birth to a life of banal *sitting*.

"Yeah, it's a wonder why I spent so much time in the nursery, raising and playing with my youngest brothers. We'd sword fight with brooms, or fish for 'exotic' fish in puddles, or trample through the garden, hunting fairies."

"You always talk like you didn't have a childhood. But it sounds like you still got to be a kid with them."

"I suppose. I wasn't the kid in that situation, though," I argued, shrugging. "I was the oldest. I was the leader. I had to be the one that made sure it didn't get too wild, and the one that thought up the games. I *provided* the wonder, rather than experienced the wonder."

She could relate. I'd seen her with Mikey, trying to keep his childhood alive while nurturing his interests. Like me, she felt his moments of wonder alongside him, but she didn't fully experience them.

"In addition to all that, I also really enjoyed flirting and playing with ladies," I explained, to lighten the mood. I let a devilish grin spread over my face.

"Oh, *really*?" she teased, rolling her eyes. "Somehow I can't see that."

"Whyever not?" I asked, my grin widening. "You think that with this face, I couldn't woo any woman? I promise, I made many women swoon with merely a turn of my lips."

"No, I believe *that*," she teased. But her eyes flicked down toward my lips for the briefest of seconds. "You're a looker. You don't need me to tell you that."

And I would prefer you didn't.

"What even was flirting back then? In books, people don't seem to really...say much."

"Mostly you smile and give pining glances. Your eyes hover a little too long, but not long enough to be creepy." I turned my head to the side and glanced at her, demonstrating the kind of look I was describing. "You appeal to their vanity, but subtly—because it's not their beauty that's drawn you in, of course. Then, they lean in a bit more, to hear more flattery, or they tease you back."

Jaimie smirked as she listened. She leaned forward, adopting the role of the woman in the situation I was describing.

"Then you go on to compliment other things about her. The things that truly make her shine." I leaned forward and placed my hands on the railing on either side of her, smirking. "Compliment her work—her art, if she's an artist. Maybe get a little carried away with your appreciation. Maybe brush her hand, soft enough it could have been an accident." Our hands rested on the railing side by side, and I brushed my thumb against her knuckles to demonstrate. Then, I released my grip on the railing and leaned back, away from her. "And then you draw it back in. She'll swoon, for certain."

As I leaned away from her, she'd started to lean forward, keeping the distance between our faces the same, but she stopped herself.

"Oh, so you've been flirting with me all along," she teased, shaking herself free of whatever hold I'd had on her. "Now that I know your ways."

"Not all along, no. But for the last few moments, yeah," I said, layering folds of silk into my teasing tone while I leaned back in. This time, I placed my hands on the railing so that they just brushed her hips. I lowered one eyelid ever so slightly, adding a hint of practiced swagger to my stance. I curled my lips into a sultry smirk. "Is it working?"

"Oh, yeah, I'm sure you'd love to know." She turned her face away but looked back with her eyes, much like I'd shown her a moment ago.

"Pray, miss, do not be coy," I pleaded, pouting. I stepped back and put a hand to my chest. "My heart could not bear it."

She grimaced and rolled her eyes.

"Oh, you wound me, Miss Jaimie, with your sharp look and your vexing humor," I continued emphatically, pulling at the front of my shirt dramatically. "Please, do not frown, for it is your smile that I so ardently adore. It is upon your smiles that my life depends. And if your frowns persist, not fate itself can save me from the grave."

"Oh my god, *stop*," she said, rolling her eyes again, but she wasn't able to keep the grin from her face.

Lucky for her, the gates opened, and it was our turn to crawl into the coaster car.

"Another one with just a bar holding you in..." she mumbled apprehensively as she pressed the bar down as far as it would go onto her lap. "I wish they had the chest rigs instead."

"It's to accentuate the *terror*," I told her, only half-kidding. "It's how you know the ride is purely drops. If it has chest rigs, you know it has flips and loops."

"Okay, I want one of those next. But I think I like the drops the best," she said. "I don't think I'll ever be one of those people that put their hands up on rides though. I'll always hold on for dear life."

Jaimie loved Goliath even more than the last one. After the ride stopped and we sat for a moment, waiting to return to the docking station, she laughed a deep throated post-terror laugh that made me fall for her even further. This girl was my other half.

• • • •

"Mikey would absolutely love this too," she said, an hour and many rides later. She was just finishing a small cup of ice cream with sprinkles that I'd bought her. She ate it slowly, not used to indulging in sweet confections.

"Yeah, I bet he would," I agreed, recalling the day Mikey almost got hit by Tristan's car and his excitement right after narrowly cheating death. "Should we have brought him with us?"

"*Hell* no," she said, surprisingly adamant. She got up and tossed her cup into a nearby trash can. "This is our thing right now. We can bring him some other time."

We, my mind repeated, awed. She'd said *our*, and *we*, and it sounded so natural. She'd also implied there would be a next time. Together.

It filled me with a kind of hope I didn't know I'd wanted in the first place, and my heart was doing jumping jacks.

CHAPTER 20

"What are all of these?" Jaimie motioned to the wall in front of her while she pulled off the cardigan she always wore.

The wall displayed original pieces from talented artists who reached greatness, and from some who *almost* reached what I determined was greatness. Just to name a few, I had signed—in person—photos of Steve Jobs, Elvis, Billy Holiday, Chris Evans as Captain America, David Tennant as Crowley, Buzz Aldrin, and Kurt Cobain.

"I collect things from people I meet who were famous or impactful, or who *I* believed would be impactful," I explained, taking her cardigan from her. I draped it carefully over the arm of my couch, resisting the urge to smell it. "Or who just...left a lingering impression."

We'd left Magic Mountain around the time that school was over and shifted back to the art studio. Jaimie wanted to put down a layer of varnish on her finished piece so it could cure overnight and be tucked away before school in the morning. She planned to photograph it after school and submit it for the contest.

Laying the varnish hadn't taken long, and Mikey was invited to Tony's house after their soccer practice, so Jaimie had nowhere to be for the first time in I didn't know how long. I was still riding a roller coaster high and didn't want our fun day to end yet, so I'd invited her to my apartment. It was another first: inviting someone home when sex wasn't the endgame.

"You've met all these people?" she said, awed, shaking her hair out over her shoulders. I could tell she recognized some of the people on my wall, but not all. She was young.

"Met all, yes," I admitted, putting my hands in my pockets to keep them from betraying me and reaching for her. I wondered if I really should share what I wanted to say next, but decided to anyway. "And slept with more than a few."

"You *do* get around," she mused, shooting me a teasing sidelong look, but she was otherwise unfazed by my admission. "Why do you collect these? Are they *conquest* trophies?"

"No, no, I'm not creepy like that," I said quickly, but bit my lip.

Technically, I kept the clothing of my lays, sometimes. Not all the time. But I didn't *keep* keep them: I washed them and offered them to some of my less-clothed lays the morning after, to erase the *shame* from their walks of shame.

"I'm just sentimental," I admitted after a beat. "I keep things to remember experiences I've had of special, important people. These people achieved greatness and everyone will remember them forever...but no one will remember *me*, even though I'll live forever. So, while I can't ever be their level of great, I can *touch* greatness. I can be in the presence of greatness, and I can collect those experiences and display them. My presence near them is never documented, but I want to remember I was there at least."

She nodded but didn't respond for a moment. Idly, she traced a finger around the frame of Elvis. "I can't help but notice that most of these 'greats' are men," she said finally, her voice light but with the slightest hint of teasing reproach.

"Yeah, and? Didn't I mention I'm pan?" I circled around her and leaned a shoulder against the wall between some of the frames.

"You didn't." She shrugged. "But I mean, don't women ever 'achieve greatness'?"

"Of course they do," I said with a laugh. "This isn't my whole collection. I have so much more in storage. A lot of it's music. And books. I have signed first editions of all of Margaret Atwood's books. And most of the *artwork* here is woman-made. Except for that one." I pointed to a large collage-like piece next to Jaimie's.

"Is that a Mark Bradford?" She leaned forward, her hand going to her mouth. "I have a whole book of his..."

"Yeah, it is. It's not an original, it's a print, but he *did* sign it when I bought it," I said, remembering that night in the gallery and the weeks following it with a smile. "And before you ask, no, I didn't sleep with him."

But I lingered for weeks while he set up his next installment, fixated. He was an interesting man, and gorgeous. In many ways, Libby's husband Colt reminded me of him, which, in hindsight, explained my attraction to him.

"I collect and buy from those I know will leave a mark on the world." I tapped the candid photo of Kurt Cobain, which I'd taken. "And it kills me when they die young. This one hurt. All of these beautiful souls left a mark on the world, like I never will."

"And what will you say about this one, then?" She pointed at her own painting, dead center in my wall of fame. "Seeing as I haven't left a mark on the world."

"*Yet*," I corrected her with a smirk. *And maybe not the world, but you've absolutely left a mark on* me. *And that's everything.* "But that one? That one is my favorite. And I'll say that she was the single greatest artist I ever met. That she could stare into a cruel world and somehow mix whimsy with its dull, bleak grays—"

"Sounds rehearsed," she chided with a snort. "I bet you say that about everyone you meet that you deem worthy of your wall."

"Maybe it's practiced because I've wanted to say it for a while now," I said, tilting my head and holding my hands up in question.

"You have?" Her eyebrows shot up and her teasing smirk vanished.

"Yeah. Every day since I first saw it." I stepped closer to her and the canvas, loving seeing both of them at the same time. "When I look at it, I can't look away. It spoke to me then, it speaks to me now. Like you could see me..."

Her mouth hung ajar in her surprise, but she closed it and blinked a few times.

"No, try again. Dig deep." Her frown twitched into a ghost of a smirk and she stepped back, leaning against the wall by the couch. "What's special about it?"

I bit my lip to keep myself from grinning. *The minx...she's teasing me,* I mused while my feet moved of their own volition, crossing the short space to her. *Challenging me to get more intimate with the compliments with each try. Then the leaning back against the wall...I wonder how she'd react if I did the wall-lean.*

"All right, how's this," I said, stopping feet from her and spreading my arms innocently. "In this case, it wasn't that I got to touch greatness, it was that I got to see greatness *dawning*. I got to witness its genesis—"

She made a sound in her throat that was a cross between a scoff and a giggle. She tried but failed to keep her face straight, and instead her mouth split into a cringe that mirrored mine. We both chuckled uncomfortably and suddenly I was even closer to her—close enough to reach out and touch her.

"Sounds even more like a line. Your first attempt was better," she said, reaching forward and nudging my shoulder as the smirk returned to her lips. "You're performing."

All right, you asked for it, I thought with mirth. Closing the distance between us, I rested an arm against the wall above her and leaned my lower body into her. My face hovered inches from hers, and my eyes narrowed in a practiced smolder.

Her eyes widened and her lips parted deliciously. I wanted to devour those lips so bad, but I held back with effort. I ached to touch her: to brush her long hair over her shoulder and nuzzle into her neck, or grab her hips and pull them to mine. Instead, I stepped back and dropped to my knees in front of her. She jumped in place at my sudden shift.

"What—"

FALLEN WOES

"How about this?" I said, looking up at her from my knees, one hand on my heart. "In addition to everything I said, this artist is my favorite because she challenged me in ways I never thought possible. She never asked anything of me, and she never made any assumptions about me, unlike everyone else. She never under *or* overestimated me. She just let me be around her..." I'd started out almost teasing, but as the words tumbled out of my mouth, they grew in sincerity and lowered in tone. I wanted to reel it in, but couldn't. I'd reached for her and pressed my hands to her hips before I realized what I was doing. I opened my mouth to apologize, but instead what came out was more horrifying truth. "This beautiful girl reached into my barbed-wire soul and stole my heart."

Oh god... I dropped my hands from her sides and ground a palm into one of my eyebrows. I wanted to disappear.

As I was lifting my head to apologize for making it weird, her hand rested on my head, her fingers splaying through my hair. I froze in surprise, and before I could check my expression, I looked up at her with huge, embarrassingly hopeful eyes, my mouth hanging open in shock.

She looked down at me, her smile half-bewildered and half-amused, but to me, she was a goddess, with honey-colored hair and eyes, and her hand threading through my hair.

The Mason from weeks ago would throw her over his shoulder and march to the bedroom where he'd tear their clothes off. And while I've been on my knees *plenty* of times, Mason from weeks ago wouldn't have said any of the things I'd just said. He'd have flirted his way out of admitting anything of substance to her. Of course, Mason from weeks ago would have scared Jaimie off in one conversation. Her eyes and expressions were fierce, but the rest of her was preciously timid and protective of her space.

As I stood, she didn't retract her hand. Instead, when I stood in front of her, her palm rested against my cheek. My hand was interlinked with her other hand at her side, but I couldn't recall who initiated that touch. I leaned a forearm against the wall above her head again and stayed perfectly still, my face inches from hers.

I glanced down at her lips, and it took effort to drag my gaze back to hers.

"I...I want to kiss you, Jaimie." I hadn't meant to say that, but I was grateful I had. The L word had been right there, poised on the tip of my tongue.

My eyes dropped from her fierce, honey eyes to her lips again, which had parted in surprise.

"I shouldn't...I know I shouldn't..." My hand tensed in hers, but I didn't let go. "But I can't move away. Because as terrifying as it was for you to steal my heart, I...I liked it—"

She lurched forward and crashed her lips onto mine. I froze once again in shock, but then all the tension left my body and I melted into her in relief, pressing my hips against hers into the wall.

I broke the kiss after a moment, both of us gasping like we were coming up for air. I rested my forehead against hers and gripped her sides, almost afraid she'd disappear. Relief inflated my chest with something resembling laughter, and I wrapped my arms around her tightly, lifting her easily off the floor and turning in a circle with her. Laughing, she wrapped her arms around my neck and instinctively hooked her ankles behind me.

Sidestepping around the coffee table, I sat down on the couch, taking her with me so she straddled my hips. She pressed her hands to the sides of my jaw and leaned in to kiss me again. My hands traveled down her legs, then back up to grip the backs of her thighs.

My heart, brain, and hands were wrestling for control as we kissed and melded into each other, like nothing was close enough. My heart was bursting with happiness, but my brain chided me, telling me I didn't need to give her her first kiss *and* bed her in the same breath. My hands, tongue, and lips also fought for the reins, gripping, brushing, licking, and nipping all the usual places: all the places I knew would make her swoon. And with every sound she made, I wanted to keep going.

I squeezed her backside, and she shivered with a silent laugh. My blunt teeth nipped at her earlobe, and her hips unwittingly ground on top of mine. My hands slipped beneath her shirt and moved slowly up her sides, and her whole torso quivered. When my thumbs brushed the band of her bra, she pulled back and I froze, waiting for her to shut me down.

But whatever indecision was going through her head, she shook it away and lifted her shirt over her head. The careless, unprompted movement surprised and perturbed me. I hoped she didn't think I expected sex immediately after her first kiss. *Jesus, Jaimie, don't think that of me. I can go slow...*

She tossed her shirt aside and turned her face back to mine, this time mimicking my actions and putting her lips to my throat, beneath my ear. My dick pressed uncomfortably against my zipper, and the heat that spread from wherever she kissed chased away most of my reservations. I yanked my lips away from hers only long enough to pull my own shirt off and throw it across the room, then I gripped her sides and pulled her closer to me, until her bare torso pressed against mine.

Brushing her hair away from her face, I slipped her bra straps off her shoulders, then traced my hands down her shoulder blades. But at the clasp at her back, I faltered, my brain finally putting up a decent fight.

"Is this okay?" I asked her in a whisper, my hands poised on her bra's clasp, and my gaze searching hers for *any* dissent.

She paused, her brow creasing. The internal battle in her eyes was fascinating, but after a beat, she offered me a small smile and a nod.

Trying not to think too hard about what those subtle facial expressions could mean, I deftly unhooked her bra and tossed it toward the growing pile of our clothes. She trembled and her legs tightened against my hips, but she didn't protest or move away to cover herself.

She nipped at my bottom lip as I cupped her small breasts in my greedy hands. She gasped against my lips when my thumbs brushed ever so softly over her nipples.

My lips left her mouth and went to her collarbone again, kissing a line down her chest until I closed them around a nipple. She wrapped her arms around my neck and clutched me there tightly as I teased it into a stiff bead, and she moaned when I gave it a hard flick with my tongue.

My dick went to full mast at her moan, but I ignored the discomfort and focused on Jaimie, only. This was about her, and only her.

Gently I eased her off my lap and onto the couch cushions and gave the same treatment to her other breast, while my thumb kept playing with the first one. After a moment of this, I shifted positions so I was beside her, my back against the back of the couch. I cupped her chin, bringing her lips back to mine, and she rested her hand on my bare side. Slowly, I grazed my hand down her neck, then her chest, then her stomach, until my fingers clasped the button of her jeans. I started to tug at it, but her hand closed around mine, halting me.

"Wait," she said breathlessly.

I splayed my fingers wide and held my hand up, into her line of sight, almost gratefully returning to the world of consent and communication. I was surprised she'd let me get even this far.

"Of course, love," I murmured settling back into the couch back. "You okay?"

"I—yeah," she said shaking herself, then biting her bottom lip adorably. "Just...before we...Is there anything I need to know about...sex with you?" Her face was already flushed from arousal, but the color deepened across her cheekbones. "Like, do we need protection?"

"No," I said, leaning into her and kissing her red cheeks. "I don't ejaculate anything, so you can't get pregnant. And I can't get any kind of VD, or spread it. But you don't have to worry about that yet, because we're not going to have sex right now."

"We're...we're not?" she said, her brow twitching inward. There were levels to the confusion in her face, and most I could only guess at. "But you said you were a slut."

"And I also said I haven't been in the mood lately," I reminded her softly, smirking. I cupped her chin gently and idly brushed my thumb along her jawline. "I'm still not. Like, I'm not saying I *won't* want it if you say 'let's do it right now!' But you said you aren't a slut like me, and that's *fine*. Don't feel like you need to say yes because you think that's what I want. Okay?"

She nodded, looking both relieved and surprised, and she pulled her arms in against her chest, covering herself. I tucked one arm beneath her head and draped the other over her torso. She nuzzled into my bare chest, and I kissed the top of her head.

I lifted her chin and kissed her long and deep again, until her arms uncoiled from her chest and she placed her palm against my cheek. I cupped her small breast again, then ran my hand down her side and around her ass. I squeezed, and she laughed against my lips. I pulled back, smiling and traced my finger around the waistband of her jeans.

"You know...we're not going to have sex, but I'm more than happy to get you off." I drummed my fingers against the zipper of her jeans. "I know you've never had sex, but have you ever..."

"Have I ever, what—" she started, but broke off when her brain caught up. She closed her eyes and bit her bottom lip hard.

"Stop, stop, stop that," I chided her, trying not to smirk at how adorable she was. I dragged my thumb down her lip so her teeth would release it from their clutches. "It's fine."

"*Look*, I share a bedroom with an eleven-year-old boy that just wants to talk about math and robotics," she said in a rush, but then trailed off, her brow creased in frustration. "It's not like I have any privacy to do anything. And it's honestly never something I think about—"

"Shhhh, I know, I know," I said, kissing her forehead and holding her head there for a moment. "Relax, okay? Stop shaming yourself. You're young. You have your whole life to explore. All I'm saying is we can explore now, if you want."

She let out a frustrated huff and butted her forehead against my chest. I chuckled and ran my hands through her hair. My dick stirred as I thought about what she'd look like in ecstasy and what those fierce honey-colored eyes would do as she came. I shifted so I was looking down at her again, and my hand rested on the button closure of her jeans.

"Do you trust me?" I asked in a murmur as she lifted her head and looked into my eyes.

She hesitated for just a beat, then nodded. I kissed her and ran my tongue along her lips, while my hand unbuttoned her jeans and slid inside. She trembled in anticipation and wariness but melted into me when I applied pressure, expertly caressing her. Her sex was soaking with arousal, giving me plenty of lubricant to massage her lower lips and slip one finger inside without any resistance. I did everything gently, and deliberately, determined to get her to a calmly cathartic orgasm for her first ever.

Her breath hitched and came faster as pressure built in her core. She rolled her hips unconsciously with my hand's movements, and when I ground the heel of my hand against her clit, she moaned her loudest one yet.

Steadily, her orgasm built inside her. Her hand gripped my shoulder tighter, and I could feel her pussy tensing and pulsing around my finger. I shifted my hand and brushed my thumb against her clit with measured precision, and her body convulsed. Her hand clenched on my shoulder and her head rolled back against the armrest of the couch, her eyes widening in surprise. She let out a strangled cry that morphed into a moan of pleasure as her orgasm crashed over her in waves.

I kept up my motions for a moment, willing her bliss to last as long as possible, before I relented and her body went limp with relief.

"I could look at that face and listen to you make those sounds for-fucking-ever," I mused softly, settling down between her and the couch back, my hand resting against her hip.

"Fuck off," she said with a huff, her chest shaking in a silent laugh.

"I *love* an empowered woman who can tell a guy to fuck off right after she gets off," I joked, idly drawing swirls against her bare skin with the lightest touch. "But you *wound* me, Jaimie."

She snorted a laugh and grabbed my hand to still it. I leaned in and kissed her cheek while she stared fiercely at the ceiling, her eyebrows drawn together.

"So that was a..."

"An orgasm, yeah," I said, grinning and poking my tongue out between my teeth.

"But we didn't..." She turned her head toward me, trying to keep the bewilderment from her face.

"No," I said, my grin widening. I kissed her lips playfully and pulled back. "The wonder of women is that you can get just as much satisfaction—if not more—outside of actual sex. Eh, men can too, but the difference is that, for men, it's messier. Did you like it?"

She huffed again and looked at the ceiling, as if it had the answer. She brought her hands to her face. "I don't know yet," she said in a frustrated whine as she pressed her fingers into her brow and temples.

I barked out a laugh and kissed her shoulder, nearly catching an elbow to the face when she laughed. I dove my supporting arm under her head and wrapped my other around her. I pulled her to me, kissing her forehead, her temple, her chin, and she laughed at each one. She was so open and blissful, I never wanted to leave this moment.

"Well, do you want me to give you another, to settle the jury?" I asked, nuzzling her ear.

"Another?" she repeated in surprise.

Adorable. Absolutely adorable.

"Another key difference between men and women. Women can have countless orgasms," I explained, shifting so I lay almost on top of her, my leg across hers and my arms crossed on her chest. I rested my chin on my hands and looked up at her. "Lapsi men can too, because we can direct and control our blood flow down there...But we're not talking about me, here. Can I show you the magnificence of being a woman?"

"I...sure," she said after a moment.

I shifted us from the couch to my bed, without changing our positions, and she tensed at the sudden location change. I lifted off her, my knee between her legs, and leaned down to kiss her lips. She returned the kiss with enthusiasm, but I didn't linger there. Instead, I moved my lips to her throat, then her collarbone, then a breast. She shuddered and dove her hands into my hair as I rolled her nipple between my lips for a moment, then I did the same to the other one.

I moved lower, kissing a line down her stomach until I reached the waistband of her panties, and I nipped at it playfully. She gasped, as if unsure whether to laugh or swat me away. I lifted into a sitting position beside her hips and gripped her jeans at her sides. I paused and glanced at her for the signal to keep going. The look she gave me was self-consciously wary, but she swallowed it down and nodded at me.

I pulled her jeans and underwear from her hips and stood at the foot of the bed to pull them down her legs. I dropped them to the side and grabbed her calves, massaging them a little before using them to pull her toward me, until her hips were at the edge of the bed. She laughed and looked like she wanted to question me but stopped when I knelt between her knees. I lifted one of her legs and draped it over my shoulder, turning to kiss her inner thigh. I kneaded the flesh with my blunt teeth and moved farther upward, to where her thigh connected to her hip, and pressed my tongue over the femoral artery, savoring the feel of her rapid pulse.

She moaned and shuddered, and my dick pulsed against my too-tight jeans. Her scent was a heady mix of sweat, spent adrenaline, and fervent arousal, and it'd been driving me wild when she was clothed, but now it was amplified tenfold. I paced myself, though, and gave the same teasing attention to her other thigh, before I couldn't stand it anymore and dove into her sex.

With my tongue, lips, and deft fingers, I gently massaged, nipped, and sucked at her trembling, pulsing clit with practiced yet fevered motions until her moans deepened and her thighs tensed. Then she was over the edge.

Her back arched off the bed, and the sight made my dick throb painfully. Her thighs squeezed my head as her orgasm gripped her and another confused cry of ecstasy escaped her lungs. The cry lost its bewilderment, though as I kept going, determined to make this one even longer and more intense than her first. She took in a breath, and the next cry she uttered was the keening moan of a woman drowning in pleasure.

I loved that sound.

When her voice faded, I slowed, and finally pulled my face away from her clit. I lowered her legs from my shoulders, allowing the aftershocks vibrating through her swollen sex to carry her, and wiped my mouth and chin on my bare forearm, laughing silently at myself over a job well done.

"Fuck," she breathed out after a moment, releasing the handfuls of my comforter from her death grip and running her hands over her face. "God damn, I see why people like this, now."

I laughed and sat back on my heels. But doing so shifted my rock-hard dick against my jeans, and I groaned at the discomfort. I shot to my feet and undid the fly of my jeans.

"You okay?" she asked, alert. She saw where my hands were and her brow creased. "What—"

"Don't worry, I'm not going back on my word," I said through gritted teeth as I reached in and adjusted myself. I groaned again and turned from her. "Just my pants are a little too tight at the moment. Fuck it, I need them off…"

Keeping my back to her, I covered myself as best I could and pulled my jeans down. I stepped out of them and kicked them aside while I searched in my dresser for a less restrictive pair of pants or shorts.

"Now *that* is a *nice* ass," Jaimie said from her position on the bed.

I threw my head back and laughed at her unguarded appreciation. I shot her a look over my shoulder, my mouth curled into a feral, lopsided grin.

CHAPTER 21

As a general, unspoken rule, I don't sleep with virgins. Vainly, I don't want to ruin their expectations of sex for the rest of their lives by setting the bar out of reach of most men. But more than that, their *timidity* puts me off.

When I flirt, or imply that we sleep together, there's fear in their eyes and gestures: fear of the unknown, fear of being seen as childish, or—worse—fear that I would go *feral* over taking their virginity.

I hate the idea of them going into it fearful. And I *hate* the connotation of "taking virginity." For so long, my idea of sex was warped by violence and selfishness, and it took a long time for me to come out of that. No matter how wild or kinky things got, I didn't want to *take*, unless I gave substantially more.

Yet with Jaimie, it was different. My soul was entwined with hers now, and I wasn't in a rush to feel that thrill of sex. We might not be forever, but we had *time*. Even if she was timid, even if she had that *pause* at the idea of sex, it was different because I wasn't just offering her one night. I wanted countless, endless nights with her. As many nights as she gave me, I would lap them up and make them last. I was hers to command, but in so many different ways than I'd been to Rosaline.

I fucking loved this girl. Deeply, confusingly, and truly, I loved Jaimie. For the first time in my life, I was in love. And even if she didn't love me back, I was her first orgasm—and her second—and I could take pride in that without feeling gross.

Enamored as I was, though, I was realistic. We had little chance of being forever.

As she got older, more adult, I would always look like a kid next to her. Anonymous sex was great at keeping this harsh reality at bay for me: having the sexual prowess of a grown man but the face of a barely adult child. But with her, it'd be hard, because she could mature and I couldn't.

I could change her, and we could appear the same age forever, but that would take her away from raising her brother or pursuing a real professional career as an artist. And more than all of that, I didn't want her to have to deal with the things *I* have to deal with. She'd constantly be underestimated, looked down on—even more so because she was a woman—and condemned to the shadows like me.

Fuck, I didn't want that for her.

"What are you thinking about?" she asked quietly, cutting through my revery before I spiraled downward too far.

"How different I feel when I'm with you," I found myself answering truthfully. "How good it feels, and how I never thought I'd feel this way about anyone...and about how I don't deserve it."

"Why don't you deserve it?" she asked.

I knew she'd ask, and I knew I'd have to tell her. After a beat I said, "Because of the things I've done. And the things I let others do..." I was just glad I'd had a few lovely moments with her before I sullied the air between us.

I took my arm from around her and sat up, resting my back against the headboard. Jaimie sat up too, her hair falling over her naked chest. She leaned into me against the headboard, and I wrapped my arm around her shoulders again. She was beautiful, and she was mine for the moment, in ways no one has ever been mine.

"See, the Lapsus that changed me...I hated her. But...I followed her." I leaned my head back against the headboard, looking at the ceiling so I didn't have to look at her. "For years I followed her: obeying her, accompanying her, fucking her, letting her fuck me, killing for her, killing with her. I've killed so many people, Jaimie. Much as I hurt myself to make up for it, much as I spiral, I can't...I can't wash all of it away."

I expected her to pull away from me, to recoil. I braced myself for the dismissal, but she didn't move. I wasn't looking at her, so I couldn't see if her face changed, but her muscles hadn't twitched. She hadn't moved her head in the slightest from where it rested between my shoulder and chest.

"What was she like?" she asked softly, carefully.

I tilted my head down and looked at her. Her eyes when they lifted to mine were placid and open.

"She's beautiful," I told her honestly but bitterly. "She's intoxicating, manipulative, brutal, merciless, *sensual*, and utterly loathsome."

"And she's still around? You told Mikey you haven't killed her," she said in that same careful, guarded tone.

God bless this girl. She was trying to be open and understanding, but she was afraid.

"I don't know if I'll ever be able to kill her," I admitted. And before she could ask me why, I answered the question I knew was coming. "I'm not strong, Jaimie. I try to be—I try to *appear* to be—and maybe I am in ways. But around her, I'm weak. Much as I hate her...I can't resist her."

I bit my bottom lip against the wince that spasmed through my jaw. "I haven't just had to quit her once." I tried not to lower my eyes from hers, but I couldn't help it. I couldn't look at her as I admitted this part. "I've been with her multiple times."

I paused, in case she had another question for me, but she stayed silent. She still didn't move away from me. So I begrudgingly continued to explain.

"The first time, she entrapped me immediately following the trauma of losing my family. Even though she killed them, and I loathed her, I stayed with her. It was a...toxic, weird, psychological, and sexual trauma-bond. But she wanted it this way. She *planned* it this way. She made me vulnerable, she sexually manipulated me, and she used sex to form me into her little monster servant."

I wanted to rub my temples and run my hands roughly through my hair, just to do something with my hands, but I didn't want to let go of Jaimie. My bare skin against hers was my lifeline, and I drew an odd, thin strength from it: just enough to allow myself to fill some of the cracks in my armor. A cathartic strength. *Please, Jaimie, don't leave me. Don't ever leave me.*

"I tore myself away from her that first time because she allowed the last thing I had of my family to be ruined. I finally woke up and fled, and spent the next half a century facing what I'd done while vexed by her."

"What...what all did you do?" she asked, unable to hide her curiosity.

"Don't ask me that," I said, my voice barely audible. I didn't want to get into the grittiness, but I had to give her something. "She was the Blood Countess. A wealthy noblewoman in the fifteen hundreds who tortured and killed hundreds of girls. She kills people—*many* people—without conscience. And when I'm with her, I'm just the same as her."

"And she can find you, can't she?" she said, trying to sound calm, but I could hear the fear in her voice.

"I've taken precautions so she can't." I fingered the ring on my right hand with my thumb. I hadn't taken it off since receiving it. "But I'll never *feel* safe from her. I can't help feeling like she can appear at any time. I'm...I'm afraid of losing myself again."

"And you're sure you'll lose yourself? Maybe you've changed."

"I haven't changed enough," I protested honestly. I felt changed, in ways I'd never expected. I was far less neutral and less ambivalent. I wanted to help and be among humans more than I ever had before. But this wouldn't necessarily help me against Rosaline. "I resist at first, but I inevitably fall. And as I fall, I realize it's *easier* to just retreat into the monster's skin than it is to face the carnage. I barely managed to tear myself away in the past, and it gets harder each time I have to rebuild my psyche."

"How long ago was the last time?" she asked, bracing herself.

"Not long enough to consider myself repaired," I told her, dropping my gaze. "When I'm away from her, I just try to straddle the line of neutrality. It was all I've managed to be before. But you've made me want to try harder. You and Mikey—and even the idiot kids at school. You've all changed me, but I'm still weak."

Jaimie didn't say anything as a response. Silently, she got up from the bed and found her underwear and jeans. Slowly, with her back to me, she put them back on. The rest of her clothes were in the other room, but she didn't move toward the door. Instead, she came back to the bed and took a seat by me. She crossed her legs in front of her and faced me, looking at me with a sad half smile.

"So, what do you think of me now?" I picked up a lock of her long hair and twirled it idly, preparing myself for the answer.

"I don't know, Mason. Really, I don't know," she said, her brow furrowed. She shook her head and shrugged at the same time. "This is all a little beyond my capacity. All I know is that you've never done *me* any harm. Everything you've done to or for me was to help me. Before you told me this, I was pretty certain that I loved you...and I'm pretty sure I still do."

To this day, I still can't accurately put into words what I felt hearing those words. I knew I loved her, but had I ever flirted with the idea that it was mutual? Not really. She liked me, yes, she let me kiss her and send her into ecstasy, yes. But *love* me?

I was over the fucking moon. I've never been a crier, but damn, I was suddenly feeling almost weepy.

Despite how emotional I felt, I was able to form the words in my mind that I'd never said to anyone. Without hesitation, I let them fall from my lips.

"I love you, Jaimie," I said softly and with an intensity that poured from my every cell.

I kissed her then, firmly and desperately. Her hands cupped the sides of my face, and I took her by the hips and pulled her on top of me. She laughed against my lips but didn't pull away. I kissed her everywhere I could reach: her lips, her chin, her neck, and her breasts, constantly reassuring myself that she was, in fact, real.

"Wow, it's been a while," Riley said, clasping forearms with me in greeting as I approached his line at the door. "I was starting to think you abandoned this place."

"Aww, Riley, baby, you *missed* me?" I teased him, grinning wide—still riding the blissful high hours after kissing Jaimie. I released his arm and stepped back, shoving my hands in my back pockets. "I've been lying low for a bit. Has anyone asked after me?"

He shrugged while he checked the ID of a young woman who was practically drooling as she gaped at me.

"Have fun in there," I told her, flashing a small smile which was hardly flirty, but her face colored immediately. She fumbled her ID into her pocket and stumbled inside.

"A woman was here a few times. She asked after you once. Other than that, I've been the only Lapsi around here," Riley told me, running a hand through his short dark hair and grabbing the ID from the next woman in line.

"Okay. Let me know the second you see her if she shows up. Or...Malcolm."

Riley's frown twitched, and his piecing blue eyes shot me a sidelong look, but he didn't ask for clarification.

He and I'd never been lovers, but he and Malcolm *had*. Riley might like the arrogant ones, but he was too soft, and Malcolm treated him appallingly. It was one of several things that had soured my relationship with the gang. I suppose part of me pitied Riley: he was a softy with sad eyes, but it wasn't all pity. Like me, he'd been through a lot, and it made us kin in many ways. We might not be close, or even friends, and he might be soft, but I trusted him to have my back—or at least warn me—if trouble came knocking.

"Thanks, friend," I told him, squeezing his elbow for a beat and winking as I edged around him.

I wasn't interested in him, but I figured if I added a little swagger to my step as I walked away, he'd keep me on his radar more than my casual request to warn me. I flipped my hair to mask my glance back over my shoulder and saw him following me with his eyes. I had him. He'd probably have his eye on me all night, even if he didn't want to.

Inside the club, I stepped straight out to the center of the dance floor and let loose. Technically, I was here to feed, but

FALLEN WOES

I wasn't in the mood for my standard flirt, fuck, and feed. All I wanted to do was dance like a fool.

I was ecstatic and exuberant, and for the first time, it wasn't because of the adrenaline thrill of ramping down a halfpipe or rocketing along a coaster track. I was riding the high of new love—and first love—and I didn't want to come down.

Jaimie was perfect. She was hardened, realistic, disenchanted, focused, and an artistic genius. And I'd earned her love. I felt unstoppable.

I danced for several songs, pausing at intervals to take a snack-sized portion of blood from a handful of patrons. I moved throughout the whole dance floor, until I was on the outskirts, nearest the front door.

A song ended, and another louder and faster song started right as my feet stopped mid-jump, and my spine straightened. I sensed another Lapsi.

Who—

Mason! Riley's voice cut through my bewildered thoughts as a fist struck the side of my face, hard enough to bring me to my knees.

My vision swam but cleared almost immediately. I started to turn and glare at my assailant, but a body rammed into my back with the force of a truck and sent me face first into the floor. I tried to get my hands under me to push off the ground, but whoever'd attacked me pressed his knee into my back, pinning me. I let out a string of curses at the top of my lungs and tried to throw him off, but I stopped short at the sharp zing of silver against my throat. I froze, hissing through my teeth.

"Mason, Mason, Mason," Malcolm purred by my ear, his beard scratching against my cheek. "Time's up, buddy. Roseline wants yeh."

My hands curled into fists against the floor as my eyes flicked everywhere around me. They landed on Riley, who was holding humans back from joining or getting too close to the crazy knife-wielding Lapsus.

There weren't any wards on this club, meaning I had only a second before Malcolm shifted me away from here to God knew where. With a groan of frustration, I thrashed once on the floor, gritting my teeth as the knife bit into the flesh of my neck.

Track me, I told Riley, hoping at least a few drops of my blood hit the floor before Malcolm whisked me away.

CHAPTER 22

Once the knife was away from my throat, I thrashed and swung out with both fists, but for once Malcolm outmatched me and wrestled me onto a twin bed with a wooden frame. He knelt painfully on my chest while my legs kicked but couldn't reach him. I struggled, but he managed to handcuff my wrists to the wooden headboard above my head.

The first time I yanked on the cuffs, a dull throb pulsed deep into my wrist bones. Silver. I stopped thrashing and lay still. I was fucking caught; it wouldn't do to break my wrists against the silver bindings.

Though maybe I should, I thought cynically. The pain would give me something to focus on other than Rosaline trying to twist my mind to her will, which undoubtedly was coming.

"Look at ye, Mason darling," Malcolm mused as he painfully rolled off my chest and stood up. He stared down at me with a malicious leer and tilted his head to the side. "Powerful, in-control Mason, all strung up like a *common whore* in over their head."

I avoided rolling my eyes at him and instead raised both of my middle fingers proudly in the air. "I never heard any complaints from you about what this *common whore* was able to do to you," I reminded him with a sultry grin.

"Cheeky, Mason," he cooed, rolling his eyes. He gripped my chin painfully in his hand, turning my head to look up at him. "Admittedly I'd much prefer to see ye ass-up rather than on your back."

"Now, now, I don't recall you voicing *any* objections to having me in charge," I chided, moving my hips suggestively to taunt him. "I'm good at what I do, aren't I? Didn't I give you some wonderous times? Why the malice now?"

"Ye're very good, Mason, I'll give ye that," Malcolm agreed calmly, releasing my face with a push. My hair fell across my face. "And this isn't personal, really. Just my greedy nature. And my *jealous* nature. Rosaline has such an interest in ye that it has me nearly unhinged with envy."

"I've told you that I don't want her. Let me go, Malcolm, and I'll disappear to where she can't find me. She'll lose interest eventually."

"Ye know she won't," he said, which I knew he would say. His eyes narrowed in a leer. "Relax, ol' boy, she says she just wants to *talk*."

I bit back my biting retort—if I had one—and turned my face away from his. After an exaggerated snicker, he left, and I was alone in the room with nothing but my thoughts and my despair.

It was time to say goodbye to my ragged patched-together soul, to the life I'd been carving out, and to the hope and exuberance of the past several hours. And to Jaimie. Damn it. I wanted more time with her.

But instead, all I had now was growing dread, the annoying ache of silver jarring my wrists every time I moved my arms, and *waiting*.

I contemplated forcing my hands through the cuffs. It'd require breaking some bones, and there was fuck-all I could do with broken wrists and thumbs. As a Lapsus, wounds and bones heal impossibly fast and we don't scar, but silver was a different story. Wounds inflicted with silver don't heal in the natural Lapsus way: they heal at *human* speed. The shallow scratch on my neck would clot and scab and heal at the speed of a human cut. And if I broke my wrists in these cuffs, it would take weeks for them to heal, and I'd be useless in the meantime.

Of course I'd only need to maim one hand...

The cuffs were looped around the ornate top rail of the wooden headboard. I could hook the chain of the cuffs into a thin section of the crowning and rub it back and forth until it split the rail in two. It'd be slow, agonizing work, but it'd keep my mind off the despair.

In two hours, I'd rubbed maybe a quarter of the way through the wood before stopping for a break. I told myself it was a break, but soon the nagging thought of "what's the damn point?" snuck in and made itself comfy.

What was the point in getting away? She'd just find me again, and it'd be a new game for her. I'd never resisted her for long, let alone made her *chase* me. She loved games, and she *always* won. So why resist the inevitable?

I shook the thought away by conjuring up Jaimie's face in my head. Jaimie who was resilient and who took the punishments meant for her brother. Who ate less so he could eat more to keep up his strength for soccer. Who wouldn't leave and save herself, which would be *easier*, because she refused to leave her brother behind. Jaimie didn't do the *easy* things. She braced for failure, but she didn't resign herself to it. I wanted to be like Jaimie.

With that in mind, I started up again, rubbing the chain back and forth over the bar. Using Jaimie's face to fuel me. Jaimie's and Mikey's, because they were equally as important to me.

After another few hours, I stopped again for a rest. My wrists were throbbing and I wasn't making much progress.

There really was no point. I wasn't going to get away. So instead, I wanted to spend my last moments as myself, thinking about the good in my life.

I imagined Jaimie. Her loveliness. Her basic, effortless prettiness. Her rare, muted smiles, her serious, furrowed brow, and her fierce eyes. Her pitying look when I used the tired platitude of "you're almost free, right?" to imply that her problems will end after graduation. Her hands as she painted. Her discerning eye that could see the light and the dark in someone and not blink at it, but rather, figure out how to *paint it*.

I closed my eyes and fantasized about touching her again. I imagined my hands running through her hair, cupping her left cheek, and her leaning into it, turning slightly to press her lips to my palm. I imagined kissing her arms on the day that the last of her bruises and the traces of the welts across her forearms fully vanished. How I'd then slowly undress her and run my fingers over every inch of her. I imagined her hair falling against my chest as she hovered above me, her knees straddling my hips, my hands traveling up the backs of her legs.

Every movement was loving, every touch a caress, and every glance was brimming with wonder and love.

And maybe in this fantasy, I offered her immortality, and she accepted it. And because it was fantasy, we wouldn't have to deal with the glances and judgments that immortal eighteen-year-olds are faced with. We're perfect, and the world is perfect.

I didn't know how many hours passed in that room while I talked myself into continuing to work at the bedframe rail in between sensual fantasies about a life I'd never have, a life I'd never deserve again.

I was fantasizing about Jaimie winning the mural contest when the door to my cell finally opened. Clenching my fists and gritting my teeth against the pain in my wrists, I pulled myself up into an uncomfortable sitting position so my head rested in front of my hands, hiding my progress on weathering the headboard.

As always, Rosaline was absolutely ethereally—or, rather, *demonically*—gorgeous with her dark blue eyes and golden hair falling in effortless curls over her shoulders. She wore a sexy wine-colored dress that hugged her ample chest and slender waist but flowed loosely from her hips to mid-thigh, with a revealing slit up the side all the way to her hip.

The sight of her brought the same polar emotions it always did. At her beauty and sensual curves, my dick reacted almost immediately, but my seething hatred tamped down on this mutiny just as quick. My nails dug into my hands to keep myself from recoiling from her and showing just how afraid I was to be in the room with her. I wasn't afraid of her so much as I was afraid of myself around her. *God, no, I don't want this.*

"Mason, Mason, Mason," she purred in her sultry voice, sending my loin stirring and recoiling simultaneously. I gritted my teeth against her voice. "What am I going to do with you?"

Kill me, I hope, I thought pessimistically, though I knew she had different ideas. I hated her tone: sultry, yet patronizing, like she was my mom and I was the kid in timeout. She took a seat on the bed beside my hip.

"You never call, you never write," she said, heaving a fake sigh that caused her breasts to bounce. She put a hand on my abdomen, slipping beneath my T-shirt. My abs contracted at her touch. "You're flat out *rude* when I drop in to say hi. Then, *this...*"

She leaned forward, her breasts pressing against my chest as she reached above me. I froze momentarily when her fingers brushed against the ring on my right hand. She tugged roughly at it, pulling it off. It *hurt*, but I was too afraid she'd see my handiwork on the top rail to notice it much. She leaned back again, rolling the ring over her knuckles like a pickpocket and slipping it onto her thumb.

"Hurtful, Mason. To block me like that? *Hurtful,*" she chided me, frowning. She put one hand on my leg and slipped her other hand under my shirt again. "Then you pick up and leave without a trace. And now this."

She removed her hand from my leg and pulled something from the bust of her dress. My phone. She opened the lock screen and scrolled through it. "For God's sake, Mason, *high school*?"

She pretended to find these things out in this moment, but I knew she'd already been through my phone. She'd had hours, after all. She'd found the texts between my classmates and me about assignments, and no doubt the sparse texts between Jaimie and me.

"A passing amusement," I told her coolly.

"And what about this *Jaimie*?" she asked, as if reading my thoughts. "Is she a passing amusement, too?"

"Yes," I said calmly, making sure my face betrayed nothing.

"Well, this amusement seems to be a little worried about you because you aren't at school today and because you're not answering," she informed me, crossing her legs and tossing her head like she was a gossiping teenager. She even giggled, which was more unsettling than her creeping hand running over my abs. "But she also just wants you to know that she's taking pictures of her painting after school and then she's free after that." She dropped the hand holding the phone onto her leg and fixed me with a disapproving scowl. "You and your artists, Mason."

My hands tensed behind me, jostling the chain of the handcuffs, but I kept my face straight and shrugged.

"I should text her back for you," she said helpfully. She took her hand from my torso so she could hold the phone in both hands, preparing to type out a text. "I should make her hate you, tell her you're done with her and back with me."

"I don't fucking care, Roz," I told her with another shrug, calling her bluff. Even if she wasn't bluffing, what did it matter if Jaimie hated me? I was never going to see her again, because *if*, in years, I came out on the other side of this, as soon as my conscience resurfaced, I was determined to kill myself.

"Oh, boo, you're no fun," she said with a fake pout, tossing the phone onto the foot of the bed. "As it happens, Mason, *I* don't care either. You can have your plaything. Bring her along."

"What?" I demanded, showing my surprise despite trying not to.

She shrugged. "Bring your pet along, Mason." Her face broke into a flirtatious smirk. She reached over and stroked her hand down the side of my face. "When have I ever denied you from introducing someone into our games? Besides, I have Malcolm currently. All I want is you on my team for this important event. Malcolm is my consort of choice: for now. You are my beautiful slutty teammate."

Her one hand caressed my face lovingly, and her other hand reached lower, cupping my crotch over my jeans. My toes curled as I suppressed the desire to recoil from her.

"Where would I be bringing her?" I asked carefully, skirting around the horrifying suggestion that I bring Jaimie into bed with us for the sake of gleaning her motives. "Where are we going?"

"Something big is coming, Mason, and I want you by my side for it. Or, rather, I want all of my favorites by my side for it," she explained with a devious smile, her eyes narrowing slyly. Her hand gripped my crotch a little more aggressively, and my dick stiffened uncomfortably, no matter how much I didn't want it to. "And you can bring your girl."

If Rosaline had her eye on something big, it wouldn't be good for any humans involved. I didn't want to be anywhere near it, and I wanted Jaimie as far away from it as possible.

She fingered the button closure of my jeans, driving me crazy with the simultaneously eager and wary sensations that spread everywhere she touched. She tilted her head to one side, like she did when she was about to say something unsettling that she found amusing.

"But I would change her as soon as possible. I have it on good authority that the thing that's coming isn't going to be all that pleasant for humans," she mused, biting her lip.

"What is it, Roz?" I said, my voice coming as a low growl as I fought to stay strong against my arousal. "What's coming that you want me so badly for?"

"Community, Mason," she said, opening the top button of my jeans, her finger tracing a distracting line above the waistband. "Community with Lapsi at last. Community and chaos."

CHAPTER 23

"There's a beautiful minx of a Lapsus who has it in her mind to take an entire city and reshape it into our very first long-standing Lapsus community," she explained slowly upon seeing my head tilt and my eyebrows draw together. She smiled and ran her hand up my torso again. "Intriguing, isn't it?"

"It sounds a bit drastic. Wouldn't it be better to start smaller? With, like, an apartment or a deserted island?" I protested, partly to distract her from going further into seducing me, and partly because I wanted to make sense of what she was saying.

"She says we must be bold in order to be taken seriously," Rosaline purred. She raked her sharp nails across my stomach slowly. I focused on the pain versus the tingling arousal the action enacted.

"Who is 'she'?" I asked huskily through gritted teeth.

"An ancient Lapsus who claims she can see the future," she mewed evasively. From that description, I already knew who she meant. I knew of only one Lapsus who could see the future. "A beautiful redhead named Cassandra."

I managed to hold in my laughter, but I couldn't stop the amusement from showing on my face. I'd met Cassandra before. She was beautiful, yes, and intense, but slightly deranged from a lifetime of trauma and loneliness. She was brutal and merciless, but she was *adamantly* opposed to sexual violence against women. And she had a soft spot for all victims of sexual assault. Therefore she *tolerated* me, even with my past actions. I found it impossible to believe that Cassandra liked Rosaline at all.

"Pray tell, Rozzy," I jeered at her, using the nickname I knew she hated. Her eye twitched, and my amusement grew. "How does Miss Cassandra feel about the whole Blood Countess thing?"

In the late sixteenth and early seventeenth centuries, Rosaline adopted the persona of Elizabeth of Báthory, a Hungarian noble. The legend states that she tortured and killed hundreds of servant girls and young noble girls. A majority believe the story was falsified by male family members who wanted her fortune. A little of both is true. When the horrors of the Blood Countess came to light, Rosaline forced another woman into her place, and this woman died in imprisonment. Cassandra wouldn't let Rosaline sit at her table with a bloody track record against women like that.

"I'm sure this scheming Lapsus would willingly turn a blind eye if it meant a strong hand behind her cause," Rosaline said with a devious smirk. "But the less she knows about it, the better, if you get my meaning."

Her hand was at my crotch again, and she pulled the zipper fly downward, torturously slowly. My dick had been starting to calm down, but now it stirred mutinously again.

"I still don't see why I'm even needed," I said, cursing my voice for sounding so husky. Her hand slipped into my jeans, coaxing my dick into a more comfortable position beneath the constricting denim.

"Every queen needs its generals," she said, tilting her head and smirking. "And every general needs its foot soldiers."

Rosaline would have the hellish playground she always craved. And I'd be her toy soldier, and fuckboy when she grew bored of Malcolm or wanted to make Malcolm jealous.

"All right. Color me intrigued, Roz. Where's this Lapsi city going to be?" I asked, pressing my luck with the questions. But if she assumed I was joining her, she'd be more open to share details with me.

"Portland, Oregon," she cooed, stroking my tip as she said it. "I want you, Mason. My beautiful Mason."

She shifted on the bed and straddled my hips. My dick rose further, eager to meet her, but it was thankfully still mostly constrained by my jeans. For now.

Her hands slid beneath my T-shirt, inching up my torso to my chest.

"Join me in this, Mason. You'll be rewarded handsomely. Just please, come over to my side."

"You've never been one to say please," I pointed out, narrowing my eyes at her. Jesus, it almost felt like my mouth was *pouting*.

"*Pleeeeaaasee.*" As she drew the word out, she moved her hips in a sensual, circular motion above my dick. A low moan tore from my throat despite my every effort to hold it back as my dick throbbed with need. My hands clenched and pulled against the cuffs. The silver caused a painful throb through my wrists as I pulled, and it thankfully drew my mind out of my horniness.

"You have plenty of muscle behind you in Malcolm," I said quickly, my voice sounding breathless despite not needing to breathe. "He told me about his past, about his change. You didn't have to sway him and bend him to your will like you did me. He worships you, and I *loathe* you."

She tilted her head back and laughed. "Don't you see though?" She walked two fingers flirtatiously up my torso, lowering herself until her chest rested against mine, giving me a clear view down her glorious cleavage. She stared up at me, pouting those irresistible lips. "You're more fun, because I *have* to bend you. It is a challenge, and oh so satisfying when I win."

She put her lips to my throat and nipped gently at the flesh there. If I had a pulse, it would be pounding in my throat now, right where her lips were.

"But what about Malcolm, love?" I reminded her, tugging on the cuffs again and focusing on the pain. "I feel like he'll object to this. He is the jealous kind, you know."

"He would join us, if I ask him to. Is that what you'd like?" she said, raising herself up just enough to look me in the eye with mirth. My jaw clenched reflexively at the suggestion, remembering his multiple threats to fuck me, whether I wanted him to or not. She smiled at my obvious unease. She reached up and ran her hand through my hair, cupping my face in her palm. "Besides, he knows what it takes to win you over. And he knows how important it is that you're at my side."

She brought her face to mine and kissed my lips for a long second, while my skin crawled and twitched with desire and revulsion. But by god, I could already feel the desire winning out. *Fuck.*

"You keep saying 'join me' as if I have a choice here," I said, pulling my head out of the spreading fog again. "Do I have the ability to say no?"

"Of course you do—"

"Then I'm saying no. No. No. No. Times infinity, fucking *no*," I said, staring into her eyes with all the conviction I had in me.

She smiled. "But just as you have the ability to say no, I have the equal ability to *ignore* it," she said. "Or at least *try* to change your mind."

She walked her fingers up the soft skin of my inner arms until she gripped my clenched hands, and again she rotated her hips over mine. As I suppressed another groan, my toes curled and my knees rose upward, trying to buck her off me so she wouldn't see the damaged headboard. When I used the cuffs to lift me, the railing gave a barely audible but morale-boosting *crack.*

I bucked harder against her, and she fell forward onto me, catching herself by planting her hands on either side of my chest. She was startled, but I could hear her soft, amused laughter.

"You won't change my mind," I choked out, shaking my hair out of my eyes. "It's a *no*, Rosaline."

"Mason, Mason, Mason," she said, kissing my neck between each word. "You can say no all you want. You and I both know it'll be a yes in the end. I know you."

"No, it won't be a yes. Even though I'll bury my conscience and rise up as a monster again, I'll still always be screaming 'no' in the back of my mind for eternity. You'll win, sure, but I will be the sorest loser in the history of—"

Out of patience now, she silenced me with her loathsome kiss, caressing my lips with her tongue. A growl rose in my throat, and I gnashed my teeth against her lips, shaking my head to get free. I managed to bite her lip after a few tries, and she jerked back, spitting blood into my mouth. She wasn't angry though; instead, she threw her head back in laughter as her lip healed immediately.

"Yes! There he is!" she exclaimed through her laughter. She looked down at me again and ran a sharp-nailed finger threateningly down the side of my face. "There's the first glimpse of the monster. Come on, Mason, let's awaken him."

I tugged violently against the cuffs again, trying to focus on the pain to keep my thoughts clear, but it was failing. The pain was dulling and the desire was winning. *Fuck. Fuck. Fuck. Fuck.*

"Untie me, and I'll let the monster loose," I growled at her as a last effort.

"Nice try, baby," she cooed through her laughter, resting her hand against my cheek. Then she whipped the hand across my face, the silver ring on her thumb striking the bone above my eye and sending delicious pain searing through my face.

As I let out a cry that was half-roar, she bent down to my neck and bit the collar of my T-shirt with her fangs, tearing it. She grabbed the ragged fabric with both hands and tore it down the middle. My dick rose, fully erect at the savage sound of tearing fabric. I moaned as she shifted the weight into her hips again.

I was gone. Irreparably, irretrievably gone. My conscience was retreating into the darkest recesses of my mind. The fear was disappearing quickly, replaced merely by apathy and resignation.

After all, I'd done this to myself, hadn't I? I'd sabotaged myself. Things were going good, so of course I had to fuck it up by hitting one of my usual clubs. Why hadn't I hidden better? All for the same reason that I never bothered to ward myself before this; I was always leaving my backdoor open because I liked the risk. I liked taunting the danger. I liked fucking around and finding out.

Rosaline and I deserved each other. Even though I hated her, she'd made me what I was. Sure, Jaimie had shown me a different way for a bit, but it hadn't trumped my weak nature.

Goodbye, Jaimie. Take Mikey to Magic Mountain for me. And buy him a skateboard the first chance you get. He could be a brilliant skateboarding mathematician. If he wears a helmet. And stay away from Tristan.

My conscience stirred.

Rosaline was sliding down my body, kissing and nipping a line from my collarbone to my naval. My hands had relaxed as I let myself give in to the ecstasy of pleasure, but now they clenched again and *pulled*. The wood of the top rail groaned quietly.

I thought of Mikey: the brainiac and the soccer player. The blunt, jedi-in-training, loyal little brother. The kid who was saving me from centuries-old grief.

Rosaline jerked my jeans open farther and wrapped her deft hand around my dick. My back arched and my toes curled as she lowered her lips onto it.

My thoughts fogged over again as I moaned, but then Jaimie's face floated into my mind.

She'd shown me there were bigger things to focus on than the bullies who wanted to break us. She showed me there was a different way to exist under adversity: by not being resigned to it but by being *resilient*.

Rosaline grabbed my hips and pulled me from my semi-sitting position, onto my back, and then tugged my jeans down to my knees. I was exposed from the knees up, my dick pointing to the sky and ready for her to pounce. If she did, I'd be done for. I'd be buried so deep in her vile harness that I wouldn't come back again.

But she'd pulled me into a position that had even more leverage on the top rail, which from this angle looked far more compromised than I'd previously thought. As Rosaline crawled over me again, pulling her slitted dress up around her hips, I let out a roar and pulled with all the strength I could muster against the silver cuffs, and I *felt* rather than heard the satisfying snap of the wood between my wrists.

Pain exploded in my wrists, and my arms were still bound together by four inches of chain, but I could *move*. I lurched violently sideways and toppled with Rosaline off the bed onto the floor. My skinny jeans were still down below my knees, essentially binding my calves together and limiting my movement, but my hands were on either side of her throat, the chain cutting into her neck.

I wasn't strangling her in the human sense—she didn't breathe—but the cuffs were silver, so a wound inflicted with silver would *hurt* and wouldn't heal. I had no idea what would happen if I snapped her neck with the chain—I doubt it's ever been documented. *What* does *a Lapsus do with a broken neck?* I mused as I applied more pressure.

She hooked her legs around mine and pulled me closer to her. She very nearly pulled me *into her*, which I'm sure was her aim. With another almost-animalistic howl, I successfully jerked away. She let out a frustrated huff and shoved me away from her.

I face-planted into the floor and rolled to the side, struggling with my stupid jeans until I managed to get one leg loose to the ankle, which gave me a *little* more range of motion. I rolled into an awkward crouch as she lunged at me, raising a ringed hand to slap me.

I grabbed the hand midstrike and tried to twist it behind her, but I couldn't block both of her hands. Her second one clawed at my face and grabbed at my hair.

We were a tangle of torn clothing, bound hands, and tangled hair. I had one of her arms in both of my hands, and she had a handful of my hair, forcing my head to stare up at the ceiling.

But then the air erupted in *noise*. I toppled backward, off balance, when her hand fell limp from my hair. I looked around wildly, my ears ringing painfully. Rosaline lay on her back, unconscious with vacant, staring eyes and blood pooling beneath her head. By the now-open door stood Riley, wide-eyed and lowering a smoking gun to his side. Beyond him, in the hallway with his back to us, was a tall blond man. And me, sprawled gracelessly on the floor, pants around my ankles, and my dick pointed at the ceiling, completed the *absurd* scene.

As my eardrums healed and the ringing stopped, a loud deranged cackle shook from my lungs and lips, and it only grew as I ran my hands through my hair and over my face in disbelief. I was still me! I hadn't succumbed as I'd feared, and someone *cared* enough about my sorry ass to rescue me!?

"She won't be out for long. I didn't have any silver bullets on hand," Riley said, coming into the room.

I rolled to my side and rearranged my tangled jeans. I pulled them up and tucked my now thankfully relaxing dick back inside. Riley offered a hand down to me, and I took it gratefully. On my feet again, I dove at him, gripping the sides of his face and very nearly pulling his lips to mine in gratitude. I stopped myself but immediately wanted to dive in again and kiss both of his reddening cheeks.

"Thank you, Riley," I said emphatically, holding onto his face for one more beat and releasing him. "How?"

I knelt by Rosaline's unconscious form, frowning. I rolled her onto her back and jammed my hand down the front of her dress, searching for the key she no doubt had hidden in her bra.

"I enlisted a witch to trace you from your blood—someone you know apparently," he explained quickly. "Sorry it took so long. You were blocked from us until a few minutes ago."

"Which sounds...suspiciously convenient," I mused, unlocking the cuffs. Once free, I rubbed my tender wrists;

pain shot through my left one and I winced. "Damn it, I think it's fractured..."

It was going to take forever to heal. With a curse, I pocketed the key and forced Rosaline's limp wrist into one of the cuffs. I looped the chain around an intricate part of the wooden bedframe and latched the other cuff around her right ankle.

"Nice," the blond said from the doorway, glancing inside at my handiwork. I vaguely recognized him as one of the guys from *that* band. He was tall with shoulder-length blond hair and golden eyes similar to Jaimie's honey-colored ones.

Jaimie. My chest inflated with relief again when I realized I would be able to see Jaimie again.

"All right, let's get out of here before Malcolm or anyone else gets back."

I got to my feet and groaned as pain throbbed through my wrist again. Would witch magic heal Lapsus wounds? I'd never asked before. It was worth a detour to Boston to visit Libby and her beautiful family again.

CHAPTER 24

As soon as Libby answered the door, I held out my raw wrists for her to see before she could comment on my crazed look and lack of shirt.

"You know, I gave you the contact info for a healer, right?" she reminded me impatiently, but she stepped aside so I could walk past her.

"I am a creature of habit," I mumbled miserably, "and I lost my phone..."

My phone had been a tragic casualty in my balls-to-the-wall brawl with Rosaline. It wasn't that bad of a loss, considering I hated the damn thing, but I wished I could text Jaimie to let her know why I was MIA at school.

"Hi, baby," I muttered to the baby, strapped into a gently bouncing cradle-thing. She looked twice as big as the last time I'd seen her, just weeks ago. "Looking healthy."

I sat on the couch cushion farthest from the rocking contraption and held my arms out for Libby to inspect. She looked something up on her laptop, then used a spell to determine that it was fractured and didn't need reset—as I expected. It would heal over time, but because of the silver-backed injury, she couldn't do anything for me.

"I can make a stiff cast for it, if you want. It'll keep you from moving it while it heals," Libby offered with an apologetic cringe. "It's about all I can do. *But* I can infuse it with magical painkillers."

"How long will that take?" I asked warily, glancing at the clock on their mantle. It was after seven here in Boston. That meant school had been out for over an hour on the West Coast. I wanted to see Jaimie before she assumed I'd abandoned her. "Any chance I can just get the drugs and be on my way?"

Her eyes narrowed, and she frowned reproachfully. I almost laughed. She had the mom-look down already.

"Or how about drugs and a splint?" I offered, holding my hands up and narrowly avoiding wincing. "You know...like two sticks and some gauze? That's the Boy Scout way, right?"

Colt snorted from the hallway entryway and tossed me a shirt. I pulled on the plain gray T-shirt—at least he understood my general monochromatic vibe. He was taller and slimmer than me, so it hugged my chest more than I usually liked, but I couldn't complain.

"Fine. But keep it wrapped, okay? I know where you live," Libby threatened, rolling her eyes and standing to retrieve supplies.

"Yeah, clear across the country." I smirked, earning a glare from her, which I worried meant the offer of drugs was about to be rescinded. I held my hands higher. "I promise I'll keep it wrapped, per doctor's orders."

She came back with a vial, a syringe, gauze, and some long, flat pieces of plastic.

"Oh, boy, Lapsi morphine," I joked, loading up the syringe.

"Basically, yeah," she said with a snort. I jabbed the loaded syringe into the vein at my elbow. "Less euphoria, I'm afraid, but it'll numb you."

"No worries, I have all the euphoria I need already," I said as I extracted the needle. I leaned against the armrest of the couch, holding my fractured wrist out for Libby to wrap.

The pain dulled almost immediately. She was right about there being no euphoria, but I didn't miss it. I felt pretty damn good all on my own. Sure, I was angry at myself for almost being ensnared by Rosaline again, but beyond the anger, I was positively *glowing*. I'd resisted when I thought it was impossible. I was still myself. And at the moment, I was indisputably thousands of miles away from her, behind heavy wards. I was *safe*.

While Libby stinted and wrapped my wrist, I eyed Colt pensively. He'd taken the baby out of her contraption and now sat with her in an armchair, bouncing her gently on his knee.

To make conversation rather than stare at them objectively, I asked Colt what he did. I'd only ever seen him supporting his wife and holding the child. I was curious what else made up this attractive man.

He told me that he was an artist by trade. *Another artist*, I mused, smirking to myself. But more than merely painting, he could use his magic to paint highly specific paintings for clients because he was a memory extractor. He could directly access people's memories and transcribe them into art.

My ears pricked when he told me this, because there was something highly specific he could help *me* with. I wanted my family's portrait back. I didn't want anything nearly as big as the original six-foot canvas: I wanted something to fit on my wall of fame but not dominate it. I'd planned on commissioning Jaimie, knowing she'd do an amazing job tying all of my favorite things into one painting. But Colt could reproduce the exact image from my memory.

I itched to commission him right away, but it could wait. I had to get back to the West Coast and see Jaimie.

I paid Libby for the single dose of drugs but left the rest with her. She protested, but I didn't mind the pain. Pain was my karma, but I kept that part to myself. I thanked them profusely and shook the baby's hand as a joke, then left Boston for Southern California.

"Hey, I'm here, I'm here! I hope you didn't worry too much," I announced when I appeared on the far side of the art studio so I didn't startle her. "I was held up for the last...twenty-odd hours, and my phone was destr—"

As I stepped into the room, my foot nudged something on the ground: her phone. I grabbed it and flipped it over. The screen was cracked more than it had been yesterday. *The hell?*

I looked up, confused. Jaimie was across the room at a sink with the water running. She was furiously scrubbing at her hands. The room around her seemed...off, but I couldn't determine *why*.

"I—I'm sorry I didn't text you, but boy, do I have so much to tell you," I said, as I walked across the studio. The elation hadn't worn off. I knew I wasn't yet *safe*, especially walking around in the open, but for the moment, Rosaline was surely still detained, and I wanted to celebrate my miraculous adventure with Jaimie. "I feel like I have a new lease on life, and I can't wait to tell you. But first—"

I'd reached the middle of the wide studio, and more things seemed wrong but not immediately alarming. The desks were pushed haphazardly out of their normal spots. Her tacklebox of art supplies was overturned in the corner, like it'd been kicked there. *That* was alarming. Brushes littered the floor, some broken, and paint tubes were strewn about, some obviously stomped on. The paint was still wet and streaked on the floor. And her painting...

"Oh, shit. What..." I couldn't finish my sentence. I took a step toward her canvas, in disbelief. It looked shiny, like it'd just been scrubbed with soap and water, but that wasn't what was horrifying. It was slashed diagonally from one corner to the opposite. My knees nearly buckled. "No. No no no no no no... Oh, Jaimie, I'm sorry..."

Sadness mixed with a slow burning anger in my chest. I reached for the slashed canvas but couldn't bring myself to touch it. I knew how much work she'd put into it and how much she had riding on it.

"I already photographed it, before it happened," she said from the sink. Over the sound of the running water, her voice sounded thick, but with anger or with tears, I couldn't gauge. "It's submitted and all that."

Thank the universe for that small victory. But this assurance did little to temper the rage as it lanced through me.

"Still though, this is property damage. This is a felony. This is damn near assault," I spewed, fuming. In my distraction and with the water running, I almost didn't catch her derisive snort at the word *assault*, but I heard it and stilled.

"Are you okay? Were you in the room when they did this? Did they hurt you?" I demanded, switching my focus at last.

I turned from the ruined painting and took in the destruction of the room. Her brushes looked intentionally snapped in half and dropped. Some tubes of paint looked deliberately stepped on, and the paint streaks looked *rolled* in.

Fuck, fuck, fuck...

Her back was still to me, and her head was shaking, but behind her thick waves, I couldn't tell if her head was moving up and down or side to side. *Jaimie, look at me,* I wanted to plead, but I stayed silent. Paint coated the bottom of her jeans, and her cardigan sleeves were rolled up to the elbows, and I could see acrylic paint staining the folds, already dried.

"Who did this?" The rage hadn't reached my voice yet, and I still sounded horrified.

"Tristan," she spat, rubbing her hands under the water with more vigor, as if she were trying to wash his name off them.

I suppose I didn't need to ask. Everyone in school picked on her, but she had only one real tormentor. Now that she'd named him, though, it was impossible to miss his scent in the air. A paint-smeared hoodie draped on a chair smelled of him, but also of someone else: like my borrowed shirt smelled of me but distinctly of Colt.

Something else tickled my nostrils, though, and sent my rage into overdrive. Beyond the testosterone, the steroids, and his musk barely held at bay by aftershave was the distinct smell of *cum*. It was faint, like she'd washed it away, but I could still smell it in the air.

"Did he..." But I couldn't say it. I just couldn't.

She abruptly shut off the water and gripped the edge of the sink. She took an agonizingly long time to collect herself. It might have only been a few seconds, but it felt like hours to my horrified brain.

"No. He didn't ra—" She also couldn't say the word. She hit her fist on the edge of the counter. "He didn't, but he—"

She came up short again. With a huff, she turned to face me, keeping her hands at her sides, but her arms twitched like she wanted to cross them over her chest.

Half of her face was red from her scrubbing it raw, mainly around her mouth and chin. She'd scrubbed her face, but stiff, dark red paint streaked in her hair by her ear. Her bottom lip was split and angrily swollen, and new bruises were on her collarbone. The front of her shirt was wrinkled and stretched, and paint was smeared across her chest, more on one side than the other. There was no pattern to it, but I could see in more than one spot what could have been *handprints*.

I was torn between storming out of there and finding Tristan, dropping to my knees in despair at not being able to stop this, and wrapping myself tightly around her, promising never to let go again. None were the right action in this moment, but I had no idea what the right action was. Much as I wanted to comfort her with touch, it was probably the *last* thing she wanted right then.

Instead, I stood with my hands clenched at my sides, transfixed by the paint handprints on her chest. My eyes drifted lower, to the handprint on the waistband of her jeans and the yellow paint smeared along her leg, like she'd dragged her leg through it.

"It's not as bad...as you probably think," she started again, getting a handle on her shaky voice. "But he held me down, and—" She snapped her mouth shut in a grimace and brought her hands up to her face. She rubbed at her eyes and temples and ran her hands through her hair. When her hand reached the paint crusted in her hair, she let out a strangled cry of frustration and threw her hands down to her sides.

"God damn it! I can't say it!" she complained, her voice almost shrill.

"You don't have to tell me," I told her honestly.

Much as my rage demanded to know what Tristan had done, it was *not* my business. Trauma is complex, and our defenses against its reign are frail. I knew from experience that forcing someone to relive something when they want to bury it can be catastrophic. So, no matter how much I wanted to know, making her talk about it wasn't the way. But I still didn't know *what* the *right* thing to do was.

"I want to, though," she snapped bitterly. "I *want* to tell you. Because you're the only person that will believe me. But I can't. Get. The. Words. Out." She hit her fists on the counter behind her between each word, her face twisted in anger at her own trauma response.

I doubted I'd be the only one to believe her. It was hard to deny that a scuffle had happened here, and her painting was ruined. Her clothes were pretty damning, and, hell, most classrooms in this school had security cameras outside the rooms *and* inside. I opened my mouth to argue this, glancing up into the corner of the ceiling, but stopped.

The lens of the camera nearest us was smeared with black paint. *Jesus, fuck.* I thought about the discarded hoodie. This wasn't a roids rage, spur of the moment, lash-out. While it might not have been a mastermind plan, it was certainly *calculated*. He was covering his tracks from the start. *Fuck.*

Jaimie let out another strangled cry that was half-frustrated-yell, half-sob, and lurched forward at me. I caught her automatically and wrapped my arms tight around her as she dove her face into my chest. She clutched fistfuls of my shirt, like she was afraid I'd vanish, and breathed heavily into me, trying to stifle the aggressive sobs fighting to get out. I rubbed her back as soothingly as I could, kissing the top of her head, but I was unsure of what else to do.

As she slowly relaxed, I carefully walked us back toward a table so she could sit atop it, with her legs on either side of mine. She stayed like that for a moment, with her forehead resting against my collarbone.

"Can you just—can you look into my head and see what happened?" she asked after a moment. She sat back and stared at her hands in her lap.

"I won't do that," I said sharply, recoiling. But I came back and lifted her chin to look at me. "I don't need to know that badly, and I'm not fucking around with your head. I promised."

Yes, I could peer into her recent memories. I could even take them away, but if I did that it would be hard to explain away her paint-smeared clothes and ruined painting. I couldn't do that to her.

"I don't want you to *take*, just look," she clarified. The fierceness returned to her eyes for a second as she looked sharply up at me. "I'm not asking you to erase anything or alter me. I want to stay angry, damn it. I just want someone to know what...happened. But I can't say it out loud. The words just won't come. So...*please*."

The longer she stared at me, the more my resolve weakened. With a sigh, I reluctantly gave in and rested my forehead against hers.

This was the last thing I wanted to do. I already knew I was going to kill Tristan for this, regardless what her memory showed me. I didn't need to see it all in 4K, from her eyes. But she was right: this was the only way she could share what happened without having to rehash it and relive the trauma.

FALLEN WOES

The following scene might be triggering for some, as it depicts attempted sexual assault.
I promise, it's not as bad as you're probably thinking, but I understand if you want to skip.
If you don't want to read Jaimie's memory, skip ahead to the next time you see this image:

*A*fter taking her photos and sending in her online application with the teacher's computer—I couldn't believe how much the teacher trusted Jaimie with the studio and her computer—*she left for a few moments to use the bathroom. When she scanned back into the studio, she was staring down at her phone and her unanswered texts to me. She shot me another text as she crossed the studio but dropped the phone to her side when she realized her brushes and paints were on the floor. She started to look around, but her eyes caught on the painting.*

In still-wet green paint, someone had scrawled the words "Kill Yourself" across the canvas. She was shocked, but only mildly irritated because, really, the joke was on the prankster. The painting was varnished and dried, so the words would be easy to scrub off. She rolled her eyes but something else caught her attention.

Splattered on the center of the canvas was a glob of what looked like milky, semi-translucent slime. She didn't immediately understand what it was, but I knew the instant her eyes fell on it. Cum.

That vile prick, I seethed.

She'd barely realized what it was and started to pull away in disgust, when a hand wrapped around her waist from behind.

"So, this *is where you hide," Tristan cooed into her ear.*

She held in a shriek as she jumped away from him. Her phone clattered facedown to the floor, and he kicked it clear across the studio before rounding on her.

"How'd you get in here?" she demanded, backing away from him and trying to put as much distance between them as she could without backing into the wall.

"Borrowed a keycard off an art nerd earlier today," he explained, smirking. He stepped toward her but sidestepped suddenly so he could stomp on one of her paint tubes. Bismuth yellow acrylic paint spurted across the floor. "Then I had to show my appreciation. What do you think?"

"It's unoriginal. And dumb," she snapped, eyeing her paints and brushes littered everywhere. He probably thought he was destroying quality art supplies that she couldn't afford to replace. But she'd bought most them secondhand for mere pennies, and she could scrub the words and his fucking cum from the canvas easily. "If you wanted it to appear more like a cry for help, and not bullying, you should have written something like 'I give up,' or 'goodbye cruel world!'"

He ground his shoe on the tube of paint with narrowed eyes. Then he stepped toward her again.

"I liked you better when you knew you were nothing. Maybe you need a reminder."

He turned and approached the canvas again, pulling a box cutter—her box cutter from her tackle box—from his jeans pocket and popping the blade out. A panicked cry leapt to her throat, and she rushed forward, grabbing his raised arm before it arced downward. He turned and, dropping the blade, hooked his leg around hers, sweeping it out from under her. He barely kept her head from smacking into the floor as he controlled their descent and crawled on top of her.

"Now, baby, you're right," he muttered savagely, his face way too close to hers. She shuddered and tried to wiggle out *from under him, but he was too heavy. His paint-covered hands pawed roughly at her chest, cupping one breast painfully. He pressed his lips to hers to silence her yell of protest.* "It's about time we address this little thing between us."

Little is certainly an apt word. It was grating and horrible to feel her powerlessness and be stuck as just a spectral visitor.

Her legs kicked out, trying to get traction on the paint-slick ground. He shifted his weight and pressed one of his legs painfully into her thigh, hard enough it would surely bruise. She cried out, but he didn't move. Instead, he pressed his forearm into her collarbone with the same bruising strength, pinning her to the floor. With his free hand, he tugged on her jeans, pulling the button open.

"No!" *She and I both yelled from the same lips, and she fought harder against him.* "Get the fuck off!"

"I'm about to, baby," *he grunted.*

His hand left her jeans and went to his, pulling himself out, but—I snickered to see it, but Jaimie didn't understand—*he was still dead soft. He cursed and rubbed himself furiously, but it stayed limp.*

Jaimie didn't know why or what was happening, but I was extremely relieved. It seemed his steroid use made him one-and-done, having sprayed his load on her painting just minutes earlier.

While he struggled and cursed, Jaimie punched at his arm and still tried to writhe out of his grip. She caught sight of the box cutter on the ground, feet from them. She reached for it while he continued trying to get himself hard, but her reach still wasn't enough. If she could stretch...so close.

FALLEN WOES

With an angry cry of frustration, he gave up and released the pressure from her collarbone. She gasped, able to take a full breath again, and she lunged the remaining half-inch for the blade. But he pulled her back and his knuckles whipped across her mouth.

She shrieked, momentarily stunned by the exquisite pain of being viciously backhanded.

"It'll have to wait until next time I guess, slut," he spat, adjusting his weight on top of her again.

He batted her hand away from her mouth, then grabbed her jaw and angled her face to look at him. He bit the cap off a tube of Alizarin crimson and squirted it in her face. She choked as the bitter and metallic paint went up her nose and rolled to the back of her throat.

My nostrils and throat burned at the residual, tangible memory and the panic of breathing it in or swallowing any of it.

He rolled off her, and she barely registered the relief of having the circulation return to her leg over the agony of inhaling acrylic paint up the nose. She sputtered and coughed and rolled onto her side, scraping as much paint out of her mouth and off her cheek as she could. She glanced with wild eyes around for Tristan, to make sure he wasn't about to pounce on her again. He was standing by her painting now, leering triumphantly at her, the box cutter in his hand.

"Wait—" she sputtered weakly, reaching uselessly toward him. "Don't—"

"You're fucking nothing, slut," he hissed, then turned and slashed a clean cut diagonally across the canvas.

I echoed the devastated cry that ripped from her lungs as I pulled out of the memory with enough force that I staggered backward on unsteady feet. I recovered after a moment and took a shaky breath to steady myself. The pain was returning to my fractured wrist, not because the meds were wearing off, but because I was clenching my fists so tight that the pain in my wrist was increasing beyond the drugs.

This cut deep into my soul, more than any of my own trauma combined. And this was my fault. I'd taunted him yesterday, despite his threat of violence toward her. I'd pushed him to do this, and he'd seized his opportunity the second I wasn't around.

Don't poke the bear, she'd said. But she didn't know I'd already hit the bear with a fucking taser.

Thankfully, Tristan was something I could easily handle.

Next time, he'd said. There wasn't going to be a next time.

CHAPTER 25

Understandably, Jaimie was adamant about not reporting anything right away. Any attempt to report it would just result in her having to explain it, over and over, constantly reliving it. And while she didn't want to forget what happened, she didn't want to give him the satisfaction of torturing her in a legal battle.

I convinced her to leave the room the way it was, though. The teacher would come in, see the destruction, the painted over cameras, and *specifically* Jaimie's supplies ruined, and would raise the alarm. Jaimie didn't have to admit that she had been in the room at all after the vandalism.

Maybe he thought he was untouchable. Maybe he thought he covered his tracks. But I'd make sure they found the hoodie he'd left behind in his car. The paint staining it would incriminate him. Posthumously, of course.

Jaimie tucked her painting into its cubby, not wanting to leave it out to be further harassed in the morning. The slash through it was clean, and she was convinced she could either glue or stitch it back together and re-stretch the canvas without issue. Later, though. For now, she didn't want to look at it.

I took her back to my place, where I had her sit in front of my sink while I studiously worked at getting the dried paint out of her hair with hot water and soap. I had to take the stint off my wrist, but I did so out of her sight. The magical meds were wearing off, but I didn't care. The pain helped keep my anger alive. I'd need her help wrapping it again, though.

While I worked, I distracted her with stories of Victorian and Edwardian England, and the clothing decade I liked the most—obviously *this* decade. I never knew clothing contentment until I donned skinny jeans and black Vans. She asked a lot of questions about the artists I'd known and who'd been the most interesting. I told her about the glass blower I'd met on Pier 39 in San Francisco in the late eighties. And my time as a low-key Kurt Cobain groupie in the nineties.

Despite the horrors of the day, I liked these moments. Talking with her was so easy and refreshing. I never just *talked* with anyone, especially not about my long life.

"I don't know what I'm going to do tomorrow at school. There are going to be questions," she said after I was finished and had grabbed her a towel. She rubbed it against her temples.

"Then don't go," I told her gently, massaging my wrist. "Put it off for a day, and let them figure out how to 'tell you.' Spend the day with me instead."

"That sounds preferable," she agreed, running one hand down my arm while the other worked her hair with the towel. "I have to face him at some point, though. That's going to fucking suck...seeing his gloating face." She grimaced and half-gagged. "For fuck's sake, I hope someone poisons his steroids some day and he dies horrifically and embarrassingly."

"That would be a fitting death," I agreed, plastering on a fake smile. I would've told her how I planned to kill him, but she'd just try to stop me. "Karma's coming for him, I guarantee it."

We fell silent for a few minutes while she patted her thick hair dry, frowning into space. She stood when she finished and pulled the chair back to its spot.

"Can I ask a favor of you?" I asked quietly, massaging my wrist again. She nodded and I grabbed the plastic pieces Libby'd used to stint my wrist. I pulled the flattened roll of gauze she'd given me from my front pocket. "I hurt my wrist earlier. Can you help me rewrap it?"

"You hurt your wrist?" she repeated, concerned. She crossed the room back to me, taking the gauze without hesitating. "I thought you couldn't get hurt."

"I can, with silver. I had to break out of silver handcuffs," I admitted tonelessly.

"Silver *what*? What happened?" I couldn't tell from her tone whether she thought I was involved in sexcapades gone wrong or had been in real trouble.

"Rosaline happened..." I said, deciding not to sugarcoat it. Her eyes widened, but before she could question me and ask why I hadn't mentioned it earlier, I dove into the story. While she stinted my wrist, much like Libby had, I told her as many details as I could, while steering away from any that would remind her of *her* assault, happening at practically the same time.

"But you got away," she said when I finished. Her honey-colored eyes were huge, and she was smiling. She gently massaged my finger which was still red and raw from Rosaline tearing the ring from it.

"She's still out there though, so I'm not safe yet. I'll have to handle it, and soon. But I bought a little time..." I assumed I had twenty-four hours *at most*, depending on how long Malcolm assumed she'd be fucking me into submission. I had to be ready when they came back for me, but that was later. Currently, Jaimie and ending Tristan's rapist ass were higher on my priority list.

"You said you wouldn't be able to if she caught you again," she said. "You said you weren't strong enough to resist, but you did."

"Barely," I scoffed, crossing my arms. "My rescue was purely a deus ex machina. I was hosed."

"But still, you're still you," she said, putting her hands to my face. "You said you wouldn't be. You're stronger than you thought. Say it."

"I...I'm not, Jaimie," I said, not able to fake it even for her. I'd been riding a high earlier, but it was long, long gone now. "I got lucky. But I...I want to be, okay? For the first time, I have hope that I can resist her." Killing her might be another story altogether, but I was going to go down saying "no" until she killed me out of annoyance.

Jaimie wanted to get out of her paint-covered clothes, so I offered her a shower and a set of clothes from one of my one-night-stands—again, I *wash* them.

While she showered, I left the apartment to get dinner for her—I told her I could get her anything she wanted, from anywhere, but she'd grown up on a slim budget and had simple tastes. She asked for mac and cheese and chicken tenders.

After showering and eating, she just wanted to sleep—with my help. We lay together on my bed, her under the sheets and me over them. At her request, I coaxed her mind into a dreamless, deep sleep.

Tristan deserved to be dissected slowly and agonizingly. He deserved to scream while he watched me remove parts of him—starting with his dick—and feed them to a lion. Then, once he expired, what was left of his body deserved to be affixed to the top of the flagpole at school, as a message to anyone else who messes with Jaimie. That was Rosaline's way.

But the media frenzy and memorialization that would follow such a horrific death was more than he deserved. If he died mysteriously or in some way that elicited pity, he'd be glorified.

Instead, I planned on killing him in one swift stroke, in a way that wouldn't be pitied. It'd be banal but still brutal: swift but karma-loaded, and—most importantly—his own damn fault. Instead of becoming a titillating unsolved mystery, he'd merely be a statistic. This was more Malcolm's way.

Still, I fantasized about all the brutal Rosaline-esque ways I could kill him while I waited for him to show. I'd tracked down his lackey, Laura, and used her phone to invite him to the park. I-as-Laura lured him with suggestive emojis and the promise of booze. And he, ever a simpleton, agreed without hesitation.

I watched from across the park as Tristan pulled into the lot, driving a car he'd borrowed off a sibling or from his parents. He parked and I shifted to just outside the car, on the passenger side. Intending to casually slide inside, I tried the door handle, but the passenger side was locked.

Fine. Violence it is.

I bent down and peered into the window, and he looked over, expecting Laura. He froze at the sight of me, but not the usual *Pause*, because I wasn't my usual, pretty, happy-go-lucky self. I was staring him down with all the dangerous malice of Rosaline's Monster.

I savored the surprise and wariness in his expression before I shattered the window with my fist, like it was nothing.

"What the shit!?" Tristan shouted, jumping in his seat as glass pebbles flew everywhere. I ignored his sputtering string of curses while I unlocked the door and slid inside. "What the hell, man? This isn't even my car!"

He let out another string of curses but didn't throw any punches my way. Instead, he was leaning away from me, pressing himself against the driver's side doorframe to put as much distance between us as he could. He was surprised enough by my boldness that it was overwriting his macho, aggressive persona. *Good.*

"Laura couldn't come after all, so you just get me," I told him calmly, putting the full bottle of bourbon on the dashboard and closing the passenger door. "I brought the promised alcohol, though. And this."

I threw the hoodie he'd left at his crime scene across the center console at him. He caught it and stared at it, dumbfounded. Then his expression closed, smugly.

"This isn't mine," he said, tossing it into his backseat. "And you're going to pay for that window, buddy."

"After what you did today, that doesn't even start to make us even, *pal*," I said with a sarcastic chuckle, regarding him with calm malevolence.

Through the dim twilight, he probably couldn't see my face very well, but I could see his perfectly. His bewilderment and most of his anger wore off at my accusation. What replaced these in his face was a guarded caution, and a dash of sick pride.

"I don't know what you're talking about," he said calmly.

"I very much think you do," I growled. "Or do you just *casually* assault women on the reg, and this one has just slipped your mind?"

"Did she tell you it was assault?" He smirked, dropping the façade of ignorance. "Sorry, pal, she came to *me*, begging me—"

I backhanded him across his cheekbone with a fraction of my strength. The force sent a shudder of pain through my fractured wrist, but it was worth it.

His head snapped to the side, and his hand flew to his face. I knew it hurt as much as a punch would have, but he let out an uneasy, giddy laugh. I wanted to hit him again but instead reached for the bourbon.

"Yeah, but unfortunately for you, you'd already blown your load, so you couldn't do what you really wanted to do to her," I murmured, slicing the seal with my thumbnail and twisting off the corked top. I looked at him with a cold, dark look. "But that'll have to wait until *next time*, I guess."

His eyes narrowed at having his exact words repeated back to him, like he didn't expect Jaimie to tell, let alone remember everything he said. He didn't open his mouth to retort but just stared me down, guarded.

"Spoiler alert," I said, holding the opened bottle out to him. "There's no next time."

"Right, and you're going to stop me?" he challenged with a scoff, nudging the neck of the bottle away from him lazily.

"Yeah. I am." I grinned viciously at him. With mesmerism, I commanded him to grab the bottle. He looked wary and confused, but he reached for it and took it from my hand. "Drink."

"I'm not going to drink this, shitstain," he snapped, but his fingers still clutched it tightly.

"*Drink it, Tristan*," I commanded aloud, with a punch of mesmerism behind the words. His mind was surprisingly strong, but it didn't matter. I didn't care how much force I had to put on his mind. I would break him, even if it drained me of all my blood-fueled energy.

He took a swig of bourbon like it was a beer and didn't even cough as it burned his throat. He lowered the bottle, still staring at me, but I shook my head. He raised the bottle again.

FALLEN WOES

After three swigs, he started to cough. He'd taken maybe three shots in less than a minute. I let him take a little break so the alcohol could have a chance to enter his system.

"I'm surprised she even told you," he said after his coughing stopped. He looked at me and grinned. "I figured she'd go and off herself immediately after."

I wanted to punch all of his perfect teeth out of his mouth and make him swallow them. But I resisted. Instead, I clenched my hands into fists and commanded him to take another drink.

"No, you vain, judgmental, cruel *fuck*. She won't do that, ever," I told him calmly. "She isn't depressed. She isn't weak. Despite constant ridicule and taunts from you and her classmates, the first thing that has phased her was *you* today. But even that, she's already rising above."

He didn't have anything to say in response. His eyes just narrowed. I commanded him to take another drink.

"She'll end up happier than all of you, in the end," I continued. "And she'll outlive many of you, I bet. She'll definitely outlive *you* at the very least."

"And why do you think that?" he asked with a skeptical yet suddenly wary expression.

"Because you're going to die tonight, Tristan."

At his scoff, I pressed into his mind and told him to drink again. He coughed after the first one, but he stifled it and took another. Some of the alcohol missed his mouth and poured down his chin. He spat some of it out on the steering wheel as he couldn't suppress another cough.

I could see the bewildered fear in his eyes as he forced more bourbon down. He couldn't explain what was happening; this kind of mesmerizing power was beyond his limited comprehension.

"You know that silly bully stunt, where you hold a kid's arm and hit him with it, saying 'stop hitting yourself!'" I mused while he continued to drink. "That's me right now, Tristan. I'm doing this. You're raising the bottle to your lips, but I'm the one controlling your arm." I turned to him with deadpan eyes and spoke in a monotone, uncaring voice. "Stop doing this, Tristan. You'll kill yourself if you do this, Tristan."

Tears squeezed from his eyes as he closed them: both out of discomfort at forcing so much burning alcohol down his esophagus and out of the spreading fear. I reached over and unbuckled his seatbelt, taking the bottle from his hand in the same motion. I held the bottle up in the fading light. About half was gone. Not enough to kill a man, but more than enough to inebriate a teenager. I set the bottle in the cupholder in the center console, but the bottle was too large. It tipped and spilled the rest of its contents at Tristan's feet. Oh well.

"Now, Tristan, we're going to go for a drive. Start the car," I instructed him while also making it impossible for him to resist my command.

He was drunk already but still able to drive with relative control. That would change soon enough once the rest of the alcohol hit his system. We drove through town recklessly, uncaring if any witnesses saw his inebriated driving. I only cared about making sure *he* was the only victim. I coaxed him onto the freeway, so we could get plenty of speed going and leave the more populated area of town.

"If you want an apology, this isn't the way to do it," he sputtered sloppily after moments of driving. "Scaring me into apologizing hardly makes it genuine, doesn't it?"

"You're right, Tristan," I agreed calmly, not reacting as he swerved and fishtailed. "But I'm not looking for an apology. I'm your karma broker, cashing out."

An exit up ahead looked straight and ended at a two-way intersection. On the other side of the intersection was a cement warehouse building. Perfect. I told him to get off at the exit, and he obeyed. But when he started to slow, I made him keep his foot on the gas.

It took a lot of my strength to force his foot onto the gas. He was inebriated, but he was resisting me out of sheer panic. He tried to turn the wheel, but I stuck out my hand to keep it straight.

"You'll die too, don't you see," he said in a last desperate attempt to reason with me.

I grinned. "Yes, but you'll be the only one that doesn't walk away after this." I glanced at him with a last devilish, maniacal look. His gaze left the road and turned to me, all-consuming fear in his eyes as the car bumped over the curb and headed straight for the cement building. My grinning, exuberant face was the last thing he saw in this life.

We hit the wall of the building, and the car accordioned around us. My arms and legs shattered, and glass flew inward, cutting my face and chest to ribbons. The seatbelt locked up and broke my collarbone. Before I blacked out from the force of the collision, I saw Tristan fly through the shattered windshield; his head smashing gruesomely into the cement wall.

It takes a lot for a Lapsus to lose consciousness, and when we do, it scrambles our brains completely. I woke up to pain and carnage, and for one terrifying moment, I thought I was back in my monster state, on a bender with Rosaline or Malcolm.

But no. No, I wasn't. I was me still. But I was in pain: lovely, body-racking, satisfying pain.

I crawled out of the broken passenger window and sprawled on the pavement below. As my bones started to realign themselves and my skin knit back together, I lay there in vindicated ecstasy, savoring the pain as it disappeared. The broken bones, the blinding, searing pain, were my punishment and my reward.

Mea culpa, the bastard's dead. Good fucking riddance.

CHAPTER 26

As soon as my bones were all realigned—except, unfortunately, the one in my wrist, which still throbbed—I shifted away before any witnesses could realize a second person had been there and had walked away unscathed.

Jaimie was thankfully still asleep when I returned to the apartment. I wanted nothing more than to crawl under the sheets and just be near her, but I was a right mess. After brushing the glass out of my hair into a trash can, I showered to scrub the blood and grime off. I finally returned to the bedroom, dressed in a pair of sweatpants, and crawled into bed.

I don't usually sleep, and when I do it's only for an hour or so. But it'd been a long, exhausting day. The stress of being captured, the horror at what had happened while I was gone, and the murder at the end of it all was too much for my mind and body. I pressed myself against Jaimie's back, draping an arm over her hip and curling my other arm beneath her pillow.

As I drifted off, I thought fleetingly that I should have fed. I hadn't been fully sated when I was abducted, and I'd used a lot of my energy in mesmerizing Tristan's surprisingly stubborn mind. My teeth were starting to itch and my muscles felt fatigued from the lack of blood energy. *Oh well.* It wasn't bad yet, and it wouldn't be bad for a while.

Jaimie wasn't in bed any longer when I woke, but my brain was so foggy I didn't realize it at first, or even remember she'd been there in the first place.

I rolled out of bed and put my feet on the floor, rubbing my forehead with both hands as if that would remove the fog. Then I heard Jaimie's voice from the living room, and most of my brain clicked back into place.

I changed into a pair of jeans, grabbed a random shirt out of a drawer and left the bedroom. I pulled the shirt on over my head as I entered the living room.

"I'm sorry I didn't come home," she said into the phone, glancing my way as I approached and giving me a half smile in greeting. "Thanks for covering for me, buddy, really. But I need you to do it again for me. Okay? Please?"

I climbed over the back of the couch and sat next to her; she leaned against me as soon as I did so. She pulled the phone away from her ear and put it on speaker.

"Yeah, just tell them that I left for school already because I had a group presentation to practice for," she said.

"But you're really at Mason's, aren't you?" Mikey's voice came through the phone, sounding oddly reprimanding for a kid. "Were you there all night?"

"Yeah, but it isn't like that, Mikey," she assured him, glancing at me and rolling her eyes. "I promise, it isn't like that. But you're going to cover for me, right? Deb's been nicer lately, but I'm not holding my breath that she won't freak out over this."

"Yeah, I'll lie to her, obviously. I'm not going to do anything to get you in trouble," he said, now sounding more like the eleven-year-old kid he really was, a kid who wants to protect his sister. "Hold on, though. I'll be back in a minute after I tell them."

He put the phone down and left it behind. I heard a door open and some muffled conversational voices. Jaimie scooted away, but then she leaned back across my legs, her head resting in my lap. She placed the phone on her stomach and put her hand in the air. I took it and put my other hand by her head, playing idly with strands of her loose hair.

"Any dreams?" I asked her softly, in case Mikey had us on speaker too.

"No, thank god," she said, shaking her head. She looked up at me, a little perplexed. "What about you? I thought you don't need to sleep."

"Usually, I don't. It was a...long day though," I said, staring at her hand in mine. "And it's far easier to sleep, apparently, when there's a beautiful girl there to snuggle with."

She snorted softly and was about to say something, but a rustling from the phone speaker signaled Mikey's return.

"You're good, and I think Deb is okay with me walking to school by myself," he said, sounding distracted. "I don't know if she was really paying attention though...her and dad were distracted, watching the news."

"Did something happen?" Jaimie asked, not sounding concerned.

"Some accident last night. A teenager was drinking heavily and ran head-on into a building with his car," Mikey explained, sounding a little wary.

My insides went still and icy as he said this. I'd thought I would have a little bit of time to think of what I was going to tell Jaimie. I hadn't expected her to find out this soon since she wasn't going to school today.

"They showed his photo when I walked in," Mikey continued. "It was dad's boss's son, that mean kid who would always pick on us at work picnics. And he's in your class, right? He was drinking...and he's dead."

I looked at our hands but watched her expression carefully out of my periphery. Her curiosity mixed with confusion and then surprise. Her brows drew together. At most, she looked perturbed.

"Oh. You're sure?" she said after a moment.

Mikey let out a low whistle. "Yeah, pretty sure. Man, two car accidents in one week for him," he said. "Karma was really chasing him down, huh?"

At the mention of karma, her eyes flicked to mine, but I couldn't read her expression. I kept my face just as impassive. She slowly extracted her hand from mine.

"You there?" Mikey said after Jaimie was silent for a moment.

"Yeah, I am," she said, recovering her voice. "I don't know how to feel. I just...I didn't like him, but...just 'oh.' That's all I have."

"Yeah, me too," Mikey agreed. "Okay, I should go make my waffles. Since I don't have you making sure I get out of here on time, I should go start figuring that out. Later!"

He ended the call without waiting for us to respond. Jaimie picked her phone up off her chest and sat up, keeping her face turned from mine. An agonizing moment of silence spread between us. I wished I'd savored that last moment, when our hands were joined and her head rested on my legs. I had a feeling it was the last time she would initiate contact or let me touch her. Dread spread through my chest, a dread that could have also been described as *heartache*.

"So, he got roaring drunk on a Tuesday night and drove himself into a building," she said flatly after a moment. It wasn't a question. She sat forward on the couch, her elbows resting on her legs.

"Would you believe he was overcome with remorse for what he did and killed himself over it?" I asked her just as flatly.

She shook her head, still not looking at me. "No, I wouldn't."

"Good, because he wasn't. And he was never going to be."

"Jesus," she said through gritted teeth, dropping her head into her hands. She didn't say anything for a long moment.

"Jaimie—"

"No. Don't talk right now. I can't think if you talk," she said, not lifting her head from her hands. She was silent for another moment. "You did this. You...you, what? Held his foot to the pedal? *Was* he drinking?"

"He was. He downed half a fifth of bourbon in a matter of minutes. Then we went for a drive." I tried to keep my voice calm as I felt her slipping away. I expected her to be mad, but why did it still hurt? "He lost control of his senses and mistook the gas pedal for the brakes—"

"Jesus, Mason," she said, her head shooting up from her hands. She turned her sharp eyes toward me. "Don't you think that was a *little* extreme?"

"No, he deserved way worse, but this was cleaner," I said, barely holding back a snort. If I was at my full mental capacity, I would have been on the floor groveling for her forgiveness, or at least I would have apologized first and then explained my justification. But I was hungry and still tired, so I let more snark seep into my voice than I intended.

"Mason..." She shook her head, like she couldn't decide how she felt.

"If I'd knifed him in an alleyway, killed him while he slept, or strung him, bloody and beaten, from a flagpole, it would have put him on some kind of pedestal," I explained, trying not to shrug or show attitude. "People would have turned him into a martyr. They would have said 'Poor Tristan.' But now, instead of 'poor Tristan,' they'll say 'Well, at least he didn't take anyone else out in the accident.'"

"You killed him, though, Mason." She stood up from the couch and turned to me. "This wasn't an accident or him being dumb. This is...this is murder."

"This was karma," I said, shaking my head. I stood up too, just so I wasn't looking up at her. "Swift, *just* karma. I refuse to feel bad for cutting him down when the justice system would never be able to touch him. He hurt you, and he would have kept—"

"You didn't kill Deb for hurting me," she said sharply. She still didn't seem entirely angry, just bewildered.

"Deb was different. You still needed the support she could offer if she changed her mindset. You didn't depend on Tristan for anything. And I couldn't change Tristan's mind. I tried." This was technically a lie. I hadn't tried to change Tristan's mind, but from the amount of power it took in the end to get him to do what I wanted, I never would've been able to do anything to his mind that would stick.

"You didn't kill Tony, the boy that hurt Mikey."

"Tony's just a kid—"

"Tristan was just a kid!" she said. "An asshole, yes, but a kid!"

"No." I shook my head. "He stopped being just a stupid annoying kid the second he touched you. *Then*, he became a monster."

"Like you?" she countered stonily. She'd been looking away in her bewilderment, but her eyes snapped sharply to mine. "Mr. I'm-a-monster? How are *you* better? What makes you less worthy of death?"

Her accusation was justified and understandable, but it still stung. It stung enough to suck the words from my mouth.

As I struggled to recover my voice, she plowed on, her voice softer. "Tell me this. In all those years of murder and death, did you ever rape anyone?"

I took a second to answer, not because I was preparing a lie, but because I didn't want to answer. This was something

I never liked to think about, and I tried to put all thoughts of it into the deepest parts of my mind. But I owed it to her to answer this.

"I don't know," I admitted honestly, my voice coming out thick. I looked away, but not before I saw her face change to dismay. She'd hoped for a different answer, and I wished I could give her one. "If I did, I did so unwittingly, unknowingly. I like to think that I never would've. I wouldn't wish my trauma on anyone else." I rubbed my neck roughly at the uncomfortable admission. I stared at her chin instead of her eyes so I didn't see whether her expression changed to pity. I didn't want to know. "Rosaline used sex to get me to submit and to follow her. And she'd force others on me, as well, depending on her mood...It fucked me up, and I wasn't always in control of my actions. But Tristan was in control. Like Rosaline, he knew exactly what he was doing. Which is why I have absolutely *no pity* for rapists.

"As for what makes me *better* than him?" I continued before she could cut in. "*Nothing*. I don't delude myself into thinking I'm redeemable. But the *difference* between him and me? I am *sorry* for *everything* I've done. And I've tried to atone." I said this part slowly, to emphasize every word. I brought my eyes back to hers, which were unreadable. "He was never going to be sorry for anything. Even if he had the centuries *I* have ahead of me to repent, he never would have. I killed him before he could hurt anyone else again. Before he could hurt *you* again. Because he *would have*."

She didn't respond but backed away from me, putting her hands to the sides of her head. She paced around the small living room. I followed her with my eyes, watching her expression.

"Are you upset that I killed him? Or are you upset that you're *not* upset that he's dead?"

"I'm upset because you keep fighting my battles for me!" she snapped, looking at me sharply. She stopped pacing. "I didn't ask you to."

"You weren't going to fight this battle yourself," I reminded her, but not aggressively. "You *couldn't* fight this battle yourself."

"Because I don't want to fight battles! I want to survive!" she exclaimed, throwing her hands up. As she brought them back down, slowly, her features softened. "I just want to *be*. And—I get it. I *do*—he got in the way of that. But so are you..."

"I'm not proud of it," I ventured cautiously, putting my hands up disarmingly. "This was *my* choice, my doing, and I'm not proud. But am I sorry that it was *him* that I killed? No. And I'll never be sorry for it. I have monsters after me, but this was a monster I could easily deal with."

"Just...stop, okay? Just stop talking for a minute," she said softly, holding a hand up.

I obeyed, and she paced again, tugging at a handful of hair that hung over her shoulder. Her face jumped between a number of expressions: from bewilderment to awe to frustration and then just exhaustion.

"I know that you're right, okay?" she said finally. She'd stopped by her shoes and her backpack. "But you shouldn't be right. And I don't know how I feel about this. I really,

really don't." She paused. After a few seconds, she huffed and glared at me. "I won't thank you."

"And you shouldn't," I told her, honestly.

She ran her hands through her hair, looking at the ceiling as if it would help her sort her thoughts.

I took a step toward her, but she shook her head sharply. "I hated him. I really did," she said. "Still, I should be horrified that he's dead, but I feel relief instead. And that's fucked up, isn't it? This is just way too fucked up for me to process right now." She slipped on her shoes without even looking down at them.

"Jaimie..." I said softly, not moving toward her, but I reached a hand out.

"I can't be here," she said, grabbing her bag. "Not right now. I need to think. I need to go."

"Jaimie, please," I said, surprised at how harrowed my voice sounded at her putting this wall up between us, at her leaving. Her hand was on the doorknob. "I love you—"

She let out a small shriek as she opened the door and barreled straight into the waiting arms of *Rosaline*, just on the other side of the door.

"Watch your step, sweetie," Rosaline cooed, gripping Jaimie's arms and forcing her back into the apartment.

I lunged forward automatically, but Malcolm stepped out from behind her and shoulder-checked me. I toppled into my kitchen counter and to the floor. Before I hit the ground, Malcolm slammed his fist into the side of my face.

"So this is the amusing curiosity that's made you so ornery? This skinny, frail-looking thing? Not your usual," Rosaline murmured. I glared up at her through my hair. She held Jaimie to her, arm wrapped around her throat as Jaimie struggled to shake her off.

"Let her go, Roz!" I growled at her, furious and terrified at the sight of Rosaline with her hands on Jaimie. She'd been waiting outside the door, unable to shift inside thanks to my wards. But how had she even found me? I'd taken precautions against that...

The ring. The goddamned ring. She'd taken it, and I'd forgotten until just now. Her taking it off me revealed my location to Riley, just as it had revealed my location to Rosaline. *Fuck.*

I lunged again, this time from the floor, but Malcolm struck me once more, clocking the side of my head with his elbow. I caught myself on my bad wrist and collapsed on top of it, barely holding in a cry of agony. Malcolm grabbed the back of my shirt and pulled me up to my knees.

"You and your artists, Mason," Rosaline chided me, then, she turned her head to address Jaimie. "You see, sweety, Mason can never resist an artist. And *I'm* never allowed to touch them. But, sweety," Jaimie flinched as Rosaline brushed her hair over her shoulder, "he can demand, all he wants, but he's never been able to *stop* me."

Rosaline's eyes were pure malice as they cut toward me. She flashed her fangs and angled her head toward Jaimie's neck.

With a roar, I dove out of Malcolm's grip. But I never made it to my feet. Jaimie screamed in terror as pain exploded in the back of my skull. I didn't remember falling, but suddenly I was face down on the tile floor. I spat out red and let out a weird kind of gargling groan as I flopped onto my back. My muscles spasmed, my fingers scrabbling at the tile by my sides for—I don't know what for.

"Night, night, Mason," Malcolm jeered above me and lifted the metal bat—which I hadn't realized he was holding before—over his head and brought it down, this time swinging it like an axe.

CHAPTER 27

Three times. Three times in eight hours, I lost consciousness, when it doesn't usually happen more than once a fortnight. Thankfully, when I woke this time, my mind skipped past the confused, befuddled stage and went straight to alert.

I was chained to a wall with silver shackles, my broken wrist pulsing against the silver cuffs, and I was hungrier than I'd been this century. The chain above my shackles had enough give that as I sat on the floor, my arms stretched high above me, but if I knelt, my wrists would rest by my shoulders. The room was cement brick and windowless, with a heavy wooden door and no furnishings. And Rosaline was in the cell with me, but not Jaimie.

Where the fuck is Jaimie? This thought, on top of my hunger, brought a low, animalistic growl from the back of my throat.

"Oh, stop that, Mason, *really*," Rosaline reprimanded, rolling her eyes and pushing away from the wall where she'd been leaning.

The last thing I wanted to be was cooperative, so I kept growling and snarling at her, increasing in volume and petulance with every second. If I was going to be chained like an animal, I was going to act like one.

"Mason, stop it," Rosaline snapped, dropping her exasperation. Her eyes flashed angrily as she took a step toward me.

Out of patience already, love? I wanted to say, but I said it in incoherent growl-speak instead.

She knelt and slapped her hand *hard* across my cheekbone, snapping my head to the side. I stopped my growling, but my lips remained curled, exposing my fangs in a silent snarl. I kept my head turned to the side.

"How did it come to this, Mason?" she bemoaned dramatically. She put her hands on either side of my face and pulled it to look at her. The right side of my head was still crusty with blood from where Malcolm had split it open—*twice*—like a melon. "My beautiful psychopath—my favorite psychopath—passes *me* up and then is caught with a girl in his room."

I gritted my teeth against simultaneously being called a psychopath and equated to a hormonal teenager in the same sentence. I could've argued that psychopathy isn't the typically violent or dangerous disorder—that's sociopathy—but I let it drop. Instead, turned my head at last and I looked her over.

Half of her long, blond curls were pulled back in a kind of bouffant and pinned to her crown—a style she seemed to like this decade, which made her resemble Cersei Lannister more than ever. She wore a shimmery top that hugged her perfect chest over tight leather-like pants, knee-high black boots. A new look for her: usually she loved body-skimming dresses and not wearing anything underneath.

"An interesting outfit you've got there, Roz," I quipped in a sultry growl, my eyes narrowing. I jangled my chains above my head. "With me constrained here and you so clothed, it's going to be much harder to do this, unless you start undressing."

"I'm afraid that ship has sailed, darling," she purred as her lips curled up into a flirtatious sneer. "For now, at least. You'll have to earn back the *privilege* of sex with me."

I couldn't help but scoff at the idea of *wanting* back in her favor, and a soft chuckle spilled from my lips. Her hand went to the top of my head and pulled my hair so that I was looking up at the ceiling, and at her.

"What happened to you?" she demanded. "You were my perfect, beautiful slave whenever I came around. Now, I have to restrain you? Now Malcolm has to bash your head in? All for some pretty little *child*."

"She's no more a child than I was, you twat," I snapped, baring my teeth at her again.

"Yes, I suppose you're right," she said, releasing my hair at last. "Which is why you should have changed her when you had the chance, like I told you to. Now it's too late."

Her words stilled me and my heart folded in on itself. Was Jaimie dead? Surely they wouldn't kill her without taunting me with her first. She couldn't be dead yet.

"Is she alive?" I asked, hiding the fear I felt behind my glare. "Did you kill her?"

"She's here, Mason, and she's still alive, for now." She smoothly got to her feet and stood over me.

Internally, I sighed with relief, but I kept it from my face.

I clenched my fists and gritted my teeth against the pain in my wrist as I pulled myself up to my knees to give my shoulders a rest.

"I suppose your next words are going to be 'that all depends entirely on you,' right?" I asked calmly.

She lifted her eyebrows once and tilted her head at me, frowning.

"I'll do whatever you want, Rosaline," I said honestly. I didn't let my voice betray that I was begging, but I put as much conviction into my voice as I could. "*Whatever* you want, if you let her go. Please, just keep her out of this."

She threw her head back and laughed a low, throaty chuckle, her hands on her hips. "How fucking *rich*." She leaned down to me, running her hands through my hair again and turning my head upward to look up at her. "You're in no position to bargain! You *will* do whatever I want, but *not* because I give you something. You'll do it simply because you have no other option." She brought her face to mine and kissed me roughly on the lips. Every muscle wanted to recoil, but there wasn't anywhere I could go. She pulled back from the kiss and glared mischievously into my eyes. "But I *like* the idea of seeing just how much I can do to this girl before you break."

My insides burned, and my hands clenched even tighter. I pulled unconsciously against the silver restraints.

"Leave her alone," I said, sounding more exhausted than angry. "She's been through enough."

FALLEN WOES

"If this young girl is so great, I bet Malcolm would love to try her out," she said with an evil glint in her eye. "Maybe even *I* will see if her nipples taste like *honey*."

I bit back a growl at the crude, horrific implication. My insides were roiling with fury and dread, but I forced myself to stare her down with the most intense, stoic look I could muster.

"I promise you, Rosaline," I told her, speaking slowly and deliberately. "I won't do a single thing you want me to do if you so much as *touch* her."

I saw her gloating smile waver at the chilling resolve in my voice. But then her lips spread into a dark, giddy smile.

"I was going to let you keep her. I really was," she said, still softly, playing the part of the reprimanding babysitter. "But now I know what needs to be done. You're going to watch her die, Mason. Like the night I changed you: you're going to watch your little life be destroyed. And you'll be *grateful* this time."

She ran a finger down the side of my face, from my temple to my chin. I wanted to recoil from her, but instead, I narrowed my eyes suspiciously at her.

"But don't worry, sweet devil," she said softly and sweetly. "We aren't going to be the ones that touch or harm her. *You* are. You'll kill her, and then you'll come back to me, to hide from your *pitiful guilt*."

"Nothing you do will make me wittingly hurt her." I shook my head against her suggestion and against the horrible realization that she was right. If I lost Jaimie, I would lose myself forever. I would bury myself in the darkness and never resurface again.

"We'll see, Mason," she cooed. "By the way, you're looking a little...well, *haggard* to be frank. When was the last time you fed?"

As if on cue, my body shook with a sudden hunger pang that vibrated through every bone and every tooth. I shuddered as it passed. I'd never been this low on blood energy before; I didn't know it would feel like this.

Rosaline was chucking softly, a deep belly laugh as the shudder dissipated. "Yes, I think if we get you hungry enough, you'll do just about anything for blood. Even kill your precious human."

"No," I said firmly, my eyes lifting to her with a determined glare.

"You will. You don't know it yet, but you will. And with her out of the way, I believe your monster side will resurface with a *beautiful* vengeance. He's been held at bay for too long, hasn't he Mason? Let him stretch his legs."

"Fuck you," I spat derisively, narrowing my eyes.

"All in good time, my love," she said, winking. She rapped her palm sharply against my cheek. "We'll be together again in good time. Because we belong together. Our blood is mixed inside you, like the blood infused in this."

From her cleavage, she withdrew a silver ring, set with a polished tiger's eye focal—the warded ring I'd bought from Libby. The one Rosaline had taken from me and I'd forgotten to retrieve before escaping, leading to Jaimie being taken.

"With this ring, I thee wed," she said mockingly, smirking darkly at me. She slipped the ring onto my left ring finger and let out a giggle. "We'll consummate it once the child slut is dead."

I wanted to snap at her with a biting comeback, but as she stood up and stepped back, another hunger pang shuddered through me with startling violence, sucking away whatever words had been on my lips. She was still chuckling derisively at me as the shudder subsided. I looked up in time to see her blond curls disappear behind the closing door.

CHAPTER 28

Up until this point in my existence, I'd lived a privileged—one might even say gluttonous—life. I was a wealthy child, so I never knew a hungry day. And I was an overindulgent young Lapsus alongside Rosaline. We feasted nightly on blood and violence and debauchery. After I left her, I didn't necessarily starve myself in repentance: I just stopped *killing* while feeding.

The first time I nearly starved, I lost control and killed my childhood best friend. I hadn't known what I was then, or that there was such a thing as control. I hadn't felt this level of hunger since, but I was feeling it now.

I tried to think back to the last time I'd fed. I'd been merely nibbling on people at the dance club, right before Malcolm abducted me the first time. Then I'd fought Rosaline, briefly, and I used a ton of power to force Tristan to drive into that wall. I didn't feed after that, and that had been twelve or more hours ago. I was *hosed*.

The thing about Lapsi hunger is that it isn't like starving for food. Your stomach doesn't growl and cramp. *Everything* cramps. And everything itches with this deep, aggravating nerve-itch that starts in your fangs and resonates in every bone.

FALLEN WOES

I've never done drugs, but I've heard some younger Lapsi describe Lapsi hunger as *withdrawal*. The chills and shakes, the body aches, the whole nine yards. It's slow and agonizing, and it only gets worse with time.

Good thing all I had was time.

At first, I worried about Jaimie. I worried about where they were keeping her. If she was cold or hungry. I worried if they were hurting her—even though Rosaline swore they would make it so that I was the only one that hurt her. I worried about her family. Surely they realized she was gone by now. Mikey might tell them where I lived. They'd break in, find her bag, the clothes she'd thrown away, and a ton of my blood in the kitchen. I knew how it would look.

I couldn't think about all of that for too long because it would have sent me into utter despair, rather than the *mild* despair I was already feeling.

Last time, I'd distracted myself with happy thoughts of Jaimie. Her smell, her looks, her smile, her skin, her tentative, inexperienced kisses. But every time I thought about her this time, it was only of her blood.

And I swear that as time went on, I could feel her. She was the closest blood, besides the rats beneath the floors and in the walls. But I can't eat rats, much as their quick little heartbeats drove me mad.

I needed to distract myself, but I had nothing. Nothing but time, an empty room, silver cuffs. And a silver ring.

And a *silver* ring.

She'd given it to me as a taunt, mocking our joining like a marriage, but she'd given me a piece of silver that wasn't restraining me and wasn't nailed down.

Was there a catch? No. You can't kill a Lapsus with a silver fucking ring. Unless you make them swallow it and then punch them. Which wouldn't kill them, but if it could debilitate them for long enough...

I doubted I could successfully use a ring as a weapon, but imagining all the ways to kill Rosaline with it was amusing enough to distract myself from the growing hunger. I was running out of death-by-ring scenarios, though, and I'd only thought of five.

I shifted to sitting on the stone floor as I struggled to think. I leaned my head against my lifted arm and blew out a sigh of frustration. The ring made a metallic tinkling chirp as I tapped the backs of my fingers against the stone wall behind me.

I froze at the sound, an idea hitting me.

I rubbed the ring sideways against the stone, pressing on it as I did so. Then I knelt, so I could look at the ring on my knuckle. The ornate filigree on the flat side of the band was marred almost flat.

I sat back down and alternated different ways of rubbing the ring against the wall, determining which direction would best serve my purpose. The tiger's eye ground to sand and fell into my hair and eyes. Slowly, one side of the ring was flattening, beveling the metal upward.

I kept at it slowly and carefully, checking every so often on my progress. It was a futile hope, and pointless, really. But it was distracting. The pangs grew more violent, but I was able to think through them if my hands were working on their task.

Carefully—ever so carefully—I pulled the ring from my finger with shaking hands. If I had a spasm while doing this and dropped the ring, I was done for. I worked the ring successfully off my finger and gingerly flipped it around and put it back on. I settled back down to the floor and continued working, scraping and milling the other side.

Slowly and surely, the ring's shape was changing. I wouldn't have called it razor sharp, but there was a definite sharp ridge along what used to be the ring setting. I rubbed the ridge with my finger and almost laughed with giddy excitement. With enough force, this could cut deeply into flesh. Not enough to kill, but enough to startle at the very least—and it wouldn't heal.

I didn't want to be finished with my silly, futile project. It'd served me well as a distraction from the pain and throb of starvation. But I couldn't work at it any further or it would dull—or worse, break the ring.

I'd worked through much of the shudders, and now they were either less violent or I'd gotten used to them. I was so tired. Grinding and honing a ring-blade with my bare hands, above my head, doesn't sound like hard work, but I'd like to see a human try it.

I had no energy left to keep me fully upright. I slumped against the stone wall, with my hands above me. It put pressure on my fractured wrist, which hurt, but if I didn't move, I almost forgot about it.

I dozed on and off, and I have no idea how long I was kept like this, whether it was just a few or several hours or days, even. All I knew was that, at my age, I couldn't last days before growing mad with hunger, and I hadn't gone *quite* mad yet.

An immeasurable amount of time later, I woke to find someone standing above me, releasing the cuffs from my wrists. Only half of my sensory processing reflexes were working, but I managed to gather my wits enough to tense my hand in such a way that one of my fingers blocked my ring-wielding finger from view.

As soon as the cuffs were released, I collapsed to the floor, groaning in relief and throbbing pain. I wanted to curl up into myself, but I didn't have the energy.

"Yeah, I'd say ye're at yer breaking point, chum." The gruff, lilting Scottish voice came from what seemed like a mile away. Hands grabbed my upper arms and lifted me onto shaking feet. My eyes unfocused and focused on the figure in front of me. I saw russet hair, grayed at the temples, and a beard I'd kill to have. *Malcolm*, I realized as my mind stirred.

He smacked his palm against my cheek, just enough to startle me and get my synapses firing. Then he marched me and my trembling legs from my cell.

I'd grown numb to my starvation in my cell. But I realized now that it had purely been sensory deprivation. Outside my cell, *everything*—every sound, every footfall, every jittering rat heartbeat—sent a throbbing shudder through me. And I could feel *blood*. Human blood was somewhere up ahead, growing nearer with each step.

I don't know exactly where I was marched to. The room was well lit, carpeted, and roomy. It could have been a lit-up movie theatre, or it could have been a common basement.

All I know is that once inside the room, I immediately smelled *her*.

Her sweat, fear, tears, and blood. And on top of it all—encompassed by it all—I smelled *her*. Jaimie. Jaime was in the room with me. *Oh god, no. No. No. No.*

They probably expected me to jump on her immediately, like a starved animal on a carcass. But I still had enough of my wits and my determination to keep myself from doing that. Instead, I threw myself to the floor, pressing my face into the carpet.

"Mason?" I heard her speak, softly and warily, from the other side of the room. She sounded so scared yet relieved to see me, even if I'd thrown myself face first into the floor.

No. No. No. I kept thinking over and over, to the sound of her rapid heartbeat. It thrummed in my ears, and my nerves pulsed along to the rhythm of it. *No, I won't do it. I am in control.*

Hands grabbed the back of my shirt, and for a heart-stopping second, I thought they were Jaimie's. I gnashed around like a rabid animal, thinking blood was nearer than it was. But it was Malcolm who'd grabbed me. He lifted me back to my staggering feet.

"Get it the fuck over with, ye weak fuck," he hissed at me.

He slapped me across the face, and the pain diverted my senses enough that my eyes were able to focus on him and his pale, hateful eyes. To think I'd once been attracted to this man, and to think I'd fucked him on a number of occasions. Now it felt vaguely *incestual*, since he was one of Rosaline's creations too.

Hatred bubbled up after he slapped me, but so did something else. I thought it would be words, but instead, I spat a satisfying glob of spittle into his face. He cursed and wiped it away, furious. He shoved me farther into the room. I caught my footing, but the world seemed to be convulsing all around me. Then I realized that *I* was the one convulsing.

"Mason!?" Jaimie's concerned voice reached me, and I cried out as the vibrations struck my eardrum.

"No," I grunted out as I dropped to my knees again. I put my hands to the floor to steady myself. "Stay away."

I said it weakly at first, and I heard a light footfall. Blood came nearer. The room tipped.

"Stay away," I said again, a little stronger. I glanced up in the blood's direction and saw her thin, fragile, blurred form several feet away. I could only imagine how *I* looked, but I tried to communicate to her with a sharp, foreboding glare what I was also saying from my mouth. "Stay back. Please, stay back."

Maybe I just looked crazed and rabid. But either way, she backed away again and out of focus.

Malcolm let out an impatient growl behind me and pulled me to my feet. I turned to swing at him, but my weak, desperate blow flew nowhere near his head. He put a hand to the back of my neck and forced me farther into the room. I could see Jaimie now, and only Jaimie. Scared Jaimie. Confused Jaimie. Beautiful Jaimie.

She was backed against the wall of the room, and as Malcolm marched me forward, she tried to run to her left, but Rosaline appeared there. She grabbed Jaimie and pulled her away from the wall, toward me. She held one of Jaimie's arms behind her back, and her other hand held a silver knife to Jaimie's throat.

"Shh, shh, it's okay, love," she purred into Jaimie's ear. Jaimie let out an involuntary whimper. "You won't feel a thing."

"No, I won't do it, you bastards," I mumbled out in a guttural growl—at least I intended to say those words. I have no idea if they actually came out as words or just a guttural jumble of nonsense.

Jaimie was in clearer focus than ever before as I was brought closer. Her hair was dirty and limp. Her face was still pretty in its effortless, normal way, but it was grimy and tear-streaked. More tears were making new trails as she grimaced in bewildered fear. I could hear the deafening sound of her heartbeat as it beat faster and faster, and I could see the delicate pulsing of her artery in her throat.

I dug my heels in and tried to stop our forward momentum, but Malcolm was stronger. Rosaline and Malcolm pushed Jaimie and me closer together until we were just a foot apart.

Malcolm wrapped a forearm around my collarbone, and I felt the poke of a silver blade at my back, right behind my heart.

"No," I still mumbled firmly, using all my strength to lean away from Jaimie and twist away from the blade in my back.

"Just do it, Mason, and it'll all be over," Rosaline said, trying to keep the impatience from her voice but failing. "You won't hurt anymore. And this poor little girl won't be terrified anymore."

Still, I shook my head and bit my lips as they tried to curl back from my teeth. *Jaimie, I'm trying so hard,* I told her telepathically, using some of the last of my mental strength to send the message into her mind. *I love you. I won't do this.* She looked at me fearfully, but her eyes changed for just a beat: she'd heard me, understood me, and forgiven me all in that instant.

Rosaline yanked on the arm she'd twisted behind Jaimie's back, and Jaimie let out another whimper, which she tried to stifle.

"Baby girl," Rosaline cooed into her ear, sounding revoltingly like Tristan. "Look at him. He's in so much pain. He's out of his mind with it. You don't want him to be in pain anymore, right?"

"Stop it," I snapped at her, gritting my teeth.

"Mason, you're just having trouble performing. It happens to even the best men," Rosaline teased. "You just need a little help, that's all. Allow me."

She kept her eyes locked on mine as she moved the hand holding the knife ever so slightly against Jaimie's throat. Jaimie hissed as a small cut formed on her neck.

Blood pooled in the cut immediately, flavoring the air with its deliciously metallic scent. I groaned as it instantly reached my nostrils. But I still found myself pushing back against the blade in my back.

"It's okay," Jaimie said, barely audibly. "It's okay."

She was numb with fear now. She might not even know what she said. I don't think she necessarily meant it was okay for me to kill her. But my will broke, both by the sounds of her consent and the overwhelming scent of her blood in the air. I leaned forward.

I took her face in my hands and felt a sob rushing up my throat as I stared into her eyes. I clamped down on it and instead tried to communicate everything I was currently thinking just using my eyes. New tears fell and she nodded ever so faintly.

"I'm sorry," I said, brushing my lips over hers as I uttered the words, barely audibly. Then, tilting her head back, I lowered my lips to the cut on her throat.

Rosaline lowered the knife to give me room enough to put my mouth over the cut. My fangs hovered over her flesh, but I didn't make a deeper cut. Instead, I took a small sip from the cut, intending my saliva to heal it. When her blood hit my tongue, however, everything went still around me, like a womb, while simultaneously everything erupted in stimulation, pleasure, and *relief*. My willpower went to shreds, sucked away like ribbon in a turbine.

But then Jaimie gave another whimper of fear and shook beneath my lips. I'd only been gone for a second, but her fear brought me nearly all the way back to my senses.

Malcolm's mistake was leaving my arms free. I steeled myself, relaxing all the right muscles to look like I was going to sink fully into the meal. Grabbing the knife in Rosaline's grip, I shoved my other hand, sharpened ring facing out, into her face as hard as I could manage. In the same beat, I reared back and buried my fangs deep into Malcolm's forearm which was still clenched around my collarbone.

I bit down hard, determined to tear a whole chunk out of his meaty arm. He jerked back and released me, swearing up a storm. Rosaline shrieked and pressed her hand to her bleeding eye. Reflexively, as she collapsed backward in agony, she wrenched the knife we still held *downward*. I clocked her movement a split second too late. I released Malcolm's arm and cried out uselessly as the sharp silver blade sliced into Jaimie's throat.

Rosaline's aim was skewed, but it still made a terrible cut, and life-giving blood colored the air with a fountain of delicious red. Jaimie fell to her knees, clutching her neck.

A tearing, wrenching pain ripped through my chest when Jaimie dropped to the ground. I'd felt this pain only once before, at discovering the bodies of my family members. A throat-shredding roar tore from me as the grief and rage overtook me, much as it had then.

I'd kept the grip on the knife as both Rosaline and Jaimie fell out of my line of sight. Blindly, I rounded on Malcolm who was still clutching his bleeding arm in fury and shock. He glanced up at me, too late to raise the knife in his own hand.

I missed his heart, and got his shoulder instead, but it brought both of us to the ground. I recovered first and crouched over him. He was too stunned to block, so I brought the knife down again and again, not realizing what I was doing. On the third stab, I finally buried the knife to its hilt into his chest, perfectly between his ribs and into his heart. He went still immediately, but I twisted the knife for good measure.

Feet behind me, Rosaline groaned in enraged agony. I turned, while pulling the knife from Malcolm's dried out chest, and got to my feet.

FALLEN WOES

Rosaline was writhing on the ground, clutching furiously at her eye, blind to the world aside from her pain. I dragged her off the ground by the throat and shoved her into the wall behind her, pressing against her, as I had done *oh* so many times.

Her right eye was destroyed. The sharpened ring had sliced clear into it and then up into her brow. It was a horrific, gruesome sight. Gone were her hellfire good looks and demure, sultry glances. Good fucking riddance.

"I wanted to be whole again, before I fucking killed you," I hissed at her, enjoying her agony and the one-eyed glare she fixed me with. "I wanted to save my soul first, and then have you look at me and *see me* as a decent fucking man again, before I ripped your heart out. But oh-fucking-well."

Before she could even muster up a deeper glare or—god forbid—any remorse in her one eye, I drove the knife up, beneath her diaphragm and into her heart.

"*His* blood in you, like yours in his. You two are wed in hell now, *bitch*!" I snarled as I twisted the knife, ending her hateful, bloodthirsty life. She was far older than Malcolm or me, so she dusted into bone fragments and long-dried skin flecks.

For parting words, they weren't my best, but I didn't care. I collapsed to the ground and dove toward Jaimie's prone form.

I pulled her into my arms, praying it wasn't as bad as I thought. There was blood everywhere, and I was still starving with bloodlust, but my concern outweighed anything else.

"Please, no, Jaimie. No, no no..." I brought my lips to the cut flesh of her throat. I did drink some of the blood pooling there, yes—I couldn't help it—but that wasn't why I brought my mouth to the cut. Lapsi saliva heals flesh wounds, so I licked away the blood there and heaved a huge sigh of relief—that might have been a sob—as the flesh started to knit back together. She was alive.

I was too late, though. Her pulse was so slow and weak, and her muscles were spasming as her brain tried to send panicked impulses to her muscles. She'd be irretrievably dead in less than a minute.

Kind, strong Jaimie. She couldn't be dead. She had a brother to keep safe and whose mind needed stimuli. She had a contest to win and so, *so much* art to put into the world. She couldn't die. I couldn't keep going in a world where she was allowed to die like this.

"I'm so sorry," I murmured into her neck as I pulled her up from my lap, hugging her close to me. "You might hate me, but I can't let you die like this."

I brought my wrist to my mouth and tore the flesh with my extended fangs. I held my wrist to her slackened mouth, letting my blood flow past her lips, over her tongue, and finally down her throat. As I held my wrist to her mouth, I brought my lips to her throat again, and slashing her flesh there for the second time, I drank the last of her life away, feeling my heart break as I did it.

I stayed with her in my arms for several agonizingly long minutes, wishing to just see her eyes one more time.

After what felt like an eternity, her arms and legs twitched, and then her mouth opened, sputtering and gasping. She breathed in a mouthful of air that she no longer needed.

CHAPTER 29

I really hate moving. Especially when it was the second time picking up everything and moving in only a matter of weeks. I prided myself too much on my collection of art prints and signed photographs to enjoy packing them all away in boxes, removing nails from walls, and fathoming hammering nails into yet another wall.

But I wouldn't be hammering nails into a new wall for a while. These were all going into storage for the foreseeable future because I didn't know where I would be living. All I knew was Portland, Oregon.

I'd just finished wrapping Jaimie's large mirror painting carefully in brown paper, plastic, and string—I couldn't be too careful—when a knock sounded on my door. I no longer had pressing enemies looking for me, that I knew of, so I called across the echoey apartment that the door was unlocked.

Mikey rocketed through the door, skidding on the slick hardwood floors as he tried to stop, and plowed into me. I wrapped my arms around him in a bear hug, savoring the feeling of his small arms around me in the brotherly hug.

"Hey, Padawan," I said in greeting, still squeezing him.

I looked past him and regarded Jaimie with a mix of tender happiness and solemnity.

Ever since our ordeal, I hadn't seen her smile in my direction much. She'd been more subdued than usual as she adjusted to her new existence.

But as I hugged Mikey and gave her a tentative smile, expecting a muted half smile, I was instead met with a light in her eyes I hadn't seen in more than a week.

She wore plain jeans and a black, loose-fitting tank top. Her wrist was still scarred from her ordeal when she was twelve, but the rest of the marks on her arms had healed with her change. She hugged her bare arms, when a week ago she would have been fiddling with the long cuffs of her cardigan. She looked like she was trying to hide her excitement about something.

"What?" I asked her as Mikey pulled out of my bear hug and stepped back.

"We have news!" Mikey said enthusiastically. He stepped over to a stack of boxes, on top of which sat my longboard.

"They picked the mural for the theatre," Jaimie said, biting her lip, as if trying to fight back a smile from her usual stoic face. But the smile won out. "They picked mine."

A stupid grin spread across my face and I opened my arms wide in my excitement. I didn't expect her to approach me and hug me—she hadn't in over a week—but she stepped forward quickly and into my arms, practically squealing with uncharacteristic delight. I lifted her off her feet and spun around in several circles while she laughed.

Through everything, I'd nearly forgotten about the contest. She'd submitted her entry right before her assault and the ensuing events. And after everything, it probably seemed less important than suddenly being made into a Lapsus. But she had been recognized for her hard work, and I couldn't be more elated.

"I told you I can sense greatness," I mumbled against her cheek as I set her back on the ground.

"I swear, if you did this, I'm going to scream," she said, looking at me sharply, but the light hadn't left her eyes.

"What? No. No, I didn't, I promise," I said adamantly. I hadn't even had a chance to consider swaying the judges—which I'd never do. I wanted the vindication when the judges saw what I saw. "This was all you and your talent."

Her smile broadened further, brightening her beautiful face with a light I'd never seen, and haven't seen since.

I took her face in my hands and kissed her. She let me for a few seconds, but then she put her hands over mine and pulled them gently from her face. She looked up at me as our faces separated, her smile waning. She looked away and quickly surveyed the room.

"Looks like you're all packed?" she said, a little too quickly, attempting to brush off the sudden awkwardness.

"Movers will be here tomorrow, but I'm leaving tonight," I said, my voice coming out much calmer than I really felt on the matter. I pressed my set of keys into her hand. "They're taking everything to storage. After that, do whatever you want with the place. Keep it or close the lease. It doesn't matter."

She could live there rent-free by mesmerizing the property manager and forging any paperwork on their computers. She could move in after graduation, treat it as her studio, or just end the lease tomorrow. I was leaving the option entirely open to her.

I moved to the large wrapped canvas and put a hand on it, motioning to Jaimie to come forward.

"This, however, I entrust completely to your care. I don't trust movers, and I don't trust storage facilities. It's just too precious," I told her, looking into her eyes so she knew I meant it. She tried to suppress the smile, but I gleaned it anyway. "I'll be back for it. So don't think you can resell it or anything."

She nodded and hugged her arms again, her new staple posture.

I walked over to Mikey, who looked positively *sullen* at the mention of movers. He slouched over the stack of boxes, his head leaning on his fist, as he idly spun the wheel of my longboard with his fingers.

"And you, Mikey-Man," I said as I walked up to him. He lifted his head from his hand but still looked sullen. I picked up my longboard, admiring it like an old friend, and held it out to him. "I want you to have this. No need to keep it safe. I want you to ride it and abuse it. Okay?"

He took it from my hands, suddenly awed. He merely nodded in response and stared down at the board in his hands.

"And for God's sake, wear a *helmet*, and no streets," I chided, looking sternly at him. I softened my face. "This isn't forever, Mikey. I'll check in."

He nodded, still looking solemn. I rubbed a hand over his messy head of hair, and he moved away to get out from under my hand. I snorted in amusement.

"Go on and try it out. We'll be right behind you," I told him. He walked out of the empty apartment, leaving the door open behind him.

I picked up my duffle that contained just a couple of outfits. I'd get more stuff later once I figured things out. I stepped over to Jaimie and brushed my hand against the back of hers.

"Come on." I motioned to the door. She followed behind me, and we left the apartment, locking it behind us.

I missed the budding romance between us, and the casual, comfortable touches, but I wasn't going to press it. I'd already overstepped by kissing her earlier. She'd pulled back from me after I changed her—before that even—but I didn't resent it. I understood.

In the first several hours of her change, I stayed near her, refusing to leave her side as she figured out her new strengths. I didn't let her go back to her family until she'd fed and gotten a handle on her Lapsi abilities.

She'd been missing for two days by the time she returned home. To explain her disappearance, she told her family about Tristan's attack and vandalism and explained that she'd left town in a trauma panic, until I found her and convinced her to come home. I showed her how to mesmerize them just enough to soften their anger and ebb their disbelief. And we worked together to mesmerize the cops into forgetting they were ever called.

To her father and stepmother, she was still human, and any erratic behavior going forward was because of her trauma. But she couldn't keep anything from her brother. He knew everything and was thrilled to have a superhero sister.

Over the past week, I'd merely been helping her with the adjustment: I took her out to feed, taught her the easiest tactics, and taught her how much to take from any one person before it became noticeable. I wanted to make sure I showed her all the ropes that so many had to navigate on their own. She resented the change at first, but she agreed that it beat the alternative. At least this way she got to see Mikey grow up, and she could open doors for him she never could have before.

I could show her the ropes of being a Lapsus. I could teach her to invest the money she'd saved now, rather than later. I could teach her how to use her mesmerism to secure housing for free. I could check all of the boxes in the Lapsus starter guide, but I couldn't help her with unpacking her experiences, because I was the cause of all of them.

I never wanted this for her—or rather, I never wanted this for her so *young*. She looked healthier and stronger than she ever had, but she was still as waifish as she had been in life, due to poor nutrition. She hadn't had a chance to put on any weight as her family grew more stable. She would always be skinny and frail looking, and she would always look young. I'd condemned her to my life of permanent adolescence. She, like me, would always be underestimated.

Because of this, I couldn't stay, and neither of us really wanted me to. I'd dragged her unintentionally through all of my shit, and she'd nearly died because of it. She forgave me for a lot: mainly for her being snatched up, held in captivity, nearly dying, and being made into a Lapsus. She hadn't yet forgiven me for Tristan, but she assured me it was because she was still wrestling with how *she* felt about his death.

She forgave me for most things, and she didn't hate me. But she wasn't ready to be *with* me.

It was too much for her. She was young, and processing a lot of horrifying information was hard for her. She'd fled when she found out that I was a Lapsus. She'd nearly fled when I killed her assailant. And now, knowing much of my bloody past, she was pulling back.

And she should. She needed to find her footing. She needed to burst through graduation, into adulthood, and accept that she would always be on the cusp of it. She needed to do this without my meddling any further.

While she did this, I intended to do some soul-searching. My physical demons were gone, but I still had some psychological demons to reckon with. I'd never reckoned with them before because there was always the *chance* that Rosaline would turn up again and undo any progress. But now I had two things I didn't have before: freedom and a goal. I was leaving Southern California for somewhere I hoped to do some good.

"Be sure to take him to theme parks. All the time," I told her, as I watched Mikey try to push himself off with the board. His balance was improving, but he was still a scrawny eleven-year-old, bordering on gawky. He had a long way to go. "You can get in for free now, no worries. And you never have to wait in line."

"I'll still wait in line, though," she told me, shaking her head and smirking. "I'm not going to let him get used to things being easy. Lines teach patience and fairness. He's not better than anyone."

I nodded and shrugged at the same time, to show that I deferred to her decision. I looked at her out of the side of my eye, and my gaze lingered for a moment.

"What?" she asked.

"I just...I love you, Jaimie. I always will," I said truthfully.

She didn't speak for a moment. "I won't thank you," she said finally, one side of her mouth twitching into a smirk.

"You shouldn't," I said after a small chuckle. It was a callback to when she'd said that after I'd killed Tristan. Was that going to be our signature thing? I kind of liked it. I turned and fully faced her, brushing my hands against hers by her sides. "I'm going to work on myself. I'm going to make you proud of me, and earn your love back."

She nodded but kept her mouth shut on any answer. Her face remained blank, guarded. That was fine.

"In the meantime, please live your life however you choose. Go out and love however many people you want. I don't care if you sleep with anyone else. I don't," I told her honestly.

We had forever to come back together as different, better people. I didn't expect her to save every part of herself for me. I wanted her to have experiences outside of me, as I'd surely have experiences outside of her. I was sexual by nature, and I knew I'd be back to my slutty ways eventually. It wouldn't change the fact that she had my whole heart.

"But, *please*, take this advice," I started again after a pause. "Only sleep with Lapsi from here on out. You can come endlessly, humans can't. Trust me. Human men: one and done. Human women: can go for a long time, and multiple times. Lapsi: *infinite* orgasms."

She rolled her eyes at the absurdity of the conversation, but she laughed a truly genuine laugh.

"Same to you, you know. I hope I haven't made you a one-woman Lapsus for eternity," she said, still smirking. "Don't abstain from sex for *me*. Get some as often as you want."

"I won't abstain—not on purpose at least," I told her honestly. "Though, I think I'm going to be a little busy. I won't be up to my usual debauchery for a while, probably."

"What are you going to be doing?" she asked, her eyebrows coming together in confusion.

"Oh, and one more thing I need you to promise me," I said, pivoting around the question. "Stay out of Oregon. Whatever you do. Something's coming, and I don't want you anywhere near it."

"Where and what are you going to be doing, Mason?" she asked, her brow completely furrowed now. Her tone suggested she already knew the answer.

Rosaline had told me about a plot in Oregon, run by Cassandra, the slightly off-putting psychic Lapsi. Undoubtedly Malcolm's crew was involved with Cassandra, and they had no idea that I no longer cared for their brand of violence and carnage. I figured I could go underground and try my hand at infiltration and espionage. I could do some good, while still being plenty enough of an asshole. That was the hope at least.

"I may or may not be in Oregon," I admitted after debating whether I should. At her wary expression, I grinned. "Being bad, but hopefully also doing a lot of good."

Feeling mischievously bold, I leaned forward and kissed her. This time she didn't pull back for a long moment.

"I'll be back for my painting, and hopefully another kiss," I told her as I pulled back from her lips. Then I shouldered my bag and disappeared.

• • • •

The End

Please Review

Please tell me and others what you thought of this book? Thank you so much for reading my story. Your eyes on the page mean the world to me. If you feel comfortable doing so, I implore you to leave a rating and review for this book on any of the e-commerce or booky platforms. Reviews (whether good, bad, or neutral) are invaluable to authors. They help us see where we need to improve, and help us get our books into more hands.

ACKNOWLEDGMENTS

This was such a wild ride! When I tell you this finished product is unrecognizable from the little story I started writing at age fourteen, it is an understatement. Only the bones of that story remain: the names of Mason, Jaimie, and Rosaline, and the ending I always planned (Inspired by Fall Out Boy's "A Little Less Sixteen Candles").

There are two main people that deserve direct acknowledgments: Megan and Erin.

Megan, I started writing this story for you, in little segments I'd print out on fancy paper and leave in your backpack, like a dork. We haven't spoken in more than fifteen years, and I have no idea how to find you, but I think of you every time I think of Mason. I wonder if he ever crosses your mind (And I'm sure you cringe whenever you think about it. The OG Mason was....problematic.) I'm sure you'd love how I rewrote his morally *dark*-gray character into my little trauma boi, and proud slut!

Erin, I'd BURIED the memory of this story. I mean, completely buried it. When I told you I was rewriting "that story I started in high school," (Fallen Idols), you said "Mason, right?" My first thought was "who the hell is Mason?" Two seconds passed, just two, before the flood gates holding him back in my brain opened and *he* stormed out, slapped me for forgetting him, and poured his real story into me.

Next, of course, I have to thank YOU, dear reader. And I apologize. I usually thank you first, but had to put Megan and Erin first this time. But this doesn't change just how important you are to me. Without you, there would be no point in this. I write for you, and only a small fraction of it is really for me.

And, as always, Thank you, Mom, Dad, and Natalie, for always supporting me and cheering for me on this journey (Even though you're never allowed to read THIS book....)

Wait! I have a surprise for you!

. . . .

Mason returns in Book 5!

. . . .

But more than that...Book 5 is <u>Riley's</u> book!!!
And everyone—I mean *everyon*e (except Jeremy.
Because fuck him)—makes an appearance in
book 5!

. . . .

And as a little treat...

Sneak Peek

Book 5 (Untitled)
Release Date Currently TBD
(Please note...This sneak peek chapter is
Unedited, and subject to change!)

CHAPTER 1

Riley

With a groan, I stopped sharing my screen and flopped backwards on the couch, rubbing my eyes.

"Wow," was the only word Felkyn uttered.

"On a scale of one to Kanye, how screwed am I?" I rubbed my eyes even harder, as if my hands could erase the terrible memory of the interview from my retinas.

"It really depends on the image you were *trying* to convey, versus the image you *did* convey," Felkyn said evasively. "Were you going for bleeding heart, stuck in the past...or were you angling more towards menace to society?"

"Just answer the question, dick," I snapped, through my hands.

"Probably an eight, dude. I'm sorry, but a solid eight."

I groaned again and yanked the pillow from behind my head, hugging it to my stomach instead.

"It started well, I thought. A bit too canned, and cheesy, but okay..." I mused, picking at the seam of the pillow's stitching.

"Yeah, your problem was going into it without a publicist," Felkyn felt the need to remind me. "It's their job to jump in when the questions become dangerous, and stop the interview from getting derailed."

"I am aware, thanks," I grumbled. "But I don't have a publicist anymore."

"Yeah, because we're not a band anymore," he snapped. "So why are you taking interviews? Are you so stuck in the past that you crave the spotlight again? Because that's what this is sounding like."

Yeah, okay, you want to play that card? I thought, irritated.

"You forget that you held onto the spotlight far longer than I did," I snapped, glaring at the laptop screen. "Remember *Long Live*? The solo single you produced after LV ended, of which *I* had no part?" He was silent in response, frowning at me through thousands of miles of internet. "And it was never about the spotlight for me."

"So what was this about then, Baby Boy?" Felkyn said, his voice softened now.

But his old term of endearment didn't soften my mood at all. I clicked my teeth together, seething, and looked away to stare at the ceiling. *Good old Felkyn, refusing to give up on calling me the baby after more than 30 years. And* I'm *the one stuck in the past.*

"I get it, though, man. You want to stay relevant. You saw *Pam & Tommy*, and—"

"Felkyn, that's enough," Danielle snapped. In my peripheral, I saw her shove into frame, but I didn't turn. "Go away until you can stop being a dick about this."

I closed my eyes while Felkyn shuffles out of view of their webcam and Danielle centers herself in the frame.

"He's being unfair. You don't need that," she said, not bothering to hide her irritation at Felkyn. I just sighed and kept my eyes on the ceiling. "Honestly, Riley, that guy was a bigot, and fuck him." Her tone softened when she spoke next. "Are you okay?"

"Yeah, I'm fine," I said flatly. Tossing the pillow aside and running a hand through my perpetually messy hair. "The interview doesn't air for two weeks. So I have a little bit before I am eight-tenths screwed."

I turned my head to look at her finally, and gave her a half smile. She'd been my solid friend for nearly thirty years now, and probably the best friend I'd ever had, next to my brother. Felkyn teased me like a brother, but she never did.

Her face on the video call looked as pretty as ever. She looked a little older than me, since she was changed at twenty-one, and me at nineteen, but I was a hundred and fifty years her elder.

"It's just a little interview, on a little podcast," I said, changing my tone to blasé. "It's not exactly hot-goss. Not likely to break the internet. I'll be fine."

"It will blow over," she agreed with a nod. "And I think most people will be more intrigued by LV than ever."

"Yeah, if anything, people will want more LV. Our sales will go through the roof. I mean, our accounts haven't exactly dried up, or been dormant, but it will be hilarious if money starts really rolling in."

"And Lorenzo will turn over in his grave for missing out on it!" Felkyn piped up from way off screen. Despite my earlier irritation at him, I grinned. Our old manager had been a fun guy, and he'd passed away just last year at the tender age of 82.

"And maybe we'll get a movie, or a TV series," he said, from closer now, but he didn't step into frame. "I bet they get Timothée Chalamet to play you and Collin."

FALLEN WOES

If only, I think to myself, feeling a little glow burn inside me at the thought.

"You'll be played by a Skarsgård, definitely. Or Evan Peters," I quipped, amused.

"I'll take Kiernan Shipka, if I can be in it," Danielle added, with a small smile.

Her big brown eyes looked at me with nothing but friendly sympathy. I caught sight of myself in the smaller window in the corner, and understood why. My smile didn't quite reach my eyes, and my expression was altogether hollow.

I knew if she asked again if I was okay, I might slip and let on that I wasn't.

Making some excuse about having to work, I ended the video call and flopped back down on the couch and dropped the pillow on my face.

If I were a real spiteful dick, I'd make Jake Santos regret that interview, I thought with a deep sigh. But as bummed as I was about the interview, I was also a masochist. A part of me wanted to see how it all played out without my interference. Stupid? Yes. Masochistic? Also yes. Likely to blow up in my face? Absolutely, but I was used to that by now.

Felkyn accused me of missing the spotlight, but it'd never been about the spotlight for me—I mean, the drummer is rarely the focal point of a band, unless you're Neil Peart, or Rick Allen. I missed being a *band*. I missed having a purpose, and being an essential piece of a unit. I loved it because I felt *wanted*.

Lonely Vagrants had been the best time of my life, even though it was only four short years out of almost two hundred. I'd been essential. I'd found a family. And no one saw my faults because I'd had Colin to hide behind.

But now that Colin's gone, what did people see in me? Surely, they think I am flighty and aloof, and a little spacy. I cut out of things early. I can't carry a conversation to save my life. I withdraw into long silences, and fade into the background.

It's strategic, though. I'd rather be just part of the landscape, than see people realize they're stuck with the lesser brother.

Colin was the well adjusted one. He wouldn't be struggling to tread water like I'd been for years. He wouldn't have been gutted about having to kill Adam twenty years later, because he wouldn't have been *involved* with Adam. And then there was Oregon, the most recent low point. I'd been there because Colin would've. He would've done so more with the last thirty years than I have.

Screw you, Colin, I muttered in my head; something I said at least once a day. *It should've been me.*

The door to the apartment slammed open, and I scrambled into a sitting position, hoisting the pillow up by my shoulder, like a weapon, before I realized how dumb that was.

The pair stumbled into the living room, a mess of locked lips and groping hands. Maon kicked the door closed behind them, sliding his hand into the man's jeans while the man tugged Mason's shirt upwards.

I dropped the pillow to my lap and, much as I wanted to disappear from this situation, I exaggeratedly cleared my throat.

Unsurprisingly, Mason failed to look embarrassed—*proud* was a more accurate term—as he noticed me finally, and retrieved his hand from the front of the man's jeans.

"Sorry, friend. I didn't expect you to be here still. This is Graham." he said, his voice husky from arousal. Mason took the man's hands to still them. "And ordinarily I'd go to *his* place, but *someone* has a roommate who doesn't know that Graham is *bicurious*..."

"The word never occurred to me until tonight," the man purred in Mason's ear, as he sidled closer to Mason and kissed his neck. Graham was several inches taller than Mason, maybe in his late twenties, with sandy hair and a goatee.

Mason pulled him in for another hungry kiss before saying, "Oh, sweet thing, I think you've been curious for a while. You just needed that last push."

His hand snaked downward again, and Graham's head rolled backwards to look at the ceiling, a quiet moan rattling from his throat. Mason gave me a mischievous look and winked.

I pressed my lips together and stood, grabbing my hoodie and turning away from them. As I shouldered it on, I tapped out the drumbeat from "YYZ" in my head to distract me from the stir the man's moans were causing below my belly button.

I wasn't mad about this intrusion, but it was a rare test of our boundaries as roommates. Mason only occasionally brought his FFFs back to our apartment, and when he did, it was almost always a woman.

We'd been rooming together since Oregon, and I often felt he only tolerated me because he felt he owed me for saving his life. We were even in that regard, though—since he saved *my* ass in Oregon in a similar situation. But still, weird as our friendship might be, I liked him. Our personalities were vastly different, but we meshed well in other ways.

This didn't mean I wanted to be in the apartment while he gave a man his first gay experience.

I patted the jacket for my keys and wallet, and mumbled something about leaving to give them space. I skirted around them awkwardly on my way to the front door, and Mason grabbed my elbow, halting me.

"You don't have to leave," he said, huskily. He took his other hand from Graham's jeans and snaked it up his chest to his hair. "You can join us, if you want. Right Graham?" He glanced briefly at Graham, but then returned his eyes to mine with a cocky smirk. "I can show him one way. And you can show him the other."

My eyes found Graham's, even though I didn't want to make eye contact. He looked both awed and wary at the idea of having two men in one night; like he didn't know if he should be into it or horrified by it.

Me too, man, me too, I thought silently, with an inner smirk.

"No. Thanks," I said, finding my voice finally. "I can find places to be. You have fun."

"Ah, right, school's back in session, right?" Mason said with a knowing grin and wink as I darted out the door.